# Bluewater
# Gold Rush

# Bluewater Gold Rush

## The Odyssey of a
## California Sea Urchin Diver

Tom Kendrick

Azalea Creek Publishing

Azalea Creek Publishing
Sebastopol, California

**Publishers Cataloging In Publication**
Kendrick, Tom, 1951 -
Bluewater Gold Rush
The Odyssey of a California Sea Urchin Diver

Includes bibliographical references
ISBN 10: 0-9677934-3-6
ISBN 13: 978-0-9677934-3-6

1. Sea Urchin—Diving
2. Salt Water Fisheries
3. Ocean Adventure
4. California Coast
5. Surfing
  I.Title.

Library of Congress Control Number (LCCN):
2006925370

910.45          LC G530          dc20

For the Piano Teacher

# Contents

# PART II

## Author Disclaimer

Bluewater Gold Rush is a work of creative nonfiction, in which I have taken literary license. Although all of the stories are true, embellishments have been made, facts have been altered, and dates have been changed in order to create a continual time flow. It is, however, an accurate portrayal of the California sea urchin fishery from 1978 through 1996, and the people involved in it. This is our story.

# Prologue

*It is not the critic who counts; not the man who points out how the strong man stumbles, or where the doer of deeds could have done them better. The credit belongs to the man who is actually in the arena, whose face is marred by dust and sweat and blood; who strives valiantly; who errs, who comes short again and again, because there is no effort without error and shortcoming; but who does actually strive to do the deeds; who knows great enthusiasms, the great devotions; who spends himself in a worthy cause; who at best knows in the end the triumph of high achievement, and who at the worst, if he fails, at least he fails while daring greatly, so that his place shall never be with those cold and timid souls who neither know victory nor defeat.*

*—Theodore Roosevelt*

# Prologue

## December Ninth 1994

Weener always suited up first, and did all the surveying. He liked to use a scuba bottle and a hand-held underwater scooter—this method allows the sea urchin diver to cover plenty of bottom area in a short time. Once he had his wetsuit and gear on, he stood up, holding on to the cabin handrail while Steve lifted the heavy tank and helped the diver strap it on.

Ward throttled down the diesel motor and shifted it into neutral. "Okay, boss. We're on our numbers—it's sixty-five feet under the boat."

"I'm in!" Moments after falling backward off the rail into the dark water, Weener cleared his mask, adjusted the tank on his back, and gave Steve the signal to hand him the scooter. "I think we finished up about fifty feet forward. Get ready with the hook while I take a quick survey." Following his captain's orders, Steve, the tender, carefully walked to the bow, keeping a firm grip on the handrail to avoid falling from the pitching boat. A few seconds later, he knelt down next to the anchor winch and pulled back on the lever, disengaging the clutch. The anchor was now ready to drop.

Weener squeezed the trigger of the scooter, activating the propeller, allowing himself to be pulled downward. Bubbles rising to the surface indicated his location and direction of travel. Up on the bow, Steve lifted his right arm, holding it thirty degrees to starboard. Ward stood inside the cabin, one hand on the wheel, the other on the throttle lever. He watched Steve's hand signals, and following the tender's directions, slowly eased the rocking boat forward. They both knew to keep the spinning prop well behind the bubbles, fifty feet or more, to keep their diver safe. The three-man team had been at this for years, and had performed the maneuver hundreds of times.

A minute later, Steve's hand clenched into a fist, the signal to stop the boat. Weener surfaced twenty feet from the bow. "Drop it!" he shouted. The chain rattled loudly as it fed off the freespooling winch, sending the thirty-pound Bruce anchor on its way to the bottom.

The boat, however, was at the mercy of the wind now that the motor was out of gear—in the twenty seconds or so that it took for the anchor to reach the bottom, they could easily drift off the spot. "I'm gonna go check the hook!" Again, he triggered the scooter and headed down the anchor chain.

Inside the wheelhouse, Ward checked the plotter numbers, thinking, "We might have drifted twenty feet or so, but I'll bet we put the hook close to where he wants it."

Ten seconds later, the anchor grabbed, causing the boat to lurch as the bow swung around into the wind. Ward killed the motor, walked out on deck, and joined Steve, who had left the bow and now stood behind the cabin, out of the cold wind. Both men hung on, steadying themselves against the pitching motion of the boat as Weener's bubbles headed back.

An immense pool of blood was the first indication of the tragedy. Weener surfaced next to the starboard rail, screaming, "I got bit by a shark! Get me on the boat!" He let go of the scooter, which immediately sank, and he floated helplessly as the crew members leaned over to grab him. "Oh, my God!" Ward whispered. Adrenaline took over, helping them to lift the nearly two-hundred-pound man with his fifty-pound scuba tank onto the boat. Both men grunted as they hauled him up, and over the rail, head first. As his body fell on to the deck, they saw his legs. Both were mutilated, with the right one skewed at an awkward angle—it hung limp, and was almost completely severed. Within seconds, the boat was red with blood—it spewed uncontrollably, covering the decks and pouring out the scuppers. Ward's eyes filled with tears as he pulled the tank off of his friend and threw it aside. Steve, having had first-aid training as a ski patrol member, ran into the cabin and pulled the belt from his jeans. Seconds later, it was wrapped around the disfigured thigh, stemming the tremendous flow of blood. Next, he ran into the cabin and grabbed the radio microphone. "Mayday, mayday, mayday! Vessel Florentia Marie! Our diver has been bit by a shark—mayday!"

"Oh God! Jesus!" Weener screamed, looking at his mangled leg. Ward cradled the diver in his arms.

"Florentia Marie, this is Coast Guard station Channel Islands—what's your position? Over!"

"Castle Rock, San Miguel Island. Over!"

"Florentia Marie, copy! A helicopter is being dispatched—he'll be on scene in thirty minutes!"

"Roger that!"

Weener had been on the boat for less than two minutes. "Ween, we gotta get you outta your suit!" Ward and Steve were both covered with blood, aghast at the gruesome sight. The scuba tank rolled from side to side on the heaving deck. Weener's voice was fainter now, but he was emphatic. "Don't take my suit off, boys. Please. It's the only thing keepin' my leg on." His friends looked at each other. "Okay, Ween. We'll leave it on."

"Vessel Florentia Marie, Coast Guard rescue helicopter six nine four. Over!"

"Florentia Marie, go ahead!"

"We're ten minutes out, how's your man?"

"Not good, please hurry!"

Ward Motyer and Steve Stickney sat with their friend on the crimson deck of the Florentia Marie. His color drained and his voice lowered to a whisper. "I love you guys." "We love you too, Weener." Both men's faces were wet with tears as their skipper faded into unconsciousness.

The rescue basket, with Weener strapped in, was winched up to the helicopter. Forty minutes had gone by. The pilot, Major Dan Lewis, looked down at the boat. "Jesus, there's blood everywhere. This is not good," he thought. Coast Guard Medic Tommy Phillips commenced CPR, working on his patient nonstop during the fifteen-minute flight to Goleta Valley Hospital. After Weener's transfer to a rolling gurney, emergency room technician Janice Tapper climbed up, continuing resuscitation efforts. His wounds were so severe that the emergency room physician would later say, "Even if it had happened on the steps of the hospital, I don't think we could have saved him."

Jim Robinson, The Weener—diver, surfer, and friend to all who knew him, died on December ninth, 1994.

# PART I

# The Early Days

*In the end, it's not the years*
*in your life that count.*
*It's the life in your years.*

—*Abraham Lincoln*

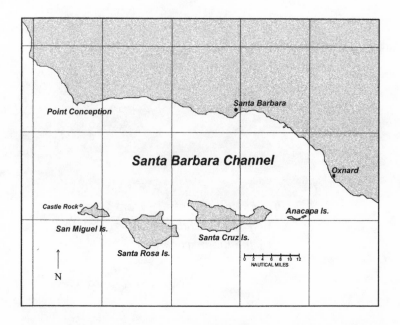

## Beginnings

Traveling south on Shoreline Drive from an area called the Mesa will take you down the hill, past Ledbetter Point, to the harbor at Santa Barbara.

In the early morning, fishermen are gassing up their boats at the fuel dock, working on their nets, and getting ready for the day. Invariably, something is broken, requiring the skipper to be down in the engine compartment of his boat, turning a wrench, skinning his knuckles, and cursing at whatever piece of equipment requires his attention. Once in a while a boat will stay tied up at the small dock long after he has taken on his fuel. Bob Meyer, who runs the place, will politely notify the skipper that a paying customer is waiting in line and to get the hell out of the way.

The small tourist shops are opening up for business, rolling out racks of tee shirts that have pictures of dolphins on them. The Harbor Maintenance crew is busily sweeping and picking up litter. Tourists from Michigan and North Dakota wait for a table at the Breakwater Restaurant while the local crowd is having a breakfast burrito and coffee from a styrofoam cup at the Minnow Café, quite possibly the smallest eatery in the world.

Fred Sloan hoses off the asphalt in front of the bait shop. He wears rubber boots and shorts every day of the year. No one knows how Fred makes money—all he ever does is hose off the asphalt and sit in his chair in front of the bait shop.

Freddy and Auggie Ghio, two old Italian brothers, occupy their seats in front of the Chandlery, as they have every morning for years. They are commercial fishermen from a time when boats were made of planks, and the only navigational aid was a compass. Now they sit on their bench and talk in a language that the new generation of fishermen don't understand. They laugh at the hulls made of fiberglass, but they secretly wish that their legs could once more hold them up on the deck of a lurching boat.

In the spring of 1978, when my story begins, the wooden docks of the marinas were narrow, and they creaked and bobbed as you walked down them to your boat. Some sections of the docks were fairly stable, but often it was necessary to be vigilant while walking on them, and every so often someone unfamiliar with their movement got seasick.

In later years, larger floats were installed and it would be like walking down any other sidewalk, except for the abundance of seagull droppings. The new docks were stable—they no longer groaned under your feet, and people stopped getting seasick on them. But some of us missed the old docks. They had personality.

### Hydroplane Hagen

Steve Hagen was fast. Everything he did was fast. He talked fast and he walked fast. His boat went fast and he was constantly trying to get it to go faster. Steve was small and skinny, with a bony, beak-like nose and eyes that were always wide open and bugged out. A nervous energy kept him in constant motion—if he wasn't busy working with his hands, his mouth was working, for he was a non-stop talker. He was new in the urchin diving business, but he was learning fast.

He was always working frantically on his boat, until whatever was wrong with it got fixed, then he worked on it some more. His wiry body was perfect for crawling around in a cramped engine box to change spark plugs, a task he could accomplish quickly. Oil stains dotted every article of clothing he owned, and anyone who shook hands with him wound up with a black, oily hand. His nickname around the harbor was Hydroplane Hagen.

Steve was the first sea urchin diver I had ever met. His boat, a twenty-four footer named the *Little Wing*, had been designed and built locally by Ron Radon, an abalone diver turned boat builder. It had a fiberglass planing hull built for speed, and a deep-vee bottom to soften the ocean chop of the Santa Barbara Channel. The small forward cabin was just large enough to accommodate two people.

An inboard-outboard, or I.O., was the most common form of power for this type of boat, and the Mercruiser V-8 motor that squeezed inside the aft engine box was the most powerful engine available, necessary to carry the heavy loads of urchins.

An outdrive, or leg, was attached to the outer transom and angled down into the water. Three feet below the waterline is the aluminum propeller, the deepest part of the boat, and usually the first thing to hit bottom in the shallows. Cables, running inside the gunnel from the steering wheel attached to the drive leg, provided a high degree of maneuverability. If driven by an experienced boat handler, this boat could easily fit into tight places.

The *Little Wing* tied up in the first slip of marina three. My old cabin cruiser, *Heidi Marie*, was almost all the way down at the end, so I had to walk by the handsome blue dive boat every day.

I formulated a plan to introduce myself to Steve and persuade him to take me out to the Channel Islands. Having made a list of qualifications that might be helpful, I was prepared to give him several reasons why I would be a good deckhand. I was strong, a hard worker, and motivated. There were no wives or kids depending on me, my income requirements were minimal, and I was a fast learner.

My opportunity presented itself the next day. Steve was curled up in a ball inside the engine compartment of the *Little Wing*, covered with grease, turning a wrench furiously.

"Nice boat," was my opening gambit.

The wrench in his hand dropped into the oily bilge. "Thanks," he offered. Although he was small, his muscles were well developed, and his dirty tee shirt bulged.

Not sure if he was thanking me for the compliment, or for making him drop his tool, I plowed on, sticking my hand out and introducing myself. "Tom Kendrick. I'm looking for a job on an urchin boat." His firm handshake blackened mine with grease.

"I'm Steve Hagen." His head was now back down in the bilge. "Ever worked on a boat?"

"No."

"Do you have a commercial fishing license?"

"No."

"You live on that old cabin cruiser, don't you?"

"Yes."

"Well, I guess I could give you a try. The weather looks good for tomorrow, so if you want to go, be on the boat at seven. I'll pay you thirty bucks a day for the first two trips. If you can hack it, buy a commercial license. Then I'll take you up to fifty a day."

I was elated! My dream of going to the Channel Islands was finally coming true, and he was going to pay me money! While lying in my bunk that night, being gently rocked, I fell into a half-sleep, dreaming of the following day's adventure to come.

My father was a military man, and to my good fortune we moved to Hawaii for four years when I was eleven. It was during this time that I developed a love for surfing and the ocean that would stay with me and eventually shape my future. In fact, surfing pretty much took over my life before I turned twelve. Schoolwork, family, and organized sports all took a backseat to the beach.

When Dad retired we moved to Santa Barbara, where I completed my high school education, and although I spent more of my time surfing than studying, the teachers at San Marcos High reluctantly saw to it that I was a member of the 1969 graduating class.

The ocean off Santa Barbara was colder than I was used to in Hawaii, and wearing a wetsuit took some getting used to, but this section of the California coast is renowned for its surfing areas, the most famous being Rincon Point and the Hollister Ranch, and I was happy to be living there.

Besides having world-class surf, Santa Barbara is also home to surfing legends Reynolds Yater and George Greenough. Surfboards built by Yater, and Al Merrick, owner of Channel Islands Surfboards, are cherished by surfers, who order them from all over the globe.

In 1973, after pumping gas at every station in town, I joined the Air Force to see the world. Four years later, after seeing Texas and Nebraska, I found my way down to the harbor, where my last three thousand dollars was spent for the purchase of a 1959 twenty-five-foot Owens cabin cruiser. I painted my niece's name on her stern—*Heidi Marie.*

Slip number B-55 of marina three became my home. It was convenient because I was able to walk across the street to the City College, where I was taking classes courtesy of the G.I. bill.

The *Heidi Marie* was an old boat. Her plywood hull was weather-beaten and warped, the paint was chipped and peeling, and some of the wood on her decks was rotten and soft where the seams met the rails. She leaked from all points as old boats do, and when the small automatic bilge pump kicked on for a few minutes every six or seven hours, it sounded like an old man with a weak bladder peeing in the harbor.

The cabin was not spacious, but there was enough room for two people to sleep, uncomfortably. When standing up, anyone taller than five feet seven inches had to cock his head to one side. The taller you were, the farther your head had to lean.

Water penetrated the cabin in great amounts during a rain, and there was only one small corner inside that stayed dry. But to me, the old boat was my little slice of heaven, and I loved her. On those cold rainy nights I lay curled up in my sleeping bag, dreaming of calm, clear waters and good waves.

Santa Barbara was a main landing port for the commercial abalone diving fleet, and for California's newest fishery, sea urchin diving. The eggs, or roe of the urchin, are a prized item in the sushi bars of Japan. Uni, as the raw gonads are called, not only have a unique flavor, but are known in Japan for their aphrodisiac qualities. The urchins that thrived in the kelp beds of the Channel Islands were in high demand. The Japanese could not get enough of the undersea delicacy.

I had heard stories of good waves, good money, and good times at the Channel Islands, and now I had found a way to get out there.

### Tender Training

We met on Steve's boat promptly at seven. After starting the motor and casting off the lines, he expertly backed the *Little Wing* out of the slip and slowly drove her down the harbor channel, around the breakwater, and out into the open sea.

Like most of the other dive boats, the two exhaust pipes of the *Little Wing* stuck straight out of her transom. The noise was loud—not like the quiet underwater bubbly exhaust of recreational boats, but the added power of the thru-hull exhaust was necessary, for this boat needed to work hard.

After we cleared the breakwater, Steve pushed the throttle lever forward. "Hang on!" he shouted. The boat gave a sudden jump as it leapt up on plane. I was thrown backward, and but for the handrail, which I now grasped with white knuckles, I would have wound up on the deck, ass first. My heart was in my throat as the bow instantly rose upward, leaving only the rear third of the boat in the water. We were flying over the waves! The engine noise I had heard back in the harbor was now behind us as we skipped over the water at twenty-five knots, on our way to Santa Cruz Island.

The *Little Wing*'s open steering area and small windshield offered minimal protection from the sea spray hitting our faces, and I could feel the wind on my teeth as a wild, uncontrollable smile spread over my face. Steve held the wheel steady while I kept a firm grip on the handrail to keep from falling backward. There were no seats, so we stood and let our legs absorb the gentle pounding.

The water was smooth and blue, and as I looked back toward the rapidly shrinking harbor I could see our wake. It streamed off the stern, fast and alive, leaving a snake-like trail as the boat sliced through the calm water. We were going so fast! Steve looked over at me, and as our eyes met, he gave me a knowing grin.

An hour later we approached the west end of Santa Cruz Island. Steve slowed the boat down, guiding us into a rocky cove, where we noticed another urchin boat. Their anchor was not yet down, and as we drifted closer one of the men on board gave a shout, "Is this your spot?"

"Yep." Steve's response was fast and short. The friendly demeanor was gone—he stared at them with narrow eyes as they left the cove.

"Those guys saw me in here last week. They were fixing to jump my spot." I wasn't sure what he was talking about, but he didn't explain, and it was quickly forgotten.

After idling the boat down, he scanned the surface of the water, studying the thick brown kelp with what looked to me to be a trained eye. "See those kelp leaves? See how some of their ends are jagged?" His eyes opened wide and a smile crept over his face. "Something's been eating 'em!"

After checking our depth on the fathometer, he walked on the narrow cap rail around the cabin, up to the bow to drop the rusty anchor, which was made of thick rebar. Four shafts angled out from the base of it to latch onto the reefs below.

Once the hook was on the bottom, Steve tied off the anchor line to the bow cleat, returned to the main deck, and turned off the motor. His movements were quick and efficient—we had been on our spot for less than a minute. And although the boat was now stationary, it bobbed and rolled from side to side. Without a constant hand-hold on something, I would have fallen over.

It was a small bay, half the size of a football field, and the rocky cliffs rising straight up out of the water to a height of roughly a hundred feet gave us the feeling of being in a large room. A harbor seal pup stuck his head out of the water and gave us several welcoming barks, which echoed as if we were in a canyon. Gulls circled in the cloudless sky above, squawking at the intruders while tiny waves lapped at the rocks, which were dotted with white bird guano. A mixture of smells assaulted my nose—the sea, the salt air, and of course, the pungent bird droppings. I was amazed and exhilarated by the little bay and all the life it held.

Steve broke my hypnotic state. "Take the cover off the air compressor. Then get the dive hose plugged in and grab the bag lines out of the cabin." I was reminded that we were here to work. Sea urchins are a product that must be delivered fresh, and Steve liked to do things fast.

In a few minutes he stood on the deck with his wetsuit on. The long air hose was connected to his breathing regulator, which hung at his side. "Get this deck organized and have a bag ready for me." In my haste to bring the lines out from the cabin, I had strewn them all over the deck—the two mesh harvesting bags sat on top of the spaghetti-like pile.

After Steve pulled on the starter cord for the fourth time, the compressor motor sputtered and sprang to life. The small engine that powered the "hookah" system was loud and obnoxious, but necessary, and now a slight vibration permeated the boat, creating tiny dimples in the water.

"I'm gonna take a survey. If I wave at you when I come up, toss me a bag." He had to shout over the noise of the motor. Then he tossed a few coils of his dive hose into the water and sat on the rail, his back to me.

"Wait!" I said, suddenly realizing that he had given me no emergency instructions. What if the air compressor quit—would he drown? We were only thirty feet from the rocks. Was the anchor holding the boat securely? But he pulled his dive mask over his head, adjusted it, and slid off the boat, disappearing below the surface.

The water was a deep blue and crystal clear. I watched him swim down, then vanish. Now only the large air bubbles were visible as they traveled up from below. His yellow hose waved at me as it followed him down on his search for urchins.

Moments later he surfaced. Taking the regulator out of his mouth, he yelled, "Toss me that bag, then get another one ready. This spot's holding!" I quickly grabbed the round steel rim of the bag and threw it toward him. Unfortunately, I was standing on the mesh so it flew three inches then fell to the deck. "Sorry." I fumbled with the net for a few seconds, eventually getting it into the water.

"If the compressor quits or the boat drifts too close to the rocks, give my hose a couple of tugs."

"But, what if …" I stammered. But he ducked his head, and with two powerful kicks of his flippers he was gone.

How close was too close to the rocks? Twenty feet? Ten feet? I sat on the lid of the engine box, watching his bubbles, keeping a wary eye on the rocks, which seemed to be inching closer. Suddenly, he broke the surface right next to me and yelled, "You're sitting on my air hose!" I jumped up from my seat, realizing that he was right. My weight had kept him from being able to pull the neatly coiled hose from the stern. "Sorry, I ..." But he quickly disappeared.

Half an hour later an orange floater ball bobbed thirty feet away. When Steve surfaced a few seconds later, he was holding his breathing regulator in his hand. "Throw me a line! Then pull the bag to the boat and tie it off!" My feeble throw made it about halfway to him, but with a quick thrust of his legs, he rocketed to it, and within seconds had attached the line to the floating bag of urchins. As I pulled the heavy bag through the water, he swam to the stern, nimbly climbing up the outdrive onto the engine lid.

After removing his fins, weight belt, mask, and gloves, Steve shut the air compressor off, which was a great relief, and began instructing me how to tend the bag, or lift it onto the deck of the boat.

First, he pulled it up a few inches out of the water and tied it off. Next, he lowered the winch line using a remote switch. Then he attached the winch line snap to the stainless steel ring on the bag and began lifting it onto the boat by pushing the "up" button on the switch. The winch groaned and the boat leaned as the full bag of urchins slowly came out of the water. Once it had reached a height necessary to clear the rail, Steve carefully grabbed the net and pulled, causing the bag to swing over to the deck, where the 500 pounds of spiny urchins were lowered into place.

As the mesh bag settled onto the deck, I stared at the animals he had captured. Hundreds of urchins were stuffed into the bag, their long spines moving in an attempt to escape back to their home under the sea. I could see varying shades of purple, black, and red as the urchins dripped with seawater and slime. Several strands of kelp accompanied them, and they seemed to be enjoying a final meal. One of them fell to the deck from atop the pile, its spiny arms alive with movement. The shell diameter was about the size of a baseball, and the pain it could inflict with the long, needle-like spines was obvious.

By late afternoon four large bags of urchins sat on the deck of the *Little Wing*, with two more on top of them. The distinct smell of fresh, raw sea urchins now permeated the air. It was a unique mixture of sea, salt, and fish, a smell I would come to love.

Steve used his picking rake to crack open an urchin, delicately scooping out a piece of the yellow roe from inside the shell. "See this?" It was about three inches long with the consistency of jello. "This is uni." And with that he popped it into his mouth. Then he handed me a piece. "Here, try some." Not wanting to disappoint him, I put it in my mouth and ate it. The taste was unique, and though it was not disgusting, it was not pleasurable. Certainly nothing I would ever pay for. Steve chuckled. "It's an acquired taste."

The deck was now completely covered, making it necessary to carefully walk on the rails of the boat. This was extremely dangerous, because with one misstep we would fall onto the spiny animals we had just captured, giving them their revenge.

Adding to the problem of space was the fact that the urchins were so far forward on the deck, leaving us less than two feet of standing room, with the dangerous spines directly behind us. I had so far been able to avoid being "urched," as Steve put it, but with the sharp spikes only inches from my back, I feared I would become a human pincushion.

After Steve got the dive hose tied down on the engine lid and started the motor, it was time to pull up the anchor. We went up to the bow for my first lesson on how to uncleat the anchor line, pull the slack from it, then cleat it off, or retie the line to the anchor cleat.

Pulling an anchor by hand is difficult and dangerous—it is an art that can only be learned with practice. First, the slack is taken out and the line is tied off. Next, the boat operator maneuvers the vessel, breaking the anchor loose from the bottom, where it is either buried in sand, or more commonly, stuck on a rock. An experienced tender is able to time his pulling and tying off so that the boat does the work and most of his pulling is on a slack line.

Inexperienced tenders make two common mistakes while pulling an anchor up: the first is getting a hand or a finger caught between the line and the anchor cleat, which can break a finger. The other problem occurs as the skipper is maneuvering the boat, attempting to pop the anchor loose from the bottom. The anchor catches, the boat lurches, and the neophyte deckhand, who is not hanging on, is thrown off the boat into the cold water. If he is not carrying a spare set of clothes he is faced with a cold, miserable ride home. Both of these things happen periodically, with a cold water dunking always being preferable to a broken finger.

This day, the anchor came up with little difficulty, and now the *Little Wing* gently rocked in the water, unattached. She sat lower, with a more pronounced roll caused by the added weight she carried. The engine exhaust was now below the waterline, and it bubbled quietly as Steve eased the shifter into gear and pointed the nose of the *Little Wing* toward the entrance of the cove. "Hold the wheel for a sec," he said, and ducked into the cabin to change out of his wetsuit.

I now stood at the helm, idling the boat out of the bay. A feeling of power and confidence swept over me for I was now in control. I experimented, turning the wheel slightly left, then right, feeling the response as I gave the boat its orders. I loved the feeling, imagining myself to be the skipper.

In less than a minute Steve emerged from the cabin. He had a four-foot-square piece of canvas that he draped over the urchins, whose sharp spines were perilously close to our backs. "Don't wanna get urched!" he said, as he displaced me from the helm and pushed the throttle forward, taking us out of the island cove.

**Heading Home**

The motor groaned and the *Little Wing* responded slowly. No longer was it a light, responsive speedboat. It labored under the nearly 3,000 pounds of urchins, but soon we were up on plane, making eighteen knots.

A light northwest wind had picked up and was hitting us from the port quarter, over our left shoulders. "Good day!" Steve said with a smile, as we began our ride home. His face had a crease in it, an outline of the dive mask he had been wearing for his four hours of bottom time. "You did good!" This surprised me, as most of the day I had stumbled around on the deck, trying to keep from falling in the water. It seemed to me that he was able to put a load on the boat in spite of his tender. Reading my thoughts, he told me that the last guy he tried out was seasick for the entire trip, and never came out of the cabin.

The afternoon sea was choppy, and Steve had to "surf" the boat, expertly guiding it down the three-foot waves, in and out of the ocean troughs. We were low in the water, being assaulted by the spray and wind.

As we made our way toward the middle of the channel, the waves grew. I made every attempt to appear as nonchalant as my skipper, but my heart pounded as we climbed slowly up the back of a wave, then shot down the face of it, the sea air feeling like pins as it hit my face. The loud motor smoked and groaned under the heavy load it now carried.

The ride home took a little over an hour and a half. My knees were stiff as we pulled into the protected harbor, and my hands had swelled up from working the bag and anchor lines. The sun was low in the sky as we tied to the pilings underneath the fish hoist. But our day was far from over.

A short, stocky man stood on the dock, looking down at us. He held a large yellow control mechanism in his hand, pushing the button, expertly guiding the hook down from fifteen feet above. "Hook up that top bag, then step aside," Steve instructed me. The hook that was attached to the large dockside hoist had a scale on it. The hoist operator lifted the heavy bag from the boat and dangled it in the air while he noted the weight, then wrote it down on a fish ticket, our receipt for the day's catch.

"As soon as you get it hooked up, get outta the way," the man yelled from above. "Every once in a while those ropes break, and believe me, you don't wanna be underneath it when that happens!"

"Have you ever seen it happen?" I asked Steve, who now stood safely on the bow.

"Yeah, last week on the *Moki*. The tender was lucky—it just grazed him. His arm was a bloody mess, though."

Twenty minutes later, the *Little Wing* once again floated high in the water, free from the weight of the sea urchins.

"Come up and meet Wes!" shouted Steve, who now stood on the dock above. I climbed the rusty ladder up to the dock, where a thick, calloused hand met me.

"Wes Carpenter, pleased to make your acquaintance!" He was a grizzly, unshaven man, unkempt and disheveled. I knew right away I would like him. "Working with Steve, huh? Sorry to hear that!" He laughed—an uninhibited, infectious guffaw, then he lit into a marketing lesson, no doubt for my benefit. "These urchins will be cracked, processed, and packed into styrofoam containers tomorrow. A piece of jelly ice, some duct tape, and within twenty-four hours they'll be on a plane to Japan. After they land in Tokyo, it's off to Tskiji, the largest fresh fish market in the world."

After we climbed the ladder back down to the *Little Wing* and drove back to the slip in marina three, it was almost dark.

Steve barked, "Hop out and tie off the stern, I'll get the bow." After the boat was secured to the dock, I was informed that it needed to be cleaned up and made ready for the next day. The deck was covered with spines, purple stains, and pieces of kelp and slime. "Throw the bags and my dive gear on the dock. Get the water hose out of the dock box and wash everything off. When you're through there, hose off the decks. Make sure you get all the spines off."

He poured a small amount of bleach into a bucket, added some water, and handed me a stiff brush. "If you don't scrub the decks down with bleach, those urchin stains will be tough to get off tomorrow." Steve chuckled. He could see I was dragging. "We're almost finished with our day, amigo." Next, I placed the equipment back onto the boat, locked the cabin door, wound up the water hose, and stowed it inside the dock box.

Our day was finally over! Fortunately, I didn't have far to go, and after a hot shower in the marina bathroom, I climbed aboard the *Heidi Marie* and fell into my bunk. My body was spent, every muscle ached and throbbed, but the events of the day still raced in my mind.

The work had been difficult and hazardous, but the island was beautiful beyond words, and working with the diver, riding in the boat, and ducking the spray, was the most exciting and adventurous thing I'd ever done.

Learning the ways of a seaman and sea urchin tender was what I wanted to do from now on, and a commercial fishing license was to be my next acquisition. On that April day in 1978, my life changed forever.

### The Hound Dog

Steve and I made two more trips together on the *Little Wing*, but then a new opportunity presented itself.

Dewey Benton owned a thirty-two-foot Radon boat named the *Hound Dog*. Dewey, along with another diver, Jerome Betts, consistently delivered between eight and ten thousand pounds of urchins per day, an average of ten to fifteen days per month.

The *Hound Dog* was a "highliner;" that is, a boat that stays out the longest, works the rough weather, and brings in the biggest loads. When Dewey offered me a job as tender, I quickly accepted, knowing that my starting wage of 10 percent of the day's catch would be at least three times what I was making on the *Little Wing*.

Dewey was tall and lean, with thick brown hair that he kept well trimmed. He had a quiet, solemn nature about him. He was a thinking man, serious, and he carried with him a sense of loneliness. At age twenty-five he had already been a builder and a real estate broker, having bought and sold several houses and commercial properties.

Dewey was a homeowner, married to a banker, and seemed to be a man on a mission. His unsmiling face hid any emotion that may have been behind it, and the creases in it belied his young age. At the time, his daily individual goal was to clear six hundred dollars, and he usually did.

Jerome was easy-going and carefree. He had a playful nature, and a mischievous sense of humor. He loved to pull little tricks on people, and being the new guy, I was the constant target of his shenanigans. But it was usually a welcome break from Dewey's serious demeanor.

Thinning blond hair and black horn-rimmed glasses made Jerome look like he would be more at home working in an office than on a fishing boat. The glasses were always slipping down his nose, which was wide but close to his face. It was not a good nose for holding glasses, so every minute or two he had to push them up with his index finger. But his short, thick body was rugged, and well suited to this line of work. Four years of high school water polo had given him great physical endurance, which he demonstrated by long stretches underwater, sometimes five and six hours without a break. He had also spent four years in the army, and had trained as a Ranger, the elite commando group. He later told me that he was sad because he did not get to go to Vietnam and that he was a frustrated warrior.

At twenty-seven, Jerome, like Dewey, was an experienced diver, and although you could not find more different work partners, the two men got along well and made a good team.

Working on the bigger boat with Dewey and Jerome, I soon learned, was different from being a tender for one diver on a smaller boat. For one thing the *Hound Dog* had a diesel motor that pushed her along at a slow but steady ten knots, which was practically stationary compared to the speedy *Little Wing*. Instead of racing out to the front side (the part of the island facing the mainland) of Santa Cruz, I was now on a boat that took from three to four hours to reach the diving grounds. We took turns at the helm, driving in one-hour shifts, while the other two crewmembers slept inside the cabin.

A typical work day with Dewey and Jerome meant getting under way at five-thirty, and starting work at nine or ten, depending on where we went that day. We almost always worked until dark, arriving at the dock at between ten and midnight. After unloading and getting the boat cleaned up, it was not unusual for me to be hitting my bunk in the *Heidi Marie* at one or two in the morning.

I was now part of a crew whose main goal was to hunt sea urchins and make money. If the weather was workable we went out, sometimes diving ten or twelve days in a row. It was hard work, and I came to value my bunk time on the *Hound Dog* .

Although we worked all of the islands in the northern chain, Dewey's favorite spot was Adams Cove on San Miguel Island. It was a long way from home, and often a tough ride out, as we had to buck straight into the seas to get there. After a sometimes grueling boat ride to the San Miguel Sandspit, at the eastern end of the island, we would turn the corner and be greeted by a calm sea as we ran up the backside toward our destination.

Adams Cove is near the western end of San Miguel Island, forty-six miles from Santa Barbara. It is home to the largest sea lion rookery on the west coast, with populations of California sea lions, harbor seals, Steller sea lions, northern fur seals, and elephant seals.

In those days, many of the reefs of the Channel Islands were virgin, which to a sea urchin diver means they had never been commercially harvested. The crew of the *Hound Dog* enjoyed many days of rich harvesting and forty-foot visibility at Adams Cove.

We were in an unregulated fishery, harvesting an animal that was considered a pest by the world's top marine biologists. Words like overfishing, catch limitations, and fishing closures were not to be heard for several years.

The first thing Dewey would do when we reached a likely dive area would be to let the boat drift for a minute or two while he studied the kelp bed—although I didn't know it at the time, the floating mass of brown seaweed has a story to tell. If the observer is experienced and patient, the kelp bed will show him where to throw his anchor.

A bed of thick kelp, with healthy, fully-grown leaves, will most likely contain few or no urchins on the bottom. The trained eye is looking for a bed that has been thinned out, with partially eaten leaves, or a thick kelp bed with holes in it—holes created by the voracious spineballs, and big enough to put a boat in. More often than not there will be a "blackout" of urchins in such a hole. And although a payday may be waiting underneath, these holes can be both profitable and deadly, for diving in the thick kelp is bothersome and dangerous. Many a diver has met his death after becoming tangled in the thick underwater leaves and panicking.

Sometimes an entire kelp bed has been eaten away and there are no strands visible on the surface, but the roe in the urchins hiding below is fat and healthy. These spots are difficult to find, but are often some of the best. An experienced skipper will sometimes idle his boat slowly along, looking for one or two strands of kelp that have escaped and reached the surface.

As always, I was full of questions, but it seemed as though Dewey had fallen into a trance as he gazed at the water. I figured he was daydreaming.

"What's up, boss?" I tried to bring him back to the present, but he ignored me, continuing to ponder the surface of the water. Jerome gently nudged me. He shook his head as if to say, "Not now, leave him alone." The techniques of reading the kelp beds and locating urchin beds are individually learned. They are secrets not to be shared, for in this business even your best friend is your competitor.

Eventually, Dewey would send me up to the bow. "Get ready." Then, after more idling and circling of the boat, he shouted my orders. "Drop it!" Down went the anchor, the thirty-foot length of chain rattling as it flew out of the open anchor locker. After being whacked in the shin once or twice by the unforgiving chain, I had learned to step aside as it rapidly made its way from boat to bottom.

Watching Dewey and Jerome jump into the water with hundreds of sea lions always made me nervous, for as soon as the divers hit the water they would be under attack. The surface became a mass of froth and boils as the curious, pesky pinnipeds welcomed their visitors, sometimes challenging them by baring their teeth and nipping at them. We'd heard a story of an abalone diver being bitten and badly injured by a sea lion at this very location several years ago, but during our time at Adams Cove no one suffered more than a few holes in his wetsuit and some frayed nerves.

Money was becoming important to me—mainly because I now had some. In days past my only requirements were a bar of wax and a surfboard. I now set my sights higher—my quiver of surfboards increased to two.

It was August 1978. I'd been an urchin tender for four months. My hands were becoming thicker, and were calloused. They now had the telltale look of a sea urchin worker, that is, multiple tiny stab wounds from the un-avoidable spines. Muscles on my arms strained against my tee shirt from pulling on hoses, bag lines, and anchor lines. It was my responsibility to keep the decks and gear of the *Hound Dog* clean and in good order, and I was learning how to repair the netting of the bags and maintain the air-compressor system.

My days of being a seasoned, experienced seaman, however, were still to come.

After a long work stretch the two divers slept while I took my turn at the helm. We were about two-thirds of the way home from Adams Cove, passing through the middle of the shipping lanes, and although we did not have radar, it was a clear night, and if one of the six-hundred-foot freighters carrying oil or imported cars were to cross our path, I could easily spot it.

The stereo headphones sat on my head. Kenny Loggins was singing, "Sweet love shining on me every night—I never seen such a beautiful sight." It occurred to me what an appropriate song to be hearing—it was truly a spectacular evening with not a breath of wind. The air was clear and crisp, the Milky Way looked down at us, and several dolphins were riding our bow wake, escorting us home across the black, greasy-smooth channel.

In my short tenure aboard the *Hound Dog* I had learned much from my teachers: I kept a vigilant eye on the temperature and oil pressure gauges, and constantly scanned the dark horizon for other boats.

The lighthouse on the coast just up from the harbor was coming into view as the noisy diesel motor chugged us along toward our destination. The lights of houses on Shore-line Drive were becoming visible, and although we were still fifteen miles out, they looked deceivingly close.

...

"Everything okay?" Dewey stuck his head out of the cabin, a curious look on his face.

"Yep, go back to sleep, boss," I shouted over the grind of the motor.

"You're sure?"

"Go back to sleep, it's another twenty minutes before your shift."

A minute or two later they both came out on deck. "Idle her down and kill the motor," Jerome shouted. A smile was on his face as I slowed the motor and turned it off. "Now bring up the drive." I pushed the actuator button and as the outdrive was coming up, Dewey went aft, opened up the engine lid and climbed down inside. When he emerged he had a spare propeller in one hand and a large wrench in the other. He shot a quick glance in my direction and shook his head. My finger was still on the button, and as the electric motor slowly continued lifting the drive, Jerome told me what was happening. "The motor sound changed. We could feel that the boat was no longer pushing water, and we knew we had lost the prop." He smiled, letting out a giggle. "We thought you would figure it out, but you didn't."

With Jerome holding his legs, and me with the flashlight, Dewey lay on his stomach and, while hovering inches from the black water, he expertly put the new propeller and keeper nut on. This was not an easy feat, as it was dark and the boat was lurching and rolling. If he dropped the nut, we could be floating out there for a long time.

After the skipper got the new prop on and we lowered the drive, his face cracked into a sideways grimace. "You had the boat on course, but we weren't going anywhere."

I sheepishly got us under way and vowed to pay better attention to the sound of the motor from then on.

## White Buffaloes

In late October of 1978, a fierce winter storm ravaged the California coast. Huge swells and gale-force winds kept even the biggest boats in the safety of the harbor for two weeks.

When we finally got back to our spot in Adams Cove the water was dirty, making for poor visibility underwater, less than ten feet. Light winds were forecast, but this day the National Weather Service was wrong. The wind blew hard all day, and by the time we headed down the backside of the island with our load, cleared the Sandspit, and got out into the channel, the white-capping wind chop, or "white buffaloes," as Jerome called the rough seas, were higher than the top of our cabin.

The thirty-two-foot *Hound Dog* felt small in the huge waves, and as we approached the shipping lanes the seas grew even bigger. Deep troughs were only slightly illuminated by a sliver of moonlight. We were taking the sea from our stern as Dewey expertly guided the boat, his hands constantly turning the wheel left, then right, trying to avoid burying the bow. Occasionally we plowed into the back of a big wave, and the motor would groan as it tried to push us through it. The *Hound Dog* unwillingly slowed almost to a full stop, then a ten-foot wave would break over the stern, filling the decks. As the water slowly drained out of the scuppers, she would wallow, and for a few seconds Dewey completely lost control of her.

At mid-channel we began taking it from our port side. "Hang on!" the skipper yelled. I braced for the shock as a large wave slammed into us, sending a shudder through the boat. White buffaloes were now smashing the left side of the cabin. "Get away from the window! If that thing comes in, you don't wanna be near it!" The port side window was taking direct hits now—if it broke, a shower of glass and water would flood the cabin.

The pile of urchins on the deck was six feet high, adding to the instability of the ship. Some of the waves rolled us so far to one side that I thought we were going over. The starboard window could not have been more than a few feet above the churning black water.

"You want me to take it for a while?" I asked. Dewey had been at the helm for over two hours. "I'll drive a while longer." His eyes bored straight ahead, trained on the black shifting mountains, trying to steer the boat around them. Looking at him in the darkness I could see the set of his jaw and the look of intensity in his eyes.

All the windows were leaking. Every item inside was soaked, and the cabin floor was like a big bowl of soup— an eight-inch puddle slogging around. Now it splashed up onto bunks and sleeping bags and nautical charts, but they were already drenched. The water could easily have been removed with the five-gallon bucket that was tied up on the back deck, but the boat was being tossed so violently it was impossible to do anything other than just hang on. Jerome was wedged into his bunk with his eyes closed. His wetsuit lay next to him, at the ready.

Now the seas no longer came out of the northwest. They were confused, hitting us from all directions. We sped down the face of a wave into darkness and buried the bow. Black water came up over the cabin and hit the forward windows, inches from our faces. Then a dark hump with a white frothy mane appeared on the port side. The white buffalo slammed into us, sending a shudder through man and boat. In an instant we pitched over at a perilous angle.

All unsecured items inside flew across the cabin, winding up either on the starboard bunk or in the puddle on the floor. I lost my grip, falling helplessly onto Dewey, who in turn fell against the starboard bulkhead, and for a brief moment our bodies pressed against each other in an awkward position. A 500 pound bag rolled off its place atop the shifting deck pile and fell into the sea. In the next instant we were slammed upright by the slosh of a wave on our starboard side, and as the boat righted itself I regained my hold on the handrail.

When we were within five miles of the coast, the seas finally calmed down to three feet. Without a word Dewey handed me the wheel, then went below and collapsed into his soggy bunk. Jerome came out and drove as I bucketed out the cabin.

"I think we came close to going over a few times," I said.

"Yep." Jerome adjusted his glasses.

"What would have happened if we had rolled over?"

"That probably would have been it for us." He stared straight ahead, then glanced down at the gauges.

. . .

The *Hound Dog* proved her seaworthiness that night, and I became a true believer in the capabilities of the thirty-two-foot Radon boat. Steve Hagen's *Little Wing* was a fine boat, but I'm not sure she would have made it.

After unloading and crawling into the cabin of the *Heidi Marie*, I felt like I was still being slammed back and forth. After a few minutes I stumbled out onto the back deck and vomited over the side.

Sleep was elusive; as I lay in my bunk reliving the perilous crossing, beads of sweat formed on my forehead, and thoughts of quitting the sea urchin business and returning to school crept into my mind.

Dewey displayed a quiet strength and determination that night as he maneuvered the *Hound Dog* through the ocean, not speaking for hours. I was glad he was the captain of our boat and I had faith he would get us home in one piece. Although I tried not to show it, I can't remember ever being more frightened.

Thankfully, we took a week off to regroup after our terrifying ride home. But two other boats had not been so lucky that night. The *Blind Faith*, a black thirty-foot Wilson owned by Tim Johnson, had flipped over in the middle of the shipping lanes. The crew managed to get off a mayday call before going over, and were rescued by a Coast Guard helicopter eight hours later. All three men were hypothermic, and after huddling together through the night while sitting on the belly of their boat, one of them was near death.

Another boat, a twenty-six-footer from Channel Islands Harbor in Oxnard, had lost all power and electronics. They had no communication and the boat was tossed around in those terrible seas for two days before being spotted by a fishing boat and towed in.

...

Jerome teased me mercilessly. He and Dewey had been working together for over a year, so things on the *Hound Dog* were fairly routine. That is, until I came along.

There are only four islands out there, but he constantly lied to me, trying to convince me that we were somewhere else. Dewey played along out of boredom.

"No, this is Santa Rosa—you can tell by that outcropping of rocks over there."

"Wait a minute, this looks like the same place we were at yesterday and you said we were at San Miguel."

"Yeah, I know—I lied. Just having some fun with you."

It was useless asking him the name of a cove, point of land, or anchorage—he always lied.

"Isn't Gull Rock on the backside of Santa Cruz Island?"

"Oh, yeah, but that's a different Gull Rock. This one's smaller, so it's not on the chart." Dewey would just nod and smirk.

Halfway to San Miguel it started getting rough. Having already driven my shift, I was now inside, curled up in my sleeping bag.

"Wedge yourself into a corner, it's gonna get bouncy for a while!" Jerome shouted to me from the steering station. I did as he suggested, and after another fifteen minutes of violent pounding, the worst was over. The seas calmed down and I was able to get some sleep.

"Okay, Tom, wake up! Get up on the bow and get ready to drop it!" I stumbled out of the cabin, and went forward, unwillingly coming out of my dreams and back to the *Hound Dog* .

The first thing I saw was a train going by up on the cliff.

"Where are we?"

"Santa Rosa Island." was Jerome's reply.

"That's a train!"

"Yeah, they use 'em to transport cattle from the west end to the ranch over by Becher's Bay."

Never having been to this island before, I had no reason to doubt him (other than the fact that he never told me the truth).

"What's that big white tank?'

"It's a water tank—it feeds off to several cattle-watering stations on the island."

It was not until late that evening, on our way home, that the truth came out. With my sharp eye and astute mind, I noticed that even after an hour of running, the island was still visible off the left side of the boat. Vehicular traffic from Highway 101 was further evidence that something was amiss.

"I guess there's a freeway on the island too, huh?" I glowered at him.

"Nah, while you were sleepin' this morning, we diverted to the coast. We were at Naples Reef."

I later found out we were at Cojo Bay, fifty miles up the coast from Santa Barbara.

Determined not to be fooled again, I studied a chart of the Santa Barbara Channel.

The California coastline takes a turn inland at Point Conception, forming what is known as the Santa Barbara Bight. Near Carpinteria, about fifty miles down the coast, the land begins its gradual turn, continuing south toward the Mexican border.

This area encompasses the towns of Goleta, Santa Barbara, Montecito, and Summerland, with the Santa Barbara Mountains rising dramatically to over four thousand feet, looking down over the entire region.

The waters here have a rich legacy of commercial fishing, pioneered by Italian immigrants such as Sebastian Larco and the Castagnola brothers in the early 1900s.

Commercial diving, in the form of abalone harvesting, got its start in the 1920s. The first to show up were the Japanese, followed by Barney Clancey's notorious Black Fleet, whose members had worked their way down the coast from Morro Bay, walking on the bottom, wearing "heavy gear," metal helmets and cumbersome canvas suits.

On a clear day the four offshore islands can be seen from land. They are San Miguel, Santa Rosa, Santa Cruz, and Anacapa, and they are the northern chain of the Channel Islands. Each island has its own unique personality, history, and diverse ecology.

San Miguel, low-lying and windswept, sticks its nose out into the open ocean farther than the other three, and receives the brunt of the weather. It is wild, and the seas around it are rough, but the diver willing to endure the pounding ride is often rewarded with clear water and rich harvesting areas. The Spanish explorer Juan Cabrillo died on San Miguel, but the exact location of his grave has remained a mystery. A monument to the adventurer over-looks Culyer Harbor.

Three miles east from the Sandspit at San Miguel is Talcott Shoals, by far the most popular dive area on the whole of Santa Rosa Island. The diving at Santa Rosa can be pristine, but murky conditions are common, and visibility sometimes suffers. Talcott, and Johnsons Lee, on the backside of the island, are known for treacherous currents. Unfortunate divers who have become discon-nected from their hose have been swept far away from their boats, some lost forever.

The stretch between the east end of Santa Rosa and the west end of Santa Cruz is called the Potato Patch. Prevailing northwesterly winds blow hard here and meet the high cliffs of Santa Cruz, making for an unfriendly sea.

Looking out the window on a dark night, seeing a large white buffalo approaching, and bracing for the shock, can be a frightening experience—the Potato Patch has claimed its fair share of boats.

Santa Cruz, the largest of the four islands, has some of the mildest waters. Its many coves and beautiful anchorages make it a favorite destination for recreational boaters and lobster divers. Mountains rise to over 2,000 feet. High cliffs climb dramatically from the sea, and hidden coves provide safe haven for both commercial and sport boats. The island is not known for its beaches, but it has several, and well-acquainted visitors know where to find the delightful stretches of pristine sand. It also has more sea caves than any island in the world, some burrowing over 1,000 feet into the cavernous rock.

Anacapa, the smallest of the four islands, and closest to land (ten miles from the Channel Islands Harbor at Oxnard), has some of the most beautiful diving on the entire California coast, though most of it is closed to commercial harvest. Steep cliffs and rapid drop-offs into deep water add to the beauty of this island and, because it is close to shore, it is a popular and accessible sport-diving area.

A loud banging on the hull of my boat, the *Heidi Marie*, abruptly brought me out of a deep sleep.

"You in there, Tom?" I recognized Jerome's voice, and slowly dragged myself out of my bunk. "Dewey's warming up the boat, let's go!"

We'd been off for nine days, but the sea had suddenly flattened out. By the time I got dressed and made my lunch, Ron had nosed the *Hound Dog* up to the stern of my boat. I climbed over and hopped on.

"Good morning!" Dewey shouted. I'd never seen him so cheerful. I think he was happy to be getting back to work. "I got a call from Yuki last night. He's screaming for uni and says he'll pay us sixteen cents a pound!"

Yuki Ogawa was one of the four Japanese processors in Los Angeles who bought our product. Our prices had always ranged from twelve to fourteen cents, so when I heard this, I began calculating.

Dewey had started me at 10 percent of the gross, but had increased my share to 12 percent after my first ten trips. As an experienced tender, I was now getting 15 percent, making around 150 dollars for a typical seventeen-hour day. But the prospects of a jump in pay had us all excited, and the three of us were in good spirits as we left the harbor and began our journey across the channel, which looked like a sheet of glass.

Jerome stuck his balding head out of the cabin and adjusted his glasses.

"The forecast is for light and variable winds the entire week, with a two-foot westerly swell. The bank's open, and we're gonna make a withdrawal!"

Rays of light split the sky over the Santa Barbara Mountains, the sea was flat as a pancake, and we were guaranteed a good price. Our six-hour boat ride through the white buffaloes the month before was forgotten, and none of us said a word about it as we settled into our work routine.

When we were thirty minutes from the diving area I went to the rear deck and began my duties, laying out the hoses, setting up nets, getting bag lines ready, and arranging the divers' wetsuits and dive gear. The cover protecting the air compressor came off, and the small gasoline motor that ran the compressor was primed and made ready for the day.

The Sandspit at San Miguel, which usually has breaking, confused waves, and can be seen from several miles away, was calm this day. As we made our way up the backside, past Crooks Point and Tyler Bight, the sun was well up into the sky. The water was a deep, clear blue, indicating perfect dive conditions.

Nine days later we were dog-tired, on our way home from San Miguel, five miles from home with 9,000 pounds stacked on the deck. The ocean was still flat, but a storm was forecast to hit that night and we were ready for some time off.

Dewey had been in a great mood all week, and had almost smiled—twice. "This is the best stretch we've ever had," he chortled. "If we have 9,000 on board, it'll give us 84,000 pounds for the nine-day stretch, and if we get our sixteen cents a pound, that'll be almost 8,000 bucks for me, 3,700 for Jerome, and 2,000 for you." We were all happy and glad to be in the business of diving and working on boats, far from the traffic and offices of the landlubbers.

Dewey joined Jerome below as I steered the *Hound Dog* toward home. We were in a thick fog bank, but were on course, and the dangers of being hit by a freighter were miles behind us.

Prior to the days of radar and electronic navigation, which was still several years in the future for us, we had a foolproof method for finding our way home in the fog. The compass heading would be set about five degrees up the coast from home, and when the fathometer indicated sixty feet, we turned the boat to the right and hugged the shore down toward the harbor. In a few minutes the sound of the foghorn told us we were close. Soon after, the beacon light at the end of the breakwater would split the fog.

Each harbor entrance has its own peculiarities—some are straightforward, and easy to find and negotiate. Others require several jogs to the right or left before one is safely inside the boat basin. The entrance to the Santa Barbara harbor can be tricky, especially in the fog. After clearing the end of the breakwater, the boat must be kept at a safe distance from the sand spit on the left, while staying parallel to Stearns Wharf, off the starboard side.

This night, as the beacon light came into view, Dewey stuck his head out of the cabin.

"How's it look?' He was bleary eyed, but always aware of what was happening aboard his boat.

"We're almost inside the harbor, go back to sleep," I replied. He flopped back on his bunk as I swung the boat around the breakwater wall. Just then, a hazy orange glow appeared off our starboard side. Now I could see—flames! Through a curtain of fog it came into view, a boat, drifting on its anchor, ablaze.

"Hey you guys, get out here. There's a boat on fire!" I hollered. Keeping the *Hound Dog* parallel to the wharf while watching the fire, I neglected to make the subtle left turn that takes you into the harbor basin. As Dewey climbed out of the cabin, we hit the beach; the boat slammed to a stop, the prop dug into the sand, and the motor died. As the three of us were pitched forward, the load shifted and the boat lurched. Dewey fell on the urchins with both hands.

The red sea urchin, the type we harvest, has long thin spines that contain a toxin poisonous to small fish and extremely irritating to humans. Every diver I've ever known has been to the hospital and gone under the knife at least once to have spines taken out of his body. Some have had long-term problems and a few have been permanently disabled.

After falling on the urchins, Dewey had two handfuls of spines. He was not a happy captain. It was midnight. All three of us were fully clothed, chest-deep in the cold smelly water of the harbor, trying to pull the boat off the sand. The harbor patrol rescue boat drove by and Dewey yelled. "Our boat is aground, we need assistance!" They replied over their loudspeaker, "Stand by. We're enroute to a burning vessel."

With the help of a rising tide we eventually got the *Hound Dog* floating, but it was four in the morning by the time we finished unloading and put her in the slip.

Dewey and I hauled the boat out the following day to flush the sand from the outdrive and make sure it was all right.

"Everything seems to be okay," Dewey said. "One of the prop blades is bent, but it's repairable. I'll send it down to Valley Prop in Ventura. They should have it back in a few days."

"Well, let me know how much I owe you, boss. That was a dumb mistake I made, driving us right up on to the beach."

A sober look was on his face. "I'll take care of it."

"How's the hand?" I stupidly asked. The multiple stab wounds had caused his left hand to swell dramatically. It was puffy and red, and he could not make a fist.

"It'll be okay." His eyes remained fixed on the propeller.

After taking care of his boat, Dewey went to the hospital to have several spines removed from his hand.

Three of them were not bad, but one had penetrated deep into the tissue. The doctor had to open up a two-inch section before he was able to remove it, putting our skipper out of commission temporarily.

## The Hunting Grounds

There is no doubt about it—Santa Barbara is a beautiful town. The entire waterfront area, with Stearns Wharf and the harbor, is spectacular, and the sparkling waters of the ocean and the Channel Islands can be seen from all over town. The whole expanse is framed by the Santa Barbara Mountains, creating a dramatic backdrop.

Cabrillo Boulevard parallels the beach; on any given day, people are walking, jogging, rollerblading, or biking along the concrete path that winds through the sand adjacent to the waves.

Across from the foot of the wharf is the bottom of State Street, the main avenue of the city, which divides it east and west. The natural geography of the area is magnificent, and the Spanish architecture and many hacienda-style buildings give the town a distinct personality that is unique along the entire West Coast.

The most attractive thing about the city are the women who reside there. Nowhere on earth is there such a collection of radiant, exquisite, and bewitching females. Their beauty is astonishing and they are ubiquitous in this wonderful city. Blondes, brunettes, redheads. Short, tall, large, and small. Intelligent, aloof, friendly, and distant. They are the most attractive women in the world, and they know it. The Santa Barbara woman knows that a snap of her fingers will bring as many suitors as she requires.

The gathering place for many of these delightful treasures is State Street, and the bars, pubs, and eateries that abound in this small but exciting area.

Just as the native Chumash Indians were blessed with Santa Barbara's rich hunting grounds, so are the men of today. Like their counterparts of the prior millennium who could gather the delicious abalone simply by walking along the tide pools at low tide and plucking them off the rocks, the men of Santa Barbara hunt their prey in places like Joe's Café, Harry's, or the infamous Rocky Galentes.

The enticing game they seek, however, is not as easy to capture as the unsuspecting shellfish or acorns gathered by the Chumash. In fact, in many cases the hunter becomes the hunted. Upon entering an establishment known for this age-old contest, a man finds himself on display. He is subjected to careful scrutiny by the very objects he is admiring.

An intelligent species, these splendid creatures can easily detect insincerity or a person of evil intent. They will accept or deny the advances of their pursuers at their whim, or sometimes toy with them, as only a supremely confident gamefish can. Often the fisherman feels sure the game he has been patiently stalking has taken his hook and is ready to be reeled in. Then, with a sudden flick of its tail, the object of his desire is gone. The poor soul is left alone. He retreats in humiliation and loneliness.

Some contenders have an advantage over others in the hunting grounds of State Street. A contestant with large amounts of money is always near the top of the list. Good looks help, and a well-conditioned body, bristling with muscles, is a plus.

There is one thing, however, one possession, that is consistently successful at landing one of these delightful prizes.

In hopes of capturing his plunder, it is necessary for the potential suitor to mention a fact about himself that he hopes will bring about interest from the object of his current quest. Phrases such as, "My new Porsche runs so much better than the old one," or "Since the trees were trimmed, the ocean view from my hot tub has really improved."

There is one thing though, one tool, the one word that in most cases clinches the outcome and sends his competitors away in defeat.

A typical conversation in a pub on State Street might go something like this:

"I'm so glad I bought that stock last year—it's gone through the roof."

"You're a stock trader?" She raises her eyebrows.

"Oh, I just dabble. My real love is real estate acquisition." Knowing that she has this one securely in her clutches, she turns to the rather weathered-looking chap at the same table who has also expressed interest in her.

"Do you have a home here, too?" She asks. He answers nonchalantly, "Yes, but I spend most of my time down at the harbor, on my boat."

A silence envelops the table as the magic word has been spoken. The secret weapon has been used. He has cast his lure. She quickly turns her head. "You have a boat?"

The eyes of the stock trader fall to the floor. With that one word, he knows he has been bested. Almost immediately his eyes begin searching the room for another target, as this one has eluded him.

The suntanned man with the jeans and tee shirt closes his trap: "Yeah, it's just a little twenty-five-footer, but it's great for trips out to the islands, and she sleeps two comfortably.

"The islands? I've always wanted to go out there. They're so beautiful! I would just die to take a trip to the islands!"

He knows his fish is caught, and he puts her in his net. "As a matter of fact, I was just heading down there to anchor up by the wharf and watch the sunset. You're welcome to join me."

For the single man in Santa Barbara, having a boat down at the harbor is almost like having an unfair advantage over the competition. I knew one urchin diver who put an ad in the local newspaper, the Santa Barbara News Press: "Female cook needed for fishing boat. Must enjoy the Channel Islands." It was shameless, but he always had a steady supply of young beauties on his boat with him, no matter that his galley consisted of a propane hot plate and a one-man barbecue.

I had owned my old cabin cruiser, the *Heidi Marie*, for about five months, and although I had done a fair amount of work on her, there was no escaping the fact that it was an old boat with a plywood hull that leaked and was for the most part not very attractive. She'd only been out of the slip a few times for two simple reasons. One, the motor tended to die. I'd changed the spark plugs and tuned it up, but the problem persisted; the other obstacle for me was that she was a difficult boat to drive. Instead of having an outdrive, like the *Little Wing* and the *Hound Dog* , my boat had a shaft, with a small rudder. This type of steering system is not as complex as an outdrive, but is more difficult to maneuver. I'd been practicing, but still had a hard time controlling her. The toughest part was avoiding the new sailboat docked next to me while putting her in the slip.

While at a crowded table at Rocky Galentes, in the heart of the hunting grounds, I was introduced to a pretty blonde who, my friend told me, was a local piano teacher. Her name was Debbie Shannon, and she seemed to express an interest in me after learning that I had a boat. As expected, she accepted an invitation for an afternoon boat ride, and we were soon walking down the squeaky dock of Marina Three toward the *Heidi Marie*.

The ocean was calm with a warm sea air as we idled out of the harbor. I had a feeling my efforts were going to be rewarded.

The area just east of Stearn's Wharf is protected from the afternoon breezes and is a favorite spot to anchor up and enjoy the company (and hopefully passion) of a friend.

My new acquaintance was enchanting. She had the lightest blue eyes I had ever seen and an alluring smile that captivated me. I swung the boat around the wharf and began looking for a likely spot to throw the anchor. "Are you from around here?" I asked.

"I grew up in San Jose and came here to attend UCSB four years ago. I love it here now, and can't imagine living anywhere else. How about you?"

I told her of my time in Hawaii and subsequent move to the central coast of California. "I can't imagine living anywhere else either."

She told me she had majored in music. She shared an apartment with a friend and was teaching piano to forty students. "I have a blue Volkswagen Beetle, but I ride my bike to most of my student's homes to save money." She had an easygoing confidence that attracted and aroused me. I liked what I was hearing, and even more so, what I was seeing.

We found a likely spot, and as I went forward to put the anchor down she gave me a knowing look. It was as though she could read my mind and agreed to what I was thinking.

"Which island is that?" She pointed offshore. I felt it was a good time to further impress her.

"That's Santa Cruz. It was named by Sebastian Viscaino, the Spanish explorer. As the story goes, a priest on Viscaino's ship left his walking stick on the island. The staff, whose end had the shape of a cross, was given up for lost, but was found and returned by the local Indians. From that day on, it was called Isla de Santa Cruz, Island of the Holy Cross."

The rusty old anchor splashed into the calm water, and as I watched it fall to the bottom, I couldn't help but be grateful for the life I was leading. I had finally found a line of work that I truly loved. There was a boat under my feet and a beautiful woman waiting for me inside the cabin. Plus my new surfboard would be ready next week. Life could not be better.

I was jolted out of my daydream just as the end of the anchor line flew over the bow. In my temporary fantasy state I had forgotten about the rope paying out from the anchor box, and I had neglected to tie it off. The last strand of anchor line waved at me as it disappeared into the depths.

Embarrassed by my blunder, I notified my guest that the anchor was lost, there was no spare, and we needed to return to the marina.

"Why don't we sit on the boat and enjoy the sunset from your slip?" Sensing there might still be hope after all, and that my hunting skills might yet be rewarded, I turned and headed back to the harbor. During the short ride, she casually put her hand on the back of my neck, gently massaging it, and in a mysterious, unspoken way, she let me know that everything was okay. I felt at ease. As she expertly tickled and rubbed my neck, a strange feeling came over me. An intangible feeling that something felt right.

As we turned into Marina Three, I concentrated on putting the boat into the slip, but just as we were safely in, the motor sputtered and died. I had shifted into reverse to stop it, but there was no power as we drifted in. We bounced off the dock and hit the sailboat next to me, where my neighbor was sitting in a chair on his back deck with a friend. His wine spilled, and as we gently crashed into him, his fetching companion almost fell over. "Sonofabitch! I can't even sit on the deck of my boat and enjoy the afternoon in peace!" He issued forth a string of colorful expletives while glaring at me menacingly. Then his gaze strayed from me to my new friend, and his anger withered as he blushed and fell under her spell.

My master plan had been a complete disaster. I had lost my anchor, put a scratch in my neighbor's boat, and embarrassed myself beyond recognition. Debbie Shannon, the piano teacher, seemed amazingly unfazed at my ineptness. She gave me a piece of paper with her telephone number on it. "I hope I'll be hearing from you soon." She whispered. Then she was gone.

My seamanship skills had failed me that day, along with my boat handling. More important though, my hunting capabilities had run aground and the prey had escaped.

On the other hand, Debbie Shannon's initial foraging had proved successful. The piano teacher had captured my heart.

## Wes

Dewey's hand was worse than suspected. The doctor had cut out as much of the spine as he could find, but after the wound healed, it got infected and had to be reopened. After another surgery and a week's worth of antibiotics though, it healed up, and seemed to be okay. A month and a half later Dewey was able to dive, and the hand worked pretty well, but unfortunately the damage had been done. He would never be able to make a fist again.

Any story of the Santa Barbara sea urchin fishery would not be complete without mentioning Wes Carpenter.

Wes was recruited by one of the original processors to coordinate things between the dock at Santa Barbara and the processing plants in Los Angeles. He was paid half a cent for every pound that he offloaded.

Divers had to call Wes early in the morning to let him know they were headed out to work. On the way home, the boat skippers would make a radio call to report when they would arrive at the dock, and how much weight they were carrying. Wes would then phone the processor and order up a truck or two, depending on the amount of product he was expecting.

In the early evening he headed down and met the boats as they arrived. Not overly prone to neatness, he usually arrived at the dock with several days worth of whiskers on his face. A growing belly, which he called his "table muscle," protruded from underneath a dirty tee shirt, and what was left of any hair on his thirty-five-year-old head had not seen a comb for years.

The trucks would be waiting on the dock. Wes's trained thumb deftly operated the hoist button, lifting bags of urchins from the boats up onto the truck. A worker carefully untied the knot on the bottom of the bag, dumping the spiny creatures onto the growing pile. After the days catch was tallied, the skipper was given a fish ticket.

Eventually, the other processors started using Wes, and it wasn't long before he was rolling in the dough.

Wes became somewhat of a father figure for the divers. If, after a night of partying, someone found himself in the drunk tank, it was Wes who got the phone call. Of course, it was in his best interest to bail out the culprit, for if one was incarcerated, he had no way of making Wes any money. But the truth was that Wes had a good heart, and could be counted on to help out if you got in a bind.

He was generous, and to our great delight he was a money spender, not a money saver. Sometimes he'd organize a group of divers to go bar hopping on State Street, and pick everyone up in a limo. Wes was well liked by all who knew him—he was honest too, sealing all his business deals with a handshake.

After four years of putting in long hours on the dock, sometimes till dawn, Wes hired a helper. He could now afford the trip to Egypt that he had always wanted to take.

"Hey, this is Wes!" The voice on the telephone was music to my ears. He had returned from his three-week vacation, and had been missed by all of us. "Get over here, and see what I bought!"

By the time I arrived, there were over twenty people crammed inside his small house on the west side of town, with a loud party in full swing. Large quantities of liquor and weed were consumed, eyes were bloodshot, rock and roll music roared. Wes was back in town and was being welcomed by his flock.

"All right, turn off the music." Wes's booming voice quieted the room. "I want you all to see the souvenir I acquired in Egypt."

As the room became silent, he opened a closet door and pulled out a cardboard box about six feet long, wrapped with twine.

"Give me a hand, Jerome." The two men carried the container into the middle of the room. "Be careful, we don't want to injure her." We all looked at each other.

Our host was clearly enjoying the suspense. The room was silent. "Turn the lights down, " he whispered. As he began to unwrap his curio, a drunken voice piped up.

"I'll bet it's a blow-up girlfriend." Nervous laughter rippled around the house.

"Are you ready for this?" Wes removed the lid, proudly displaying his trophy.

Upon seeing the vaguely human form, it took a few seconds to register.

"What the hell?" I said.

"It's a dead body!" one of the wives screamed, nearly fainting.

Immediate sobriety overtook the room as we gazed at the gray figure wrapped in tattered, decomposing rags. No one breathed.

"It's a mummy!" Wes exclaimed. "I bought it on the black market and smuggled it out," he bellowed with undeniable pride. "Look, you can see the fingers!"

One of the girls puked.

Finally, someone spoke. "Jesus Christ, Wes! That's gross!" We inched forward for closer inspection.

"Unbelievable." Hydroplane Steve Hagen spoke up. "You're one in a million, Wes. What the hell are you gonna do with it?"

"Keep it in my closet, show it to my friends!" came the reply. "Ain't it cool?"

People came from near and far to see the mummy in Wes's closet.

Wes disappeared one day. The rumor on the dock was that it was part of his tax-planning strategy.

I got a call from him about six months later from, sure enough, Costa Rica. He told me he was brokering fish, and he could set me up down there. I've always regretted not going down to check it out.

Wes was in Central America for several years, but we had not seen the last of him.

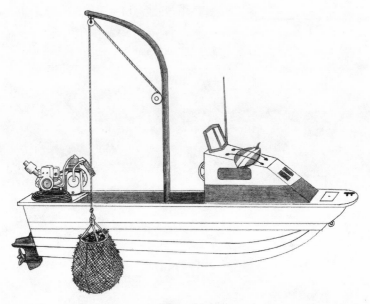

*1979 Radon 24´ dive boat*

## The Dive Team

The preferred dive hose of a 1970s urchin diver was a Gates 33HB. The inner diameter, the part that air flows through, is three-eighths of an inch. The outer dimension is seven-eighths of an inch, similar to a garden hose, only much stiffer. It is a black, multi-sheathed hose, heavy, and will not kink. It is difficult for the diver to pull off of the boat; the farther you get from the boat, the harder it is to pull. Handling the hose above water is not easy either— a three-hundred-foot hose, coiled in a four-foot area, stands two-feet high and weighs eighty pounds.

Hydroplane Steve Hagen was the first diver I knew of to switch to the thin-walled, lightweight plastic Keflex hose. Intended for industrial spraying, the two-ply hose feeds off of the boat easily, its yellow color is easy to spot, and it only weighs fifteen pounds. When a diver first uses the light hose he discovers a new freedom—his once cumbersome tether is gone. His new hose slides easily through the water, slipping smoothly off of the kelp leaves. At times he is unaware there is even a hose attached to him.

There are two disadvantages in using this hose. First, the skin is not as tough as the Gates hose so it damages more easily. If it gets hung up on something sharp, such as a propeller blade or an underwater reef, it can be cut. Rarely will the damage to the hose be severe, but periodically sections of hose need to be removed, and new sections spliced in, using a portable banding tool. A new hose only has two bands—one at each end. After five years it might have twenty bands from all the splicing.

Another, more serious problem with the thinner hose is kinking. A hose can kink from grabbing a cleat on the boat above, or by getting caught on an underwater reef. An improperly coiled hose or a tangle can cause a kink as well.

The diver with a kinked hose simply backtracks a few feet which usually relieves the tautness on the hose, allowing air to once more flow freely through it. A kinked hose does not always fix itself though, and the sudden loss of air can be terrifying. All sea urchin divers have stories of losing their air and having to quickly disconnect and bail out to the surface. These rapid ascents are performed only as a last resort for they invite the possibility of internal injury or death from the bends. But even with the periodic kinking that occurs with the lighter hose, their comfort and ease of use caused the majority of divers to switch to them by the early 1980s.

A properly coiled dive hose will feed off of the boat by itself as the diver pulls on it from below. Two types of hose coils are used. The figure-eight coil lays the hose down in the shape of an eight, using an area of deck covering about five feet. On the Radon and Wilson Boats, the hose sits on the engine lid, in the aft section. A figure-eight coil feeds nicely off of the boat, rarely getting tangled. However, it uses a large area and this type of coil is normally only used with a single diver operation.

The more common coil is the over-under. The hose is laid in a circle, with each coil alternating over and under. When the hose is properly coiled, it feeds off of the boat adequately, and it takes up less space, allowing for two hoses side by side.

The duties of a seasoned tender are many. Upon reaching the dive location, wetsuits and dive gear are laid out on the engine lid, ready for use. Hoses have been untied and positioned to the rear of the lid, with the Hansen quick-disconnect fitting in sight, and ready for the diver to grab. The first mesh bags of the day are standing by, ready for use, with the remaining bags stowed on the cabin roof. After removing the waterproof cover of the air system, the gas in the compressor motor is topped off. Bag lines are made ready, neatly coiled and ready to throw.

When the divers hit the water and start harvesting, the tender shifts to another mode: he now has a watchful eye on the hoses, keeping them free and loose and helping the divers by tossing a few coils in the water as the hose is leaving the boat. Bubbles from below mark the diver's location. A good tender always knows where his divers are.

Large volumes of bubbles hitting the surface indicate the diver is filling his floater ball with air and will be up momentarily. Now, the tender pulls all slack from the hose. The diver surfaces and gives a hand signal for the tender to pull him in. Divers like to hang on to their bag and be pulled quickly through the water, pushing kelp leaves out of the way, cutting them with a blade that is welded onto their picking rake, or simply biting through them with his teeth. The tender braces his feet and pulls hard as the full bag smoothly glides through the water. When diver and bag are within twenty feet of the boat, a bag line, which has been thrown by the tender, is snapped to the lifting ring of the bag. An experienced tender is able to throw the line thirty feet or more, placing the snap within a foot or two of his diver. The diver now leaves his bag floating and swims toward the boat. A hand signal will tell the tender if another bag is wanted, in which case it is thrown to the diver. In an instant, he is on his way back down.

The filled bag is pulled toward the boat, cleated off, attached to the lifting boom and winched onto the deck. While performing his duties on deck, a watchful eye is kept on the hoses and bubbles, for if one of his divers surfaces, the tender must be ready to stop what he is doing and take care of him.

Urchin diving is competitive. All divers want to out-pick their partners, no matter how good of friends they are. Once they are in the water working, the game is on and they are moving fast. If both divers surface simultaneously and are screaming for a bag line, the tender has to make a quick decision who to handle first. The logical choice of course, is the skipper, who writes the checks.

Several times a day the boat must be moved, sometimes five or more, in order to stay in decent picking. It's the tender's job to make sure all hoses and lines are out of the water, to pull the anchor up, and to be ready to drop it when given the signal. All movements on a day-tripping boat have to be fast and efficient, for time is of the essence.

After the last bag of the day is aboard, the tender neatly coils the hoses, ties them on to the engine lid handle, and covers the compressor. Now the captain is at the helm and the motor is running. He stays in his suit in case the anchor gets stuck, which seems to happen every month or two. The tender scampers forward, walking gingerly on the rail to avoid the urchins. He pulls up the hook, then climbs into the steering area to take the helm. The divers are now up on the bow peeling off their wetsuits, which they toss to the tender, who stows them. The three-man crew is now on its way home.

When the boat is in the slip, the engine room is usually the owner's domain. Everyplace else belongs to the tender. The walk–on diver has no responsibilities other than showing up for work on time and diving.

The harvesting bags are kept neatly stacked on deck, with four tightly wound thirty-foot bag lines sitting on top of the pile. Wetsuits are laid out on top of the hoses, which are neatly coiled on the engine lid. From a distance they look like two black bodies side by side, arms splayed outward.

Each diver owns a mesh gear bag that holds his mask, fins, gloves, picking tool, and any gauges he wears. These might be a decompression meter (bendomatic), depth gauge, and sometimes a compass. The gear bags are kept locked inside the cabin, but the suits remain outside, due mostly to the smell, for try as they might there is not a bladder in the fleet that can hold on for several hours underwater. It's only a matter of time before a brand new suit takes on the faint smell of urine.

Once in a while a diver worries about his suit getting stolen off the boat, so he locks it inside the cabin. After opening the door the next day though, and stepping into a cabin that smells like a giant diaper, he decides to risk stowing the suit outside. Stealing items off of a boat is a cowardly practice that sometimes happens, but in my nine years of working out of the Santa Barbara Harbor, I cannot recall anything ever being stolen off of an urchin boat.

Once a week the cover is taken off of the air-compressor unit, which is bolted to the rear deck, on the port side. A thorough soaking with WD-40 ensues, followed by a fresh water rinse and a paper towel wipe down. This exercise is a feeble attempt at staving off the inevitable rust and seizing up and breakage of anything kept outside in a salt air environment.

Every few weeks the cabin needs to be cleaned out. Sleeping bags and foam bunk pads are placed on the deck and aired out to prevent mildew from forming. Soggy tortilla chips are disposed of and the cabin is wiped down with a mild disinfectant. A few hours later the dried out foam pads and sleeping bags are returned to the now clean cabin.

Some of the more seasoned tenders are allowed to take the boat to the fuel dock for gas. This is considered a privilege; only the most competent and deserving tender is given this job. An experienced tender in the 1970s was usually paid 15 percent of the load for the many tasks he was expected to perform, but being the low man on the totem pole, he was also expected to shoulder the blame for any problems that arose during the course of a work day. Simply put, whatever goes wrong is always the tender's fault.

My pay as tender ranged from eighty to two hundred and fifty dollars per day, depending on the price, and our poundage. But my sights were now set in a new direction. I yearned for the day when I would put on the wetsuit and be a diver. And although the pay was more, that wasn't the only reason. I wanted to be swimming in the ocean, not stuck up on the boat.

# New Directions

*We must let go of the life we have planned, so as to accept the one that is waiting for us.*

—Joseph Campbell

## Jumping In

I was feeling terribly guilty about running the *Hound Dog* up on the beach. No harm had come to the boat though, and the expense to clean out the outdrive and fix the bent prop was minor. Dewey's hand was another matter. He never spoke of it though, so I didn't either.

We were back at it in late January, on the fourth day of a good stretch. By now, we were a well-honed team. The three of us got along well and the *Hound Dog* was one of the top producers in the fleet—a highliner. We were one of about twenty boats working out of Santa Barbara at the time, with maybe ten boats out of Channel Islands Harbor in Oxnard, to the south of us. The coastal kelp beds in San Diego were being harvested by five or six boats.

Tyler Bight, a large cove east of Adams, had become our new spot. The picking was good, and the lack of sea lions made things a little easier on our nerves.

The anchor was down. It was time to go to work. "Rise and shine, you two. We're in twenty feet of water and I see polka dots on the bottom." Prying those two out of their bunks on a chilly morning was sometimes the hardest part of my job.

Jerome finally made it out on deck and began suiting up. Dewey was still curled up inside and wasn't moving. When he got up, he looked bad. "I think I might be sick," he murmured quietly. "My wife has a bad cold. I think I'm coming down with it." Then he went back inside the cabin and fell into his bunk. A few minutes later he stuck his head out. "I'm down for the day. You can use my gear if you want to do some diving."

I was stunned. "You sure?" I asked.

"Go for it. My suit should fit you fine. Just don't drown, and try to make me some money. I'm going back to sleep."

I'd trained as a scuba diver at the Diver's Den over on Anacapa Street, received my certification, and had made several dives with tanks, but never with a hookah rig. "It's a lot nicer," Jerome chuckled. "You don't have the weight or the bulkiness of the tank on your back. You'll have a much lighter feeling, and more freedom."

Jerome helped me with the gear. Dewey and I were about the same height and weight, making it easy for me. His weight belt was a little heavier than what I was used to, but only by a few pounds, so I didn't bother removing any weights.

After coating my body with a thin layer of sweet-smelling hair conditioner and slipping into the wetsuit, Jerome checked me out on the regulator harness, showed me how to put it on, and explained the quick-disconnect fitting that attaches the diver to his hose. "If for any reason you need to get free of your hose, just grab the Hanson fitting and pop it off, like this." Fortunately, my feet were the same size as the skippers, making it unnecessary to readjust the swim fin straps. His mask did not seal against my face perfectly, but it was adequate.

Jerome got the finicky air compressor started after three pulls on the cord. "Jump in and take a look around. Get comfortable, then come up and I'll toss you a bag. Break open an urchin every few minutes and make sure the roe inside is yellow and fat. A piece of roe should be about the size of your thumb. If it's brown, or skinny, don't pick in that area. Move to where the kelp is thicker." He was clearly enjoying his new role of dive instructor, and he was giggling as I flopped over the side into the clear water of Tyler Bight.

Suddenly I was in a new world. Gone was the noise of the compressor motor; all was quiet now, except for the sound of my breathing and the bubbles escaping from the regulator in my mouth. Hundreds of brightly colored fish darted about. Rockfish of all types—China cod, chucklehead, vermillion. A big ugly sheepshead with deformed teeth swam by, oblivious to the large black rubber newcomer. A small bright orange spot flitted about in the distance. As it came closer I could see that it was a Garibaldi, one of the prettiest fish in the sea, and the California State Saltwater Fish.

Kelp stalks swayed lazily in the underwater breeze. Calico bass hovered around the large brown leaves of the floating kelp canopy. The water was shallow—twenty feet, and crystal clear, with visibility close to forty feet.

After swimming down to the bottom, I spotted the anchor safely burrowed into a small sand channel. Sparkling rays of light shown down from above, and looking up, I could see the misshapen image of the boat floating above.

A sharp tug on my hose brought me out of my underwater stupor. After slowly swimming to the surface, I saw Jerome standing on the back deck. "What are you doing down there, let's get to work!" he shouted. I had forgotten all about urchin harvesting and had been sightseeing for ten minutes. "Toss me a bag!" I shouted confidently. I was ready to start picking. He handed me the large mesh bag off the side of the boat. "Don't pick the babies, nothing smaller than a baseball." He then jumped in with his bag off the other side of the boat.

I began my descent, but before getting halfway to the bottom, I got tangled in the mesh of the bag. The rake, which was in my right hand, got stuck in the net and I was unable to free it. Next, I managed to get wrapped up in a kelp stalk, and although I was kicking furiously, the hose seemed to tie itself around the underwater trees. The extra weight of Dewey's belt took over, speeding my descent. I landed on the bottom, upside down in a tangled mess of kelp, dive hose, and net. Fortunately, I was in a sand channel and had not landed on a rock, or worse, a sea urchin. As I attempted to escape from my self imposed trap, my breathing sped up, and I began to hyperventilate.

Jerome was about twenty feet away, watching in amusement. He swam over, helped me out of my mess, and put a few urchins in my bag. Pointing me in the direction of a good patch, he then went back to his area and resumed his work. He swam back to check on me periodically to make sure I was okay. Once, he snuck up behind me and gave one of my fins a yank, almost giving me a heart attack. Another time, he gathered a handful of small rocks, hovered above me, and released them. It was raining rocks on my head, courtesy of Jerome, the underwater prankster.

It wasn't long before I became acclimated and began to get the hang of it. The urchins were clinging to the reef tightly though, and I broke several of them before figuring out how to dislodge the delicate creatures.

Jerome swam by. I stopped and watched in wonder as he glided effortlessly through the kelp jungle, quickly snatching up urchin after urchin, deftly placing them into his bag. Sometimes he quickly tapped three or four at a time with his rake, breaking their hold on the reef. Then, with one smooth motion he swept them into the bag. His one year of harvesting had given him the skill necessary to efficiently capture the urchins without breaking their thin shells.

He never touched the bottom. Only the tips of his rake, which acted as an extension of his arm, swiftly darted out from his body in rapid succession, careful to take only what he came for. Watching him made me feel clumsy and slow, but I kept plodding away, eventually filling my bag.

My transition from deckhand to diver that day at Tyler Bight was less than spectacular, but I had managed to harvest almost two thousand pounds in spite of myself. It was a fair amount of weight for my first day, but was due more to the perfect weather conditions and abundance of urchins rather than any skill on my part. Dewey knew the kelp beds of San Miguel, and he had put the boat in a virgin area—easy picking.

Jerome landed almost five thousand pounds for his efforts, which was quite amazing, as he had to climb out of the water every hour to winch the bags up, and make ready new ones. He out-picked me three to one, plus he did all the tending.

On the way home that night, Dewey was feeling better, and he drove his shift while listening to my stories of net traps and raining rocks.

"Do I need a special license for diving?" I asked Dewey.

"No, your commercial fishing license is all you need." Then he glanced at me. " I have a feeling I may have lost my tender."

"Yup."

Debbie Shannon, the piano teacher, and now my girlfriend, was waiting on the dock when we arrived. "I had cookies and juice for you guys, but I made the mistake of offering some to the other boats that unloaded before you. They ate them all!"

"Those pirates!" Jerome shouted. "I'm starving!"

"I'll bring more next time."

The next day I drove to the Wetsuit Factory on Haley Street, where all the divers had their suits custom made. Walking into the large room, I was greeted by a unique smell, the combination of toxic wetsuit glue coupled with cigar smoke. An old man with short white hair sat hunched over a table in a corner; a pair of scissors in his hand carefully followed the pattern on the large piece of rubber spread out in front of him. A cloud of smoke encircled his head from a three-inch cigar stub that was clamped in his teeth. "Can I help you?" he said out of the side of his mouth, keeping his head down and the scissors moving.

I told him I needed a suit for diving urchins.

"Uh huh. Been getting quite a few of those lately. The sport guys use quarter-inch rubber, but they're only on the bottom for thirty minutes at a time. You need three-eighths. Take your shirt off, I'll be with you in a minute."

After finishing cutting on the piece of rubber, he laid the scissors on the table and turned to face me. He looked over the top of his glasses, but only his eyes moved. His head stayed down and his shoulders remained hunched.

He was not a small man, but years of being in this position made him seem so, for I think that standing up straight was no longer an option for him. An arthritic hand reached out. "I'm Don." The words came from the left side of his mouth, while the right side remained firmly clenched on the stogie. "I make two-piece suits—a farmer john-style bottom, and a hooded top with a beaver tail. If you want, I can sew on a quarter-inch face piece, which will butt up against your mask, keeping any skin contact with the water at a minimum. Some of the guys like pockets in the farmer john legs—they put a few pounds of lead in them to help distribute their weight—helps to keep from getting a backache after three or four hours underwater. I charge two hundred for the basic suit. Face seams and pockets are twenty dollars each. What size shoe do you wear?" Size twelve I told him. "You need extra-large booties—they're thirty dollars."

The next five minutes were spent measuring me—arms, legs, head circumference, neck, inseam. He must have taken over twenty measurements, carefully writing each one down on an order sheet.

"Okay, that's it. I need a hundred dollars. Your suit should be ready in a week. What boat are you on?" Upon learning I was with Dewey and Jerome, he glanced up over the top of his glasses. His head bobbed with a short nod of approval. "Hard workers, those two. I'll give you a call next week." He turned and shuffled back to his cutting table.

This was my first encounter with Don Duckett, founder of the Wetsuit Factory, whose high quality suits were to become the preferred work uniform of commercial divers worldwide.

I walked outside, happy to be away from the noxious fumes of the shop, and took in a refreshing breath of the automobile traffic on Haley Street.

"Crazy" Harold Shrout was the man to see for regulator whips and picking rakes. After locating his house in Goleta and waiting my turn behind another diver, I introduced myself and told him of my needs. He kept a few of his standard three piece regulator whips made up and ready to go—all that was needed was to adjust the belt to fit me.

Choosing a picking rake was another story—there were many different styles to choose from. There is no standard for this tool, they are as individual as the diver wielding them. A one-piece rake, consisting of a length of stainless rod that had been bent into a U shape, was light and comfortable. Jerome used this type. Another style, which was a bit more complicated, was a welded contraption, with an angled hand grip and a blade for cutting kelp. Other rakes were essentially garden tools that had been modified. I quickly gravitated to the welded rake, since it was the type used by Dewey, and the only style I had used in my one day of being an urchin diver.

A pair of industrial gloves made of thick green rubber were purchased from Harold as well. All I needed now was a gear bag, depth gauge and a mask, which were purchased at the Divers Den in town.

Acquiring these items, the tools of the diving trade, solidified my entrance into the world of urchin diving. The total cost of my gear in 1979 was almost $600, a substantial amount indicating a high level of commitment.

Tenders come and go. A single trip to the islands is enough for some, and they quickly realize that working on the ocean is not for them. There is no real responsibility, financially or verbally. If a tender wants to quit, he simply does not show up on the boat. A diver assumes a new level of obligation. He now has a monetary stake. His gear is stowed on the boat he is working on—he is expected to show up for work.

Up to now, when the waves got good, I could drop everything and go surfing—it was my lifestyle. I was now a diver, and had to assume the new, deeper responsibilities that came with it.

## The Curse of the Chumash

The sea urchin trade was growing, becoming a viable business for adventurous young entrepreneurs who were willing to take risks. More dive boats were being built, most of them at the Radon yard across the street from Stearns Wharf. Radons were the most popular dive boat, due to their strength, comfortable ride, and ability to pack the heavy urchin loads.

A forward-thinking abalone diver, Harold Shrout, converted his Goleta garage into a workshop and began building air-compressor systems for the rapidly expanding urchin fleet. His eccentric ways soon earned him the dubious title "Crazy Harold."

It was about this time, in the spring of 1979, that the crew of the *Hound Dog* disbanded. Jerome had gone out on his own and was having a boat built by Brian Wilson, a new boat builder on the scene. Dewey was also building a new boat, an innovative mid-engine design with a high-speed diesel engine. He was doing most of the work himself, so the diving on the *Hound Dog* slowed down.

I was on my own now. My diving skills had reached an adequate level of proficiency, allowing me to feel comfortable working on other boats in the fleet. The training Dewey and Jerome had given me on the *Hound Dog* was invaluable, but it was now time to move on.

After making a few trips on other boats, the *Spirit* became my steady home. There was nothing particularly special about the *Spirit*, in fact in some ways it was a step down from my prior accommodations.

Also a Radon thirty-two, she was gray, with a large cabin. She was one of the original Radons, built of fiberglass over wood, and heavier than the new molded fiberglass hulls. A well-stocked built-in galley and propane stove sat between the bunks, which were side by side. Another bunk was built overhead, allowing the *Spirit* to sleep three. It was the first overnighter I worked on and it was on this boat that I discovered the joy of being gently rocked to sleep at night under the stars, and waking to the smell of bacon, and bright, blinding sunlight reflecting off the water.

Several stress cracks on the decks of the *Spirit* required constant patching. Instead of a mast-and-boom system such as the *Hound Dog* had, the *Spirit* used a davit, and could load bags from only one side of the boat. This was a minor inconvenience, sometimes requiring the diver to swim his full bag of urchins under the boat, or be pulled around by the tender, in order to hook it up.

The redeeming quality of the *Spirit* was its crew, Duane and Robin Brown. Duane, owner and captain, was a recreational diver who saw the promise of the new sea urchin fishery early on. He was one of the first urchin divers in the state, having broken in at the very beginning, 1973, working for a nickel a pound. At fifty years old, Duane was a seasoned veteran diver of the Channel Islands. He had little formal education, and for the most part spoke in very simple terms, but his knowledge of the islands and boats was limitless.

Duane was a little on the heavy side. The man loved to eat; it was his hobby. His favorite food was spaghetti with canned meat sauce, and he could eat it by the barrel. He was not a fast eater—he paced himself, sometimes requiring up to two hours to complete an evening meal. The cabins of most dive boats smelled of wetsuits and moldy cushions, but the *Spirit* had an overpowering aroma of spaghetti sauce.

Short, with a ruddy complexion and perpetual smile, Duane was a joy to be around. His words were usually accompanied by hand and arm gestures. It was impossible for him to tell a story without flailing them around. He was the Scoutmaster on the boat, being the oldest and most experienced, and after a day of work and a good dinner, the crewmembers of the *Spirit* were always treated to several of his stories, which were accompanied by wild gestures and arm waving. Later, as we crawled into our sleeping bags and turned out the lights, I would fall asleep to the sound of Duane's spoon scraping out the last bit of spaghetti from the bottom of the pan.

Nothing bothered him. The term "easygoing" would be an understatement in describing this man, who was so mellow that you would think he had just awakened from a nap. This was a logical supposition as his bunk was comfortable and well used.

Our skipper was a thoughtful sort. In the course of a conversation, when it was his turn to speak, there was always a lull. He formulated his words carefully before they escaped from his mouth, as though we were discussing matters of great importance.

Robin Brown, Duane's son, was twenty-two years old. He stood six feet tall, wore a well-trimmed beard, and had been blessed with the body of a Greek God. His chin jutted out, his face was hard and chiseled. A perpetual scowl belied his likeable personality. Robin attracted women like a magnet. He was the envy of all the contenders in the hunting grounds of State Street.

An able sea hand as well as an experienced diver, Robin ran the *Spirit* whenever Duane took time off, which was often. He was a good skipper but a little more on the serious side than his dad, so when Robin ran the boat, it was all business. A fish lover and a good cook, Robin always whipped us up a welcome break from Duane's spaghetti.

Santa Rosa Island was the *Spirit's* domain. No other dive boat had worked there as much, or knew the reefs and kelp beds better than Duane. Even with the confusing wind and current patterns that are associated with this island, he always knew where to find good pickings.

Once, while we anchored up on the back side of Santa Rosa Island, a boat appeared, slowly circling the *Spirit*. It was an East-Coast lobster style, white, about thirty feet long. The unwritten code among the dive fleet stated that you should never get any closer than two or three hose lengths from another boat. Any distance within the six or seven hundred foot range was considered bad manners. Phrases like "he jumped my spot today" or "that guy's a spot jumper" became part of our vocabulary. Bad feelings were associated with spot jumping, and violence erupted on the docks periodically due to this cowardly practice.

This day, as the unwanted guests encroached on our spot, we scowled at them and they scowled back. I wondered how our easygoing skipper was going to handle this situation, for no one had ever seen him upset or angry.

Both arms left his side and began waving in the air. "Howdy fellers!" he shouted to the scoundrels. As they idled their boat closer, one of them sneered. He spoke with a foreign accent. "Nice day, huh? You guys doing any good here?"

What cowards, I thought. Not only could they not go find their own diving spot, but they were inquiring about ours. This was crossing the line. Something had to be done to banish these spineless invertebrates.

Robin stared with narrow eyes, "I know that guy" he said quietly. "His name is Dominic. He's from down south, and I can tell you first-hand he's an asshole and a blatant spot jumper. He'd just as soon cut your throat as look at you. He carries a short-barreled shotgun on his boat, and he's been known to use it."

Duane scratched his head and thought for a minute. Then he waved his arms. "We're doin' good!" he shouted. "There's plenty here for everybody. You can join us if you like."

Clearly perplexed by Duane's reaction, the trespassers slowly backed away. After a few minutes of deliberation, their skipper gave an unsmiling nod of his head and headed his boat up the line.

The only thing I could figure is that the evildoers suspected that the amiable old sea dog was setting some sort of trap for them. Duane, our hero, had thwarted the villains.

The underwater makeup of Santa Rosa Island is such that it contains less reef and more sand, making for murkier waters than the other islands. On the *Spirit,* we accepted this fact, and much of our diving was done in eight-to-twelve foot visibility. Currents are also prevalent, sometimes so strong they are impossible to swim against, requiring the diver to crawl down the anchor line to the bottom. If he allows himself to get behind the boat, the tender has the back-breaking job of pulling him back. On the *Spirit*, we took turns tending, so we all encouraged each other to keep well forward of the boat if we were working in a current.

After anchoring up, Robin usually got in the water for an initial survey.

"How's it look?" we would ask when he surfaced.

"Not too good, the viz is about six to ten feet."

"Any current?"

"It's smokin'. I had to crawl down the anchor line."

"Great. Any good news?"

"The urchins are so thick you can't see the bottom. Toss me a bag." That began a mad scramble for the other diver to get his gear on and get started.

Jerome was spending most of his time these days at the Wilson yard overseeing construction of his new boat, but whenever Duane took a break, Jerome hopped on the *Spirit* for a trip or two.

Jerome, Robin, and I were on board as the anchor of the *Spirit* sat on the bottom in Johnson's Lee, which at fifty miles is about as far from the harbor as you can get. Our first jump of the day had been at East Point, but two-foot viz sent us packing. Next, we tried Ford Point, further up the line. A big northwest swell was pounding the entire back side, rendering this area hopeless as well.

So here we sat, in the relative calm of Johnson's Lee, with the swell building, wishing we had stayed home. We could find no spot where there was any visibility, and with the wind and swell picking up, the day looked like it was going to be a bust. We didn't strike out often but sometimes Mother Nature just says, "Not today." While we pondered our fate, Robin hung a baited line over the side in hopes of catching dinner.

"The boat's safe here. Let's swim to the island and go for a hike, then see what the ocean does tomorrow." Our young skipper was an adventurer, and did not like to be idle, so the three of us stuffed our clothes into garbage bags and swam to the beach in our wetsuits. After changing and stashing our gear we took off straight up a hill toward the top of the island with Robin taking the lead, setting a furious pace. After thirty minutes of nonstop climbing we were all panting and sweating, but when we stopped for a breather and looked behind us, we were astonished at the view.

Far below us in the large emerald bay that was Johnson's Lee, sat the *Spirit*, a small speck floating in a sea of green. A distinguishable wind line could be seen outside the protected cove—the ocean beyond was a frothing cauldron of mist and herds of white buffaloes.

From our vantage point we could see in all directions. The rough waters of the Potato Patch, off the west end of Santa Cruz, were visible in the distance. Prevailing northwesterly seas hit the high cliffs there, making for a confused sea—we did not look forward to negotiating this treacherous area on the way home tomorrow.

Looking north and west, the hills and valleys of the island stretched out before us. The mid-afternoon sun cast a beautiful but eerie sheen on the land. The three of us were spellbound. We did not speak for a full minute.

"The Chumash had encampments somewhere around here." Robin, the historian piped up. "Keep your eyes peeled for artifacts, but don't touch anything or you'll be cursed." We continued on, happy in our quest for adventure, and wondering what treasures lay before us.

...

Human settlement of the area from Malibu to Paso Robles, including the Channel Islands, began about 13,000 years ago. With the passage of time the natives thrived and at their peak enjoyed a population of almost 20,000. The Chumash Indians, as they came to be known, were skilled fishermen and hunters, using bows and arrows and throw spears to hunt seals and fish.

Two thousand years ago the Chumash designed and built boats made from hand-hewn planks. The canoes were well built and able to make the crossing to the Channel Islands in mild sea conditions.

Food on the islands was plentiful. The large kelp beds were abundant with fish, and abalone lined the shallow tide pools. Sea lions provided meat and furs.

The Chumash way of life gradually came to an end with the arrival of the Spaniards in the early 1700s. The spread of European disease ended the reign of the original natives of Santa Barbara and the Channel Islands by the mid-1800s.

After an hour of tramping around the island, the only thing we saw was a large herd of elk in the distance.

"Anybody getting hungry?" Robin suggested we head back to the boat before the sun went down. We turned around but had not been walking for more than a few minutes when Jerome stopped. His eyes were glued to the ground in front of him.

Hundreds of years ago the Chumash Indians made spears to hunt with. At our feet, gleaming in the afternoon sun, was an arrowhead about five inches long, intricately tooled, and in flawless condition. Before anyone had a chance to speak, Jerome picked it up. The three of us carefully examined it, taking turns holding it.

After several minutes of scrutiny, Jerome put it in his pocket. "The curse, Jerome, the curse!" I sputtered.

"You've put the hex on us, lad. We're doomed now," Robin chimed in. The two of us admonished him for the evil deed he was committing, but secretly we both wished that we had discovered the prize.

By the time we made it back to the beach the sun was down, so we swam to the boat by the light of a three-quarter moon. A two-pound chucklehead waited for us on Robin's line, providing a fine dinner, after which we swapped a few stories then crawled into our bunks. But as he turned out the light, Robin put on his pirate face. He closed one eye and turned to Jerome. "Ye've put the curse of the Chumash on yerself, lad. From now on, wherever you go ye'll be plagued by trouble and torment. Woe is you." With those words we all cackled and doused the light.

The morning brought light winds and a calm sea. The water was clear, giving us good diving conditions so Robin took a quick survey and found a blackout right under the boat. By late afternoon 9,000 pounds were stacked on the deck of the *Spirit* without ever having to move her, and by the time we pulled the anchor up and got under way, the channel had calmed down to a manageable two-foot chop. Congratulating ourselves on our good fortune, we enjoyed a pleasant ride home.

Six months later Jerome's new boat was in the water. He called her the *Sea Roamer*, and she was a honey—the cabin was well forward, with tilt-forward windows and two large fish holds aft. A Volvo turbo-diesel was his choice for power, the first engine of its kind in the fleet. The *Sea Roamer* would have a radar unit, also a first for the urchin boats of the day.

By the time she was floating, Jerome was broke. The fathometer was installed and working, but he had to make a few trips before he could afford to pay for the radar, which sat in a box at Ocean Aire Electronics.

But now, the curse of the Chumash was about to strike.

On his first trip, Jerome hit the one-mile buoy while coming in on a moonless night, a most improbable accident. Fortunately it was a glancing blow, and the damage was minor—the four-foot scrape along the hull was easily fixed. If he had hit the large steel can head-on though, he could have been killed. The worst injury, though, was to his ego, for other than driving your boat up on the beach, hitting a stationary buoy is a most embarrassing thing to do.

Over the years we've lost touch with each other, but our paths occasionally cross. Jerome grimaces when he sees one of us because he knows what's coming. One eye will close, and a pirate-like voice will say, "You shoulda left that arrowhead be, lad."

# The Journey

### January 9, 1979

Hiro Yanagida has completed a long day of work at the Design Center of Kyoto, Japan. As a mid-level manager he oversees the work of twenty employees. Now, this Friday evening, Hiro meets some friends for dinner and a few drinks at his favorite restaurant before the long train ride home. Looking at the splendid assortment of sushi and sashimi before him, he ponders their origin. The red meat of hamachi, the yellowtail tuna, he knows, comes from local ocean waters, and increasingly from fish farms. Unagi, eel, is harvested from fresh water streams. But now his eyes have fallen upon the bright yellow piece of uni. The gonad of the sea urchin is his favorite item, but he is not sure of its origin. "How did this small piece of uni come to be here in front of me?" He asks himself. "Where did it come from, and what travels has it been through to arrive on this tray?"

### October 29, 1929

On Wall Street in New York City, stock traders were only slightly concerned at early morning selling and sharply declining prices. Throughout the South, prohibition agents chased moonshine bootleggers. President Hoover preached prosperity for the nation.

On the west coast of Vancouver Island, near the Nasparti Inlet, a small bed of sea urchins have reached their springtime spawning cycle. Here, over a hundred million sperm are released by the males. Close to a million eggs from nearby females are fertilized, and their journey begins. Most of them, over nine hundred thousand, are taken out to sea, and are quickly consumed by microscopic predators. The remaining larvae drift into the North Pacific Current and begin their journey down the west coast of North America.

Off the Washington coast they are fed into the California Current, and continue southward. Ten days later more than three-quarters of them have been eaten by seagoing competitors. After three weeks of drifting in the swirling currents, fifty thousand of the creatures reach the waters of California, where again, animals higher on the food chain devour them in great numbers. At the reefs of the Channel Islands, five thousand remaining animals settle to the shallow ocean floor. Here, bottom dwelling anemones, as well as filter feeders ingest the still invisible newcomers.

Sixty days after settling onto the reefs, the remaining five hundred urchins have become visible to the human eye, measuring one centimeter. The tiny urchins make their way into the protection of cracks and crevices on the reef bottom where, as their growth continues, they feed on drifting organisms smaller than themselves. Crabs, snails, and starfish descend upon the still helpless echinoderms, reducing their numbers to one hundred by the end of their first year. After three years, thirty juveniles have made their home on the reef. They are now one inch in diameter.

### December 6, 1941

Admiral Hirohito's attack fleet has managed to maintain the element of surprise as it closes in on Pearl Harbor. Artie Shaw's "Stardust" is the most requested song of the year. Bob Hope and Bing Crosby filmed *The Road to Zanzibar*.

Tyler Bight, San Miguel Island: Thirty feet below the ocean surface, fifteen urchins from the 1929 spawn have burrowed into permanent positions in the reef under a thick canopy of kelp. The adults are almost four inches across, and are able to defend themselves against most predators. Their sharp spines contain poison, and act as a strong deterrent to attackers. Having been adults for five years, they have each produced millions of spawn of their own, which have traveled to destinations in Mexico and South America. Crab and lobster are able to pry them from their homes though, and their numbers continue to dwindle.

### September 9, 1961

President John F. Kennedy ponders the troubling situation in Southeast Asia. Mickey Mantle and Roger Maris race to beat Babe Ruth's home run record. Decca Records rejects a singing group who call themselves "The Beatles."

Four urchins have survived since their birth at Vancouver Island. They are part of a large bed of several thousand, all at various stages of development. At over thirty years of age, their shells are thick and strong. Thirty percent of their bodies are now imbedded in the holes they have burrowed in the reef, Two of the four are in a crack, one is on a rock wall, and one is under a reef ledge. Only a small number of animals are able to dislodge the sturdy creatures. A sea otter, with his intelligence and ability to use rocks as tools, could easily capture one, but the furry mammals will not reach these waters for thirty more years. The thick kelp, however, has attracted many varieties of fish, among them the sheepshead, a large predator with powerful teeth. More urchins would fall prey in the coming years.

### December 16, 1978

President Carter, Anwar Sadat, and Menachem Begin sign the historic Camp David Accord, ending conflict between Egypt and Israel. Smallpox has been completely eradicated from the world. College dropout Bill Gate's young company, Microsoft, reaches annual sales of $900,000.

From the population of a million fertilized eggs nearly five decades ago, only one remains. It is a male. He has produced fifty million sperm of his own, eaten hundreds of pounds of kelp, and can now look forward to many more years of adulthood, for he is deep in a crack, and safe from all predators

All but one.

A thin stainless steel tool reaches into the crack and quickly dislodges him. With a flick of his wrist, Jerome Betts sweeps his catch into a mesh bag, where it joins five thousand others that the diver has captured this day.

### December 17, 1978

The forty-nine year old adult sea urchin is one of fifty thousand others being unloaded from a truck at the Los Angeles processing plant. It reaches an assembly line, where a person wielding a special tool cracks open the shell, exposing the five pieces of yellow roe inside. Next, the pieces are quickly and carefully removed with a thin spoon, and placed into a tray of salt water. Now a person with tweezers removes excess material from the gonad, preparing it for its next station, a special liquid mixture of alum and water. Here it is soaked for a set time, in this case, two hours. The solution makes the roe firmer, and now it is removed and placed on paper towels to dry and drain. A final tweezer cleaning takes place, and the product is now ready for packing. Due to their high degree of manual dexterity and patience, women are used for the placing of the roe into the wooden trays, for the carefully packed tray must be attractive to the overseas buyers. Roe pieces must be intact. Any broken pieces are used for a lesser valued secondary market. Ten wooden trays are packed into a styrofoam container, along with a square of blue ice, a temporary coolant. The container lid is put on with a wrap of tape, and is on its way to the airport.

### December 18, 1978

Styrofoam containers are removed from the plane and transported to the Tskiji market in Tokyo, the world's largest wholesale fish market. After their arrival and unpacking, the wooden trays are put on display, and the product is open for bid.

Now the uni is taken on its final journey to stores and restaraunts, and that night, one piece of roe from the single survivor of the Vancouver Island spawn of 1929 is deftly lifted from its place atop a square of pressed rice and seaweed, and placed into the mouth of Hiro Yanagida.

## Crazy Harold

The man I had purchased my regulator whip and picking rake from was Harold Shrout, known by all as Crazy Harold. He is a bonafide legend in the commercial diving community of Santa Barbara, and although he was educated as an engineer, an office job was not in his future. Harold became one of the top abalone divers throughout the sixties and seventies. He was one of the new breed of divers who, instead of using the bulky, hard-hat "heavy gear," used by earlier commercial divers, wore the "light gear"; that is, a wetsuit, swim fins, and scuba breathing regulator.

Crazy Harold's garage was long ago converted into a shop that he could do just about anything in. Old regulators were modified to deliver more air. Davits were manufactured and custom fit to the individual boat. He shaped custom molds for his "hip weights." After melting down old lead and pouring the hot liquid into his molds, he produced weights with a bend in them. After sliding the two opposing weights onto a belt, they rested comfortably above the diver's hips, affording hours of bottom time without the conventional flat weights digging into his back.

His specialty, though, was air systems: high-volume compressors, belt driven by eight-horsepower gasoline motors (usually Kohler or Briggs and Stratton), mounted on custom-made lightweight fiberglass stands. The big compressors were heavy, and added a slight list to a small boat. But they were preferred over the smaller, lighter compressors, which needed to be run at higher speeds, putting stress on the internal workings of both motor and compressor.

The units were mounted to the deck with early model Chevrolet motor mounts, which acted as vibration dampeners. Slots cut in the mounting holes of the stands provided for belt tension adjustments, and copper cooling tubes kept the compressed air from superheating as it left the compressor head.

Early designs used no air filters. Eventually, however, particulate filters were incorporated into the system, keeping any solid material from reaching the diver.

A potential hazard with the air system is the exhaust from the gasoline motor. If the toxic carbon monoxide gas is allowed to enter the intake of the compressor, the results can be sudden, and deadly. Crazy's simple solution to this potentially lethal problem was to mount the air system so that the compressor intake faced forward, and the motor aft. Next, a muffler, two feet long, and angled upward at forty-five degrees, was attached to the motor. The exhaust is directed up and away, downwind from the air intake.

Harold stayed busy in his shop, and on any given day you could see a boat in his driveway, one in the street, and two or three divers waiting patiently for the Guru of Goleta to render his advice on their project.

Harold was, to say the least, a bit on the quirky side. It could not be said that his conversation was laced with profanities. A more accurate description would be to say his profanities were laced with conversation, often times mentioning your family members or farm animals. Personal insults aimed at his customers were commonplace and most of his sentences were prefaced by the phrase, "You Dummy!" He spoke in a unique scornful code that few understood. However, if the recipient could withstand the verbal barrage, he would greatly benefit from Harold's expertise.

Prior to visiting the Goleta Garage, a Crazy Harold dictionary might be helpful:

*Ya!*
Hello, may I help you?

*You fuckem up, I fixem up*
I'm open for business

*Gitchyer dumb ass over here*
I have time to work on your project

*Bring hundreds*
I prefer cash

*He's cheap*
He prefers to do his own work

*Skinny*
Crazy's wife, who is normal

*Dummy*
*Everybody*

*See yer dumb-ass later*
Goodbye

The compressor motor on the *Spirit* had been acting up for the last several trips. We had an eight-horsepower gasoline powered Briggs & Stratton, a fine motor for a lawnmower. But given the salt water environment the "Briggs & Scrap Iron," as we called them, quickly became unreliable. They required constant maintenance.

Our "popper" had developed a flooding problem when we tried to start it. After two or three pulls on the cord it became necessary to remove the spark plug and blow some air into the compression chamber. Then it would start right up.

Since this task had become a daily routine, I took the initiative to mount a small plastic tool box on the stern, just forward of the air system. The box was about ten inches long, large enough to hold the spark plug tool and a screwdriver, but not so big as to interfere with our space. Duane and Robin approved of my invention, for now it was no longer necessary to dig through the heavy tool box in the forward cabin to find the few tools needed for this simple task. Our daily ritual of removing the plug and drying out the chamber was made easier by my little box mounted next to the Briggs.

The fuel dock was as much a social club as it was a gas station. This was the place where the fishermen got caught up on the latest harbor gossip. If someone's boat was broken down, or an inattentive driver ran his boat up on the beach, the fuel dock was the place we learned of it. It was our "knitting club".

"Take this line, you can side tie to the *Outlaw*." Fuel Dock Bob tossed Robin a line and helped us snug up to the other boat. The space around the fuel dock is small and often crowded, this day being no exception.

As we waited for the gas hose, I spotted Crazy Harold yakking with a couple of other divers, imparting valuable information to them in between insults.

"Hey Crazy, check this out." I was proud of my invention and was anxious to show it to him. Who knows, it could become a trend—small boxes with tools for specific tasks mounted on boat sterns.

At forty-two years old, Harold was a physical wonder. He was small and wiry with a full head of gray hair that was so thick it resembled a wire brush. Twenty-five years of diving were behind him, but he nimbly climbed over the *Outlaw* and hopped onto the *Spirit* like he was a teenager.

"Hey, Dummy!" he greeted me cordially. "What have you fucked up now?"

"Check out this little box I mounted next to the popper. It carries a few essential tools for when the thing floods out and we need to work on it." My pride at this simple but effective innovation was obvious.

The fuel dock was more crowded than usual, with at least ten boats tied up and rafted to each other. All conversation stopped when Harold bellowed, "You fucking dummy! Instead of putting a toolbox back here, why don't you fix the fucking motor?"

As I began to shrink and look for a place to hide, people gathered to admire the contraption that was causing Crazy Harold to turn red with laughter. "Jesus Christ, give me twenty bucks, I'll fix it for you!" he shrieked. A month or so later the snickers and guffaws began to subside.

Several years later, after moving up north, I was passing through Santa Barbara, on my way to Mexico with my wife and two small children. Ignoring my spouse's objections, our truck found its way to Crazy Harold's house. It had been a long time, but he recognized me immediately. "Hey, dummy!" The familiar warm greeting.

The kids, aged seven and four, hid behind me and

clung to my legs in fear as the old gray haired bean pole disappeared briefly. When he reappeared he handed each of them a bag of cookies. "Quick, eat as many as you can, 'till your Mom makes you stop."

After a short visit with Harold and Skinny we continued our journey. It's been over ten years now, but the kids still have fond memories of Crazy Harold, the strange man with the cookies.

## Two Wives

Jerome pulled me aside at the fuel dock. "Have you been over to the Radon yard lately?"

"No, why?"

"There's a twenty-four-footer for sale cheap. The guy built it for diving urchins, then on his first trip he got his picking rake stuck in a rock and broke his arm. He went back to boat building, and the boat is up on barrels."

We hopped in his truck and drove over to the boat yard.

When I saw her, it was love at first sight—a brand new white molded hull with a tan cabin, large enough for two people, and room on top for two surfboards. I even

110

liked the name, *Coyote*. It had a Volvo small block gas V-8 motor with an outdrive and had less than two hundred hours on it. A Crazy Harold air compressor system was mounted aft behind a galvanized steel davit. A turn key urchin boat! The guy wanted $8,000 for the boat, which sounded like a bargain to me. I asked Jerome what he thought. "It's a steal. Buy it." He said.

"I can't leave Duane and Robin in the lurch. They've treated me great."

"If you want to move up in the business, your time is now. They'll understand."

"I don't have eight thousand bucks!"

"Give him five hundred to hold it for a week, and go find the money. You won't regret it." Jerome had never steered me wrong before (other than constantly lying to me), and I trusted his judgment.

I now went on a desperate search for money. My first stop was Santa Barbara Savings, where my checking account contained a grand total of three hundred and eleven dollars. After listening patiently to the assistant manager, I learned the concept of collateral, down payments, and financial track records—none of which I had. My dismal situation was further compounded by my assets, which consisted of two surfboards and a twenty-year-old plywood boat that had rotten decks and leaked. The assistant manager at the bank smiled and wished me luck.

My next stop (and last resort), was my father, who was not a wealthy man but he was a good man. And he was a wise man, for he correctly foresaw that by lending me the money for the boat he could accomplish several things. At a reasonable interest rate he could turn a respectable profit on his investment. Also, he would be helping me in my new career that he had been following with no small amount of interest. And finally, if I could indeed make as much money as I claimed, his refrigerator would be forever safe from my midnight plundering.

So, with a generous heart and a promise from me not to get myself killed, he drew up a five-year note and I was in business. My first load on the *Coyote* was delivered on April 12, 1979. Upon receiving my check my dad got his first payment.

At twenty-seven years of age, I now considered myself a man of means. The old *Heidi Marie* had been sold—a sleek new dive boat sat in her place in slip 3-B-55. Money was coming in. I bought a new compressor cover from the sail-maker and ordered a new surfboard.

Debbie Shannon, the piano teacher I had met that fateful day on State Street, was now my fiancée. We had discovered though, that our differences were many—she was college educated and had her own business. She was responsible. Fair skinned, the summer sun was not her friend. Frugal to a fault, she never bought anything unless it was on sale, and her idea of an exciting day was going for a two-mile hike.

I, on the other hand, had not completed college. In fact the teachers at San Marcos High School, I suspect, had permitted me to graduate only for fear of seeing me again the next year. I was unfamiliar with the concept of legitimate employment or saving money. All I wanted to do was surf, dive, and surf.

If opposites attract, it was a match made in heaven. Even Debbie's parents approved of me (her previous boyfriend was a sullen, egotistical snob—they were desperate).

On June 2, 1979, family and friends gathered at the little church in Summerland, a small town four miles south of Santa Barbara. Looking at the guests, it was easy to see which ones belonged to whom. On the right side of the aisle people wore suits, or were nicely dressed. They looked responsible, and they were quiet and well behaved. The pews on the left were populated with divers, surfers, and pirates. They wore jeans, aloha shirts, tee shirts, and flip-flops. Half of them celebrated early and came to the wedding drunk.

Everyone in the church knew I was marrying up. They also knew Debbie had a project.

In those early years my wife was a familiar sight down at the docks. Almost every night when we came in, she was there with cookies for everyone, even the guys on other boats. If the *Coyote* was broken down, Debbie was there, making trips to the parts store or bringing me lunch.

My new wife was five feet four, twenty-five years old, and weighed one hundred and eight pounds. She had a well-established business with over forty  piano students, and within two months she had us on a savings plan, putting away a hundred bucks a month for our future. Once a week, I was told, we were going for a hike.

## South Swell

My new bride arranged a low budget honeymoon package to Hawaii. We visited Wahiawa, the small town on Oahu where I had lived as a kid, and drove by my old house. Most of our time was spent on Kauai, where we looked up Pat Haynes, a surfer pal from Santa Barbara, and stayed at his house on Tunnels Beach. Debbie and Pat's wife, Lani, combed the pristine beaches for shells while Pat and I surfed, but no matter how tired or sunburned I was, every evening after dinner I was taken for a hike.

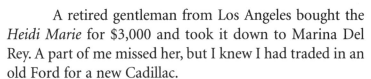

A retired gentleman from Los Angeles bought the *Heidi Marie* for $3,000 and took it down to Marina Del Rey. A part of me missed her, but I knew I had traded in an old Ford for a new Cadillac.

With the three grand from the sale of the *Heidi Marie*, plus $5,000 from Debbie's piano money, we were able to put a down payment on a small house on the west side of town. The two-bedroom Spanish-style home at 1903 Mountain Avenue was old, built in 1936, but we loved it. Before long our living room had a piano in it, and the house was filled with music from students. Debbie quickly increased her number of pupils to fifty.

The *Coyote* performed flawlessly. She was fast, easy to handle, and had no problems packing 4,000 pounds of urchins across the channel.

Lenny Marcus, a friend from high school, had gotten into the diving business about the same time as I did. He was a perfect choice to have on the boat for one simple reason—Lenny surfed.

Although he was short and a bit on the heavy side, Lenny was not pudgy—four years of high school football had hardened every inch of him, and his skin was brown from years of surfing and being on the beach.

Lenny accepted a spot on the *Coyote*—his pay as a split diver would be the standard 55 percent of his catch. Considered an independent contractor, the "walk on" diver would be responsible for his own taxes. A walk-on diver (the diver who does not own the boat), receives a percentage of his catch, usually between 50 and 60 percent. In 1979, when prices were around sixteen cents per pound, an experienced diver who harvested 3,000 pounds, made roughly $250 per day.

Lenny had been diving on a small boat without the benefit of a tender, and convinced me it was not necessary to carry the extra baggage. "They take up too much room on a twenty-four-foot boat with two divers," he said. "Besides, that's an extra mouth to feed. Hell, most of 'em just get in the way."

Diving without a tender took some getting used to, and in the beginning it was difficult. I was used to having a bag line tossed to me—now I had to get the urchins back to the boat by myself.

It didn't take long to acclimate, though, and before long, the dual job of diving and tending became second nature. Watching Lenny, I learned little tricks, like using the hose to pull myself back to the boat. Several snap lines were hung off the sides—full bags were attached, and floated next to the boat, waiting to be tended. Extra bags leaned up against the rails, easy to reach up and grab.

Santa Cruz Island would be our initial diving area. As a neophyte skipper, I liked the idea of being close to the harbor—if there were any problems with the new boat, we were only twenty-five miles from home. The calmer weather, common to this island, also helped to minimize my fretting. And although the other islands have more spots, the roe found inside the urchins of Santa Cruz is known for it's consistent high quality. The bright yellow eggs are firm, with a distinctive sweet flavor.

Working at Santa Cruz, and with Lenny, was a joy. The natural beauty created by the high cliffs rising from the sea, and the clear blue water were welcome sights compared to the unpredictable conditions of Santa Rosa Island, my prior workplace on the *Spirit*. It had only been ten months since my first visit there on the *Little Wing* with Hydroplane Steve Hagen, but it seemed like a lifetime ago.

Being long time wave chasers, the two of us agreed that as soon as our bank accounts had been built up to a comfortable level, our next priority would be to make some surf trips on the *Coyote*. We knew that the south swell season was approaching.

From the months July through October, southerly ocean swells, spawned by low-pressure systems in the southwest Pacific, arrive at the California coast. Unlike the winter swells that originate in the Gulf of Alaska, south swells often are accompanied by warm weather and no wind— perfect conditions for surfing.

Most of the Santa Barbara coastline is in the "shadow" of the islands, and thereby protected from south swells, but the backside of the islands are exposed. There are a few places that have reasonably good waves—and one place with a near perfect wave.

The weather channel crackled, listing the current observations from the offshore buoys. "Santa Monica basin buoy, wave height, five feet, seventeen seconds, wind calm." The south swell we had been expecting had arrived; the conditions were perfect.

"Lenny, its happening!" I shouted into the phone.

"What's the Santa Monica buoy say?"

"Five at seventeen, no wind."

"I'm on my way!"

Twenty minutes after receiving my frantic phone call Lenny showed up at the slip, his surfboard under one arm, a loaf of bread and a jar of peanut butter in the other.

The radio gave a more recent observation as we left the harbor—longer interval, swell-size increasing. After only three months of working together, our bank accounts were healthy, Debbie's business was going well, and I had doubled up on my dad's payments. Life was good.

From the moment I laid eyes on the Channel Islands I had dreamed of surfing out there. In fact, the original motivating factor behind my purchase of the *Heidi Marie* was to access the waves of the Islands and the Hollister Ranch, a private coastal enclave. The skippers I had previously worked for, Steve, Dewey, and Duane, didn't surf, but I knew someday my time would come. And the time was now.

The channel was like grease, and an hour later we were cruising past Smugglers Cove, turning the corner at the east end of Santa Cruz Island. Soon after, the *Coyote* was climbing over long smooth lines of thick blue water. As we streaked by Yellowbanks in twenty feet of water, the bottom was clearly visible. A squadron of sting rays lay perched in the sand with only their tails and wingtips touching the bottom, and as we flew over them, they took off with a flap of their wings.

Lenny knew I'd never been to this particular spot, which in those days was still relatively unknown. "Don't tell anybody I was the one who turned you on to this place," he said.

"Mum's the word, amigo."

"Okay, head for that canyon. Get ready to idle down."

We pulled up to the spot, slowing down to an idle so our wake wouldn't disturb the waves. Three commercial dive boats were anchored up—the *Otra Vez*, the *Vanilla*, and the *Hard On*. Their crews were already in the lineup.

"Let's toss the hook a little further out from those guys, Lenny." I was taking no chances with my new boat.

After securing the *Coyote* we had a sandwich and watched for awhile. It was big.

My dive partner and I had done some surfing together at Rincon Point and Haskell's over the years. We were of similar abilities—neither one of us could be considered world class surfers but we could hold our own, and we both liked big waves, up to ten or twelve feet. That day it looked like it was about six to eight feet, with ten-foot cleanup sets.

The water was a beautiful dark blue. As we jumped off of the boat and began paddling, we could see twenty feet down the kelp stalks. Bright orange Garibaldi fish glittered underneath. The glare of the noonday sun stung our eyes.

Every fiber of my body was now alive, for my longtime dream was becoming a reality. Paddling toward the waves, I briefly reflected on the life I was living. A beautiful, independent woman who loved me was my partner in life. The ocean was where I made my living, working with people I liked and admired. And now I owned a twenty-four-foot Radon boat with a rack to hold my surfboard. Life could not possibly have been better. My heart began to pound as Lenny and I lowered our heads and stroked toward the booming surf.

Waves are created by wind. The closer the wind, the shorter the wave interval. Wind from a close proximity to the area—say within a few hundred miles, creates what are known as "wind waves." When the wind is farther out—say 1,000 miles, the waves generated are called "groundswells."

If you are driving up the coast and see long lines rolling in, you are looking at a groundswell.

The strength of the wind and the longer it blows determines swell size. The distance it has to travel to get to its final destination determines the interval, or time between swells. A hurricane six hundred miles away might have an interval of thirteen seconds. A swell generated in the Gulf of Alaska could have an interval of seventeen to twenty-five seconds.

Ground swell waves arrive in sets and are sometimes very predictable. An experienced surfer might let the first two waves of the set go by and target the third wave, because he knows it will be the biggest. Then, just when he has the pattern all figured out, a monster set comes along. It is bigger than the other sets and breaks further out, often trapping the surfers who are waiting for waves. The unfortunates are ambushed and get caught inside by the "cleanup sets," so named for obvious reasons.

Making our way closer to the lineup, Lenny and I noticed everybody paddling furiously out towards us! A quick glance behind told me why—a cleanup set was upon us!

The guys in the lineup never had a chance. Two of them scratched over the first wave, but then they were faced with a thick monster that broke hard, enveloping them. There were probably six guys in the water, all getting creamed.

"Go! You're in the slot!" cried Lenny. There was no time to think—a ten foot wave was right behind me, and with two quick strokes, I had it.

Half of the crew was on the beach, with the rest floundering in the whitewater as I streaked down the face of a perfect Santa Cruz Island wave. Dropping to the bottom,

I leaned hard to my right and cranked a turn, my eyes focusing on the feathering lip twenty feet down the line. It folded over me and there I was, deep inside a huge barrel, looking out a big hole far ahead of me, and seeing a waterfall on my left.

When inside the tube of a breaking wave, time freezes. It's as though you're standing in a crouch on your board, and although every muscle in your body is tensed and you're flying through space, you have the illusory feeling of standing still—a passenger behind the waterfall. For a few fleeting seconds the powerful vortex has been harnessed. You are riding in the eye of the storm. The violent noise of a crashing wave has been replaced by a quieter, distant sound, like wind rushing through a canyon. This elusive, temporary place is known by surfers as the "Green Room," and there is no place on earth like it.

The smooth vertical wave face was inches away from me. I held out my right hand and touched it, allowing my finger to lightly drag through the fast moving water. Suddenly, the thick lip of the wave hit me square on the back, slamming my face down into my board. In an instant I was underwater, being pulverized—the salt water washing machine held me down for what seemed like an eternity.

Gasping for air, I surfaced just in time to see Lenny tucking into the barrel of the next wave which was even bigger than mine. He flew by me, deep in the tube, an intense, focused look on his face. I raised both arms in the air and tried to scream out a hoot of approval, but I was still choking and gasping for breath. All I could do was smile and gurgle.

We made it back to the lineup at the same time. "Epic!" Lenny was ecstatic. "I was so deep in that thing! I can't believe I made it out!" The guys on the beach, victims of the large set, had seen his wave. They were hooting and applauding with praise.

"What happened to you? He was so excited he didn't realize that he was screaming at the top of his lungs. I thought his eyes were going to pop out of his head.

"I got hammered, but the view was nice for a few seconds," I replied, still hacking up a lungful of seawater.

Three hours later we paddled back to the boat, our bodies aching and spent.

The deck of the *Coyote* was warm. We stripped our suits off and basked in the sun, intoxicated by our experience. As we lay on the boat and napped, our dreamlike state was periodically interrupted by the sound of thundering waves and hooting in the distance.

"Wake up, sleeping beauty." Lenny had hold of my foot and was shaking it. The boat was tied up in the slip, the sun was down. I had slept all the way home.

We both agreed that it was an all time surf session, one that would go down in history. And with firm resolve, the two of us vowed never to allow our work to interfere with surf.

That extraordinary August day in 1979 was the fulfillment of a dream, for I had finally tasted the Island waves. But just as one dream ends, another begins. The Islands held many more surf spots, some fairly well known, some secret. Over the next eight years, my time at the Channel Islands, I would know them all.

Music played somewhere off in the distance. The faraway sound of a piano entered my dream. Then it stopped. I rolled over and went back to sleep.

Soft hands were now massaging my neck and shoulders. A sweet voice whispered in my ear. "It's eight o'clock, honey. Are you going to sleep all day? I've already had two students this morning." Reaching up, I grabbed her small shoulders, pulling her down for a morning hug. "I dreamed I was in a piano concert." I yawned.

"That was no dream, dude. Remember, I told you I'm hosting my first recital in our living room next month. You heard Timmy practicing his piece."

"Oh yeah, that's right." I pulled the pillow over my head. "Will I have to do anything?"

"Yes, husband. You will be greeting parents at the door—dressed nicely, cordial and clean shaven."

"Mmmmm. Okay, honey. cordial ... clean shaven ... man, those waves yesterday were something."

"They must have been—I've never seen you sleep so late." She dove on top of me. "But now it's time to get up! No surfing today. No diving. And no spending time with that other woman."

"Huh?"

"Oh, I know all about her. You spend all your time with her, and I'm getting tired of it." She had hold of my foot, trying to pull me off the bed.

"And this woman, pray tell. What might her name be?"

"Her name is *Coyote*. And I'm getting jealous!"

"But baby. She has such sweet lines."

"Ahhhhhhh!" I was now fending off a full attack. There was only one way out. I grabbed her and planted a big wet kiss on her lips.

"Yuk! Go brush your teeth! And be quiet, I've got a student coming in five minutes. Remember, today's my day—we're going to Shoreline Park, then shopping for a new piano bench, then dinner at Brophy's tonight with Steve and Lori Hagen. By the way, you might think about mowing the lawn sometime this month."

"Hey now! Who's the man in this house, anyway?"

"I am! Now get up!"

## Weener

In California's relatively small band of underwater harvesters, we all shared an unspoken desire. Our unique lifestyle shaped in our minds that intangible thing that we all strove for—to be rugged individualists, successful, and respected by our peers.

We were a fun-loving group who did not take life too seriously. How could we? We flirted with death and danger on a daily basis! If asked by family members or land-loving acquaintances about the perils of our work, we always gave the same cocky answers: "I laugh in the face of death!" or, "Danger is my business!"

If there was one person who captured the totality, the mystique, of our endeavors, it would have to be Jim Robinson. To me, he was the ultimate sea urchin diver: waterman, surfer, diver, and all-around athlete. He had mechanical aptitude and could fix any problem on a boat. But most of all, he was an adventurer, always looking for the next virgin reef, the uncharted surf spot. I both liked and admired him, and we quickly became good friends.

After growing up in Newport Beach, he attended the new commercial dive school at Santa Barbara City College, and then headed for the oil rigs of the North Sea. When he arrived at the harbor, in 1979, his stories of saturation diving at 800 feet for a week at a time, with hundred-knot winds on the surface, made me feel safe spending my days at fifty feet, only thirty miles from home.

A mop of long curly blonde hair added three inches to his lean six-foot frame. Always in motion, he was the type who could not sit still even while sitting still. His blue eyes darted about, sparkling with mischief, always busy. He was a planner, drawing out an idea for his boat, studying charts for a new urchin spot, or arranging a foreign surfing adventure. He was an accomplished pianist and a music lover, his favorite pieces being the throaty, emotional ballads of Tom Waits. And he was a partier, able to consume copious amounts of tequila while still maintaining some slight semblance of propriety.

Upon entering a room, his presence was felt by all who were in attendance, for his good looks and strong personality were overwhelming. Women loved him, not just for his body, but in large part I suspect, because of his behavior toward them. All females were treated equally—like goddesses. Raised by strict parents, he was well mannered, and carried with him a level of good form and politeness that was rare indeed among the waterfront crowd.

Another thing that set him apart from the rest of the divers was his nonchalance at displaying his affection, not only towards women, but for his male friends as well. He was not effeminate, far from it. In fact, he was in many ways "a man's man," but he was known to profess his love for his friends, male or female, and give them warm hugs. Or call them on the phone. "Yo ho ho! It's Weener, I love you!"

Jim had four names he went by. And he could have had more. A hard worker, his natural leadership abilities soon earned him a foreman's role within his work crew on the North Sea oil platforms. He had a way of gently commanding his peers, insuring the task at hand was accomplished quickly and efficiently. "Yes, Bwana," became the rallying cry within the ranks of his dive team when he issued an order. "Look lively, here comes Bwana!"

His superiors quickly spotted the charismatic foreman, and gave him new responsibilities. The lead job of divemaster, the person who runs the job, assuming overall authority for the current task, was his. "Big Gun" became his new moniker within the ranks of the divers off the coast of Scotland. Periodically the job phone would ring; a team leader on another rig needed assistance. "We got a coupling job over here, it's deep, and it might get hairy. Can you send the Big Gun?" Soon a helicopter sat on the pad, waiting for Jim Robinson.

But the name that stuck forever came after he left the oil field business. On a surf trip with two other pals to the Gold Coast of Australia, a group of Aussies had befriended the likeable Yanks at a small village pub, where stories of surf exploits, fueled by vast amounts of tequila, got the foreigners an invitation for a wave expedition the following day.

"Wike up, mite—the wives aw gude! wire off!" At sunup, the bleary-eyed crew made its way to an uncrowded cove known only to the local inhabitants. After removing boards from the van, the group of wave soldiers began changing into their wetsuits. At the moment of complete nakedness, one of them spotted Jim's substantial manhood. "Crikey! Loogathot weener!" He shouted. The blushing American quickly donned his suit and the group began the climb down the cliff to the beach. The friends made the long paddle out, and introductions were made to the small contingent in the lineup.

A bold surfing style soon earned him respect among the Aussie crew, and, with his big personality, the American and his friends were quickly accepted into the tight knit band.

"Ah heeah Sonta Bawbara has gude saf!"

"Some of the best in the world. But it's not any better than these waves we're on right now!"

"Yah, it's ah grite dye. Glod ya cud mike it."

A long lull brought the entire pack of eight together, bobbing on their boards, enjoying the calm, glassy water. Jim's favorite new friend, a small, dark haired chap who had equaled his alcohol ingestion abilities the previous night, spoke up. "Yu shude see this gaws weener! It's a regulaw snike!" An outbreak of guffaws and laughter belched forth from the crowd.

"Well, ah'll tell ya" one of the Aussies chuckled "The weener can suf!"

"Ya, he con. Thot was good one the weener had in the lost set!" More uncontrolled laughter ensued, as a new name was born. It followed him back to his home continent, and to the harbor at Santa Barbara, where Jim Robinson was to be forever known as Weener.

In the winter of 1979 Weener bought his first urchin boat, a blue Wilson twenty-six he named the *Paula Marie*, after his current girlfriend. It wasn't long before he discovered one of the best island surf spots, Chinese Harbor. Chinese, on the front side of Santa Cruz, sits directly across from Rincon Point, with waves that are sometimes just as spectacular as the world-famous "Queen of the Coast."

Weener, Lenny, and I were on the *Paula Marie* one day, blazing out to Chinese for some surf. The fog was thick, cutting visibility to less than an eighth of a mile.

"No worries," said the Weener. "I can read my compass so good, the first thing you guys see will be a six-foot tube." He was almost right.

We tore into Chinese at over twenty knots and just missed running over the three guys in the lineup. As further insult, a big set came along that did two things: first, we almost got put on the beach (in fact, we were so shallow the prop got dinged); second, the wake from our boat ruined the waves for the guys in the water.

We finally got the *Paula Marie* anchored up, but we were so rattled we had to wait thirty minutes for our nerves to calm down. Paddling in to the lineup, we were greeted by scowls from our surf compadres. "Thanks a lot. You almost killed us!" We hung our heads in shame.

"Sorry." Weener offered meekly. They loosened up after a while though, and we all had a good chuckle and good waves. No one ever doubted Weener's compass reading skills after that.

His second boat was a thirty-four-foot Radon that he named *Florentia Marie*, again after a girlfriend. Apparently he didn't know the old fisherman's rule about naming your boat—wives and girlfriends come and go. Always name your boat after your mother.

Weener worked all of the islands, but his favorite spot, by far, was the desolate and untamed Foul Area of San Miguel.

The cabin of the *Florentia Marie* was spacious, and it was common to see several boats side-tied to "Hotel Weener" in Cuyler Harbor, San Miguel Island, with a wild party raging inside.

"*Florentia Marie*, this is the *Hot Chocolate*, channel sixteen, over."

"*Florentia Marie*, this is the *Hot Chocolate*, channel sixteen, over."

"Weener! Channel sixteen!"

"Hey Paul! What's up?"

"It's two o'fucking clock! Turn the fucking music down so we can get some fucking sleep over here!"

"Sorry buddy, will comply."

"*Hot Chocolate* out."

Weener's generosity was renowned. The guy would literally give you the shirt off his back.

At a wedding, he learned that a good friend was going to drive to Rosarito, northern Baja, for his honeymoon.

"You're not taking your car, are you?" Weener was concerned.

"Yeah, it'll be okay." The groom had faith in his 1966 Oldsmobile.

"Take my Pathfinder. It's got four-wheel drive and you just never know down there."

"Weener! You want us to take your brand new Nissan to Baja! No way, man!"

"Take it, that car of yours worries me. Consider it a wedding present."

Ten days later his telephone rang. "Hey, Weener! Is it okay if we drive a little farther down the peninsula?" The car was returned three weeks later, after making the full trip down to Cabo San Lucas and back. Weener said it had a few new squeaks, but that it was fine, and he was happy to do it.

With the *Florentia Marie*, a good strong crew, and his powerful work ethic, Weener became a highliner. He would remain at or near the top of the heap for many years.

## The Spaniard

The first time I laid eyes on The Spaniard was one night on the dock while we were waiting to offload.

Santa Barbara in the late summer has balmy, almost tropical evenings. The harbor is bustling with fishermen, tourists, colorful characters, and beautiful women, the kind of women you are looking at as you walk off the dock and fall in the water. It's a great place to hang out, especially if you just offloaded a boatload of urchins and knew you had a fat paycheck coming.

There we were, a crew of tired, smelly divers at the tail end of a fifteen-hour day, drinking coffee, and looking forward to a hot shower and a pillow. Here comes this guy strutting down the dock, wearing a suit and an overcoat, a leather purse slung over his shoulder, a pipe in his mouth, and a gorgeous woman on each arm.

Andreas Martinez had recently arrived from Spain, and was about to take the urchin business by storm. He became a diver, acquired a boat, and went to work. But he was different from the rest of us. He was an innovator, who had ten new ideas every day, and although nine of them were catastrophes, one would be a resounding success.

The Spaniard was shaped like a fire hydrant, short and thick. Scars littered his body from years of soccer in his homeland. His speech was obscured by a thick Castilian accent, making it difficult to understand what he was saying. In fact his success could be partly attributed to his habit of standing six inches from you as he spoke in a dialect that was unintelligible. That, coupled with the fact that his breath was unbearable made it necessary for people to constantly try to escape from his verbal grasp. As his oratory was rapid and nonstop, the recipient might agree to whatever was being pitched just to get away from him. It is quite possible therefore, that agreements were made without knowing what was said.

Andreas acquired a slip in the harbor. His boat, which was named the *Josefina*, after his mother, was too long for the slip, so he took a chainsaw to it, cutting two feet off the bow to make it fit. The boat weighed eight thousand pounds, and was set up to haul seven thousand pounds of urchins.

He convinced one of the top outboard motor companies, Evinrude, that he was a genius, and he negotiated a contract that would supply him with free motors for life. The plan (he always had a plan), was that everybody would see him carrying huge amounts of weight at fifty miles per hour and the Evinrude people would sit back and watch the orders come rolling in.

The boat performed beautifully—empty. But as soon as she got any serious weight on her, she would bog down and wallow at about five knots. It was common practice for Andreas to throw five hundred pounds of urchins back into the ocean, so he could get his boat up on plane. On the *Coyote*, whenever we found a really good spot, we would joke that we must have stumbled across one of Andreas' dumping grounds.

Those outboards would blow up at the rate of about one every three months, but Evinrude kept them coming. After giving him five or six motors, they finally got fed up and wiggled out of the deal.

This taught me two things about Andreas: one, he was a bullshitter; two, he was a good one.

In the early eighties there were five urchin processors, all Japanese, all in Los Angeles. They were in cahoots, making sure that the same price was paid to all of us, within a few cents per pound. My first three years in the business saw prices from twelve to fifteen cents per pound, but I never squawked much about it—I was diving, surfing, we had fresh fish in the frig, and I was making three to five hundred bucks a day.

"I yam gon to shange theeth beethnith."

"Huh?" Weener wasn't sure what he was saying, this foreigner with the unusual clothing. But he saw energy and focus.

"I kav a plan! Joo are gon to make twithe ath mush money! I need won good boat to yoin me—zee reth weel follow."

"I don't know. I'm pretty happy selling to Yuki."

"I kaf all thee tholushons to jour prolems! Joo need to troth me. An I weel troth joo—together we weel rule zee world!"

Weener, the eternal optimist, took an immediate liking to the strange newcomer.

"Okay, I'm in. I hope you know what you're doing."

"I wone forgeet theeth—joo weel be my nomber won boat. Breeng me good thee urchins, and I weel perthonally thee zat joo geet zee higheth pritheths of anybody een zee fleet. Joo kaf my word." The two men, who had only known each other for ten minutes shook hands. The new partnership would change the future of the urchin business, and they would remain friends forever.

Andreas said he was going to change things, and he did. Wearing the nice suit and overcoat, and carrying his purse, he went down to Los Angeles to have meetings with the processors. Eventually he made a contract with the largest processor, Ocean Queen, to let him be their supplier. He would buy the product from the divers and pay them according to the quality and freshness of their load. He leased a brand-new eighteen-wheeler to transport his urchins, the first of a fleet that would eventually grow to five.

Competition within the dive fleet rose to a new level as boats contended for the higher prices. We learned new phrases such as A-grade, B-grade, tray pack, and bulk pack. Ocean Queen paid Andreas a set price for one year, then they would renegotiate for the upcoming year. We never knew what that price was, and I didn't care. All I knew was that I was making more money. Kako, Ocean Queen's owner, was happy—she no longer had to deal with the barbarian divers, she had no more trucking hassles, and with Weener on the *Florentia Marie* leading the way, she knew she would have a steady supply of high-quality urchins.

The Josefina Fish Company was formed. Members received jackets with his logo and their boat name embossed on the sleeves. One of the offloading hoists at the dock was reserved exclusively for Team Josefina boats—a pot of hot coffee for his crews was waiting, and the first three boats in got doughnuts. The average time to offload a boat and send his crews on their way was a speedy fifteen minutes, unheard of in those days. Higher prices were promised, and received, written on checks with the Josefina Fish Company logo.

At this time there were about thirty-five urchin boats in the harbor. Within a few months after seeing the prices that Weener was being paid, half the fleet signed on with Andreas, including me.

Almost overnight, fierce competition arose among the processors, who had to pay higher prices to keep their boats from defecting to Andreas. Our prices skyrocketed from sixteen to twenty-five cents a pound within a year.

The other processors were not pleased with Ocean Queen, for she'd opened the door to a non-Asian. The Japanese hold on the uni market was still in place, but it had a crack in it.

The Spaniard enjoyed many years of success. He bought a powder blue Mercedes and threw a big party every year. One year he rented the exclusive Montecito Country Club for a bash. A ninety-foot party boat, complete with live band and full sushi bar, was hired the next year.

Not everyone liked the loud, arrogant entrepreneur, but there is no doubt that with the competition he created among the processors, Andreas Martinez  played a major role in putting the lowly sea urchin at the very top of California's seafood exports.

## We're All Liars

Every sea urchin skipper on the coast owns a pair of high-quality seven by fifties. They are stored on the boat, in an easily accessible location where he can quickly grab them.

When a piece of flotsam is spotted off in the distance, a glance through the binoculars will tell if it is something that needs to be further explored.

Observing the horizon of the channel, looking for saw-teeth, can give an indication of surface conditions, aiding in the decision whether to go to work or stay in. But the most important reason everyone carries seven by fifties is to keep an eye on each other.

Upon spotting another dive boat, the seasoned skipper immediately takes a look through his glasses, mentally recording the area, jotting it down in his notebook, or punching in the coordinates on his plotter. It's important to know where the competition is diving. It's an honorable thing to find your own spot, and for the most part, this is the standard method of finding urchins. But if you know that the *Keoki* had a good load last night, and you know where he was working, and you know that his boat is broken, and you know that he is sitting in his slip, cursing at his engine …. you know where some urchins are.

We're all liars. In fact, instead of being called the fuel dock, it should be called the Liars' Club.

"Hey Bob, hand me the hose, will ya?" Hydroplane Hagen, on the *Little Wing,* had the gas hose. Weener, on the *Florentia Marie,* was tied behind him, and Jerome was pumping diesel fuel into the tank of the *Sea Roamer.* All three boats had delivered sizable loads of high-quality urchins the previous evening. All three skippers knew exactly how much weight the others had offloaded; all three skippers had been promised high prices from their buyers, and all three skippers had been paid nineteen cents for their last loads.

"How'd you do yesterday?" Weener sipped strong Minnow coffee from a styrofoam cup.

"Not so good." Jerome adjusted his glasses. "We found some, but they were skinny. How 'bout you?"

"Aw, my popper was givin' me fits. We knocked off early."

"Get it fixed?"

"Nah, I'll probably stay in and work on it. You headin' out?"

"I don't think so—sounds like the winds coming. It looks bumpy out there."

"Yeah."

Speedy Steve Hagen's head popped out of his engine box. "How's Yuki treating you, Jerome?"

"Aw, he reamed me on my last load. I'm hoping for seventeen cents for last night. What's the Spaniard saying?"

"Aw, you know—there's a three cent difference between what he says and what I get in my pocket. I'm hopin' for sixteen cents."

"Yeah. How's it look for today?"

"Lori's sister's in town. I gotta do a family day."

Thirty minutes later, all three boats have cleared the breakwater, on their way to the islands.

The Japanese processors were no better.

"Hey, Yuki, this is Jerome."

"Oh! Herro!"

"Just calling to see how the market looks."

Oh! Velly bad, velly bad! Too much uni—mokket frooded!"

"Great. Are you sending checks up today?"

"Oh! Yes, checks coming today!"

"What'd I get?"

Oh! Ret's see … Sea Lomah … you got nineteen cents for rast road. Velly skinny loe!"

"Nineteen! Jesus, Yuki! You promised me twenty-two!"

"Oh! So solly, Jelome. Mokket frooded light now. Too much uni!"

"Well, okay. I'm gonna take a day or two off."

"No! We need uni!"

"I thought you said the market was flooded?"

Oh! Yes! But we need to … retain mokket share! Need uni! I pay you good. You my favolit boat!"

"Okay, I'll go out.

"Oh! Jelome! Prease dive same alea!"

"Same area? I thought you said they were skinny?"

"Yes! Skinny—a few good—dive same alea prease!"

We were always looking for a friend who would give us a truthful report or a processor who would treat us fairly. Maybe fishing and honesty are opposing concepts.

## Belly Up

December 15, 1980. A high pressure system centered in Idaho had created a mild offshore flow that made for an unseasonably calm ocean. Lenny and I had been slaying 'em on the front side of Santa Rosa Island.

The water had been so clear at Talcott Shoals that I was able to use the "stay dry" survey technique. Lenny stood at the helm, idling the boat around in the large beds of kelp, while I lay on my stomach up on the bow. As we slowly crept through the calm waters of Talcott, I hung my head off and looked down at the bottom, thirty feet below.

These conditions—no wind, no swell, and water visibility up to fifty feet— are extremely rare at the Channel Islands, especially in the often murky waters of Talcott Shoals. But on this warm sunny day, our fourth in a row, I gazed at the bottom, which was perfectly visible from the boat.

Polka dots were what I was looking for, and now, as a large field of black spots came into view, my hand went up. "Okay, stop the boat!"

I felt the slight clunk as Lenny pulled the shifter down into reverse, bringing the *Coyote* to a stop. And although my view of the bottom was now obscured by the milky bubbles caused by the counter rotating propeller, I knew we were on a good spot. I quickly pulled the hook from the open anchor locker and threw it toward the edge of the large kelp paddy.

Once the anchor line was secured to the bow cleat, we took a minute to survey our surroundings—three other urchin boats were in sight. The *Hot Chocolate* was closest, anchored up in the next kelp bed over, about a quarter mile away. They had two bags on deck.

The *Debra Ann* sat in a shallow kelp bed down toward Brockway Point, about two miles east of us. Her decks were empty, a sign that the urchins were eluding them.

Weener was about a half mile outside of us, toward the mainland. As usual, a big pile sat on the deck of the *Florentia Marie*.

As with the previous three days, the conditions, as well as the urchins, cooperated, and by three o'clock the *Coyote* had a good load on her deck. We had about 4,000 pounds aboard, but the prices were good, and I knew we'd have an easy ride home across the smooth channel, so I elected to get one more five hundred pound bag. That mistake, borne only of greed, would haunt me for years to come.

"Fire up the popper, Lenny. I wanna get one more quick bag."

"You got it, Captain!" He had already changed into his clothes but he didn't mind. The weather had been splendid and we were in high spirits.

A twenty-four-foot Radon boat can safely carry about 4,000 pounds of urchins, depending on the layout of the deck, and the ocean conditions. After that, the boat becomes unstable. The *Coyote's* record load was 5,200 pounds, but after that harrowing ride in, I decided 4,000 pounds was all she would carry.

I was only down for about twenty minutes. After I surfaced Lenny pulled on the dive hose, dragging our final bag through the kelp, with me hanging on to it. When he tossed me a bag line that almost hit me in the head, I snapped it onto the bag, swam to the boat, and climbed on. Lenny shut the popper off and hooked the winch line to the floating bag. I gave him a hand as he brought it up out of the water.

We got the bag up on top of the pile, but the boat was leaning a little. "Easy, partner, bring it up a touch—let's get this boat level" The entire deck was filled with urchin bags. Lenny stood on the engine lid holding the winch button, keeping his distance from the sharp spines (his hand was swollen from being stuck the previous day, but it was a minor injury). I was standing on the narrow rail. I had a good grip on  the mesh of the bag, and was pulling on it, easing it closer to middle of the stack as Lenny worked the winch.

As his finger held the control button down, the boat lurched. The bag I had hold of lifted up off of the pile, but it got away from me. "Let her down!" I yelled—but it was too late. I released my hold on the netting to avoid falling on the spiny urchins. A split-second later the bag slid off the pile, wildly swinging out over the water.

The neatly coiled dive hose slid off the stern as the *Coyote* leaned farther and farther. My mask, fins, and weight belt fell into the water—time slowed to a standstill as the Coyote started to roll.  "She's going over!" I yelled. When she reached ninety degrees, I dove off. Lenny clung to the rail, trying to avoid the inevitable.

Floating in the water, a few feet away, I watched helplessly as 4,500 pounds of sea urchins splashed into the sea, and my boat rolled over.

Large bubbles gurgled to the surface as she awkwardly settled into her new position, and although the watertight bulkheads kept her afloat, my boat was now upside down.

Dazed, I swam over and joined my friend who was sitting on the belly of our floating craft.

Lenny's eyes were wide with disbelief. "What happened?" he wailed.

I was too stunned to speak.

The urchins, of course, went straight to the bottom, along with everything else. Anything that could float started popping up all around us: sleeping bags, soda pop cans, a bag of tortilla chips. Always alert, Lenny snagged the chips and started eating dinner.

A mix of emotions swept over me. I was mad at myself for being greedy and overloading the boat. Sadly, the engine, wiring, and electronics would be ruined. But the scene was so ridiculous looking—things floating all over the place, Lenny munching on tortilla chips. The humor of our predicament overtook us. A few minutes later, we were laughing our heads off.

"You're not even wet?" I stared at his unblemished clothing.

"It rolled so slow, I just crawled right over." He grinned, tortilla chips stuffed in both cheeks.

The thought of sitting on the boat all night tempered our laughter. We needed to contact the *Hot Chocolate*, who was the closest to us. That's when we looked up and saw that they were gone! So was the *Debra Ann*. The only boat in sight was the *Florentia Marie*, two kelpbeds away.

The unpleasant thought of midnight hypothermia was in my mind as I jumped in the water, swimming as fast as I could toward Weener. Shortly, to my great relief, I could see them headed our way. I stopped swimming and floated on my back, looking up at the evening sky. Weener, our hero, was coming to the rescue.

It was almost dark by the time we were safely aboard the *Florentia*. My boat was upside down at anchor, and all the urchins were on the bottom, but we were happy to be rescued and on our way home.

"I was watching you guys with my binoculars. I couldn't believe it! As soon as your boat rolled, we started scrambling to get our bags aboard and come get you." Weener handed us each a cup of hot coffee.

"You were the last boat on the island, pal." I said. "It would have been a cold, lonely night for us."

"Yeah, this is December, too." Weener gave me an ominous look. We both knew that the outcome could have been disastrous.

...

In return for rescuing us, I gave Weener salvage rights to the *Coyote*. He contracted with my insurance company, and we headed out the next morning aboard the *Florentia Marie* to get my boat. Jerome offered to bring the *Sea Roamer* and lend a hand, so I told him he could dive up the urchins that were under the boat and keep half the profits. But that's not how it worked out.

I wasn't worried about the *Coyote*. She was still at anchor, and there hadn't been any wind. It was another beautiful day. As we idled out of the harbor the fleet was either stacked up at the fuel dock, or on their way to work.

When our two boats were about forty five minutes from Talcott, we got a call on the radio. "*Florentia Marie*, this is the *Maalea* on channel sixteen. Switch and meet me on seventy two, over."

"*Florentia*, switching."

"Hey, you guys, did you give permission for somebody to take Tom's boat? Over." Weener and I looked at each other in disbelief.

"Huh?"

"There's a blue Wilson boat out here and he's got the *Coyote* under tow, trying to get it upright. Over."

"What's the name of the boat? Over."

"I don't know, there's no name on the stern. It's that new guy with the thirty-footer. Over."

"Thanks, buddy."

"Maalea, out."

Jerome, who'd been keeping us company, cruising along at fourteen knots, heard the radio transmission. He instantly kicked his turbo diesel up to speed, and took off like a rocket.

At nine-thirty we arrived on the scene. Sure enough, the strangers in the blue boat had the *Coyote* under tow about a mile from where I had left her. They were trying to get her flipped over, but so far had been unsuccessful.

Jerome motored over to us, came out on deck, and yelled. "I'm not sure what the laws are on salvage rights, but I think those guys have possession of your boat illegally. Can you contact the insurance guys?"

These were pre-cellphone days, so I got on channel twenty-five and hailed the marine operator to put a ship-to-shore call through to Tom Caesar, my insurance agent. We all knew that maritime law was different from land law—I needed some direction.

"They what?" Tom was dumfounded, but he was also unsure about how to proceed—this had never happened before to him. "Stand by on this channel—I'm calling the lawyers in Los Angeles."

After waiting about five minutes, he came back on the radio. "Okay, maritime law states that if the vessel is secured at anchor, which it was, and for a period of less than thirty days, which it was, it is not considered abandoned, and therefore is still the property of the owner. When the persons possessing the vessel arrive in Santa Barbara, they will be arrested."

By now, the *Sea Roamer* and the *Florentia Marie* had moved to within thirty yards of the thieves. Jerome disappeared inside his cabin, and when he reappeared, no one could believe what they were seeing. He wore a camouflage hat, aviator sunglasses, and was cradling an M16 in his arms, weapon of choice for the United States Army Rangers. He walked back to his engine lid, laid the rifle down on it, and stood there staring at the thieves with his arms folded. Then he reached up and adjusted his glasses with his index finger.

The blue boat had been monitoring their radio, along with just about everyone else in the fleet—it was the best show in town. I think they'd been trying to figure out how to make a graceful exit, but after seeing Jerome the commando, they quickly cast off the tow line, and hailed us on channel sixteen.

Apologies were made, along with weak excuses—they claimed they were under the impression the boat had been abandoned, and that they were entitled to salvage rights, being the first boat on the scene. My dive gear was on their boat. It was transferred over in silence.

The urchins were gone. They probably stole them as well, but we had no way of proving it. Besides, my boat was adrift upside down—we needed to get to work. I thanked Jerome, and he headed off to do some diving while Weener and I got busy getting the *Coyote* upright.

The technique for flipping over an upside-down boat is to swim a line underneath it, secure it to the opposite rail cleat, then put the tow boat at the proper angle—about thirty degrees, and the proper distance—about forty feet away, and give it full power. The first three times we tried it, Weener didn't slow down fast enough, and the *Coyote* came over, but she kept rolling, ending up upside down again. Finally, on the fourth attempt, she stayed upright. I took the helm of the *Florentia* while Weener jumped on the *Coyote* with a gas operated bilge pump and pumped out the cabin. Thirty minutes later, the *Coyote* was stable, a tow line was secured, and the slow ride home began.

"I was getting worried about you guys." Debbie was on the dock with hot coffee and cookies. It was nine o'clock. "You said you'd be home before dark."

"It took forever to get her flipped over, but we finally figured it out. Plus, we could only make about five knots coming home."

Two thousand dollars was Weener's pay from the insurance company—a nice payday. And since the boat was delivered in good order, they promised him future contracts. But they determined it would cost more to get the boat fixed than to cash me out, so after owning the *Coyote* for less than two years, I was left with a check for ten grand and no boat.

I didn't know the owner of the blue boat, but I ran into him at the fuel dock a couple of weeks later. It wasn't necessary to say anything—everybody in the harbor knew what had happened.

Two months later, while returning from the islands with a full load of urchins, a blade flew off his propeller, ripped through the bottom of the shaft-driven boat, and she sank. The rumor was that he had no insurance; he quit the business and we never saw him again.

# It's All Good

*It has been said that man is a rational animal. All my life I have been searching for evidence which could support this.*

—Bertrand Russell

### Boats

A decision needed to be made. The eight thousand dollars I had paid for the *Coyote* was a once in a lifetime deal. Urchin diving was becoming popular; boats were expensive.

I knew that I wanted a boat, but which one? Using the insurance money for a down payment on a bigger boat, say a thirty–two footer, made some sense. Of course that meant the commitment of hiring a full-time crew. Also, it would be difficult to find a slip for it. 3-B-55 could only accommodate up to twenty–six. I still owed my dad 4,000 bucks, and I offered to pay him off, but he knew I would need every penny for the purchase of a new boat. "Just keep making your payments," he told me.

Debbie and I talked it over. We decided I should look at different boats, work on some of them, and take a few months to make the final determination.

So, I began my search.

Ron Radon, Sr. was a man with a vision. In the early days of abalone diving, one of the main problems was the high sides of the boats. They had to build stern platforms and ladders in order to have a way to climb up on deck.

Radon designed a boat with decks low to the water. The diver would be able to swim up and climb onto his boat easily. He built a deep-vee shaped hull to cushion the rough seas of the Santa Barbara channel, and he put lifting chines to help get the boat up on plane. Decks were made with a large working area. The new boats were fast, strong, and reliable.

The early designs worked well. Within a few short years jigs were being built to make one piece, molded hulls, and by the mid-seventies, the twenty-four, and thirty-two foot Radon boats were the standards of the industry.

Ron's son, Don took over the business in the eighties. His small boatyard in Goleta now delivers ten boats per year, still incorporating his father's original design. The Radon boats have earned wide respect in the watercraft community, and today they can be seen in harbors all over the world.

Brian Wilson, another abalone diver, also became a popular boat builder. His boats had a sharper bow entry than the Radon's, and the sides were slightly higher. The Wilson boat yard, also located in Goleta, soon began getting orders from urchin divers.

For a ten-year period beginning in the late seventies, eighty percent of all dive boats on the California coast were from one of the Goleta yards.

For me, the year of 1981 was spent diving on different boats, trying to figure out which type to buy.

The *Francesca* was one of the East-Coast-style lobster boats that were beginning to show up in California. She was thirty-foot, diesel powered, with a shaft. Her hull was white, with a large forward cabin that could sleep three comfortably. At $60,000 it was an expensive boat, but reliable, and able to carry the weight.

Domenic Pasquini was Italian. Short, and skinny as a rail, he had an explosive temper and no sense of humor. During my tenure on the *Francesca*, I don't recall ever seeing Dom laugh—he just looked angry all the time.

For such a small man, Dom had an extremely loud voice. He spoke in accusatory tones, trusting no one, and he always had a way of implying that you were guilty of something when he was talking to you.

"Good morning, Dom." I'd been diving on the *Francesca* for a month.

He cast an angry stare my way. "What's so good about it?"

"Well, Captain, it's a beautiful day. We're on the fourth day of a good stretch, and that spot we found yesterday at Cluster Point should give us another day or two of good picking if we're lucky."

His eyes narrowed. "Don't call me captain."

Dom was not a person who was well liked—his abrasive manner made people steer clear of him. I lasted three months with him, which may be a record, but there were good reasons for my long stay on the *Francesca*.

No longer being a boat owner, money became a prime motivator. Debbie and I were paying the bills just fine, but the boats I was shopping for were expensive. We were trying to tuck away as much as possible.

Dom had a habit of accusing other boats of jumping his spots. The following was a routine occurrence on the *Francesca*.

As we approached the kelp beds, Dom would spot a boat, whereupon he would point and scream, "The motherfucker is right on my spot! He's right on my spot!" His face turned various shades of red and purple and large veins protruded from his neck.

"Uh, Dom, I think our spot is over there, about a mile further down." He would then turn to face me, and snarl, "You don't know what the fuck you're talking about! He's right on my spot! That's the *Keoki*! That guy's a friend of yours, huh? You told him we were working here, didn't you? After I kick his ass, I might have to kick your ass too!"

"No, I'm pretty sure we were down a little further, Dom."

Ten minutes later we would drop our anchor, right where we had left off the previous day, a mile from the *Keoki*. A loaded short-barreled shotgun was kept on his bunk, and I saw him threaten to use it more than once. In fact, he was always telling someone he was either going to shoot them or kick their ass.

I only saw him get into one fight though, and it didn't last long.

One night on the dock, Dom was trying to get a tourist, an older gentleman, to move his car, which was parked near the end of the dock, blocking the truck access.

"Hey! Move your goddamned car! My truck can't get out on the dock!"

"Oh yes, sorry," the man responded. He was about seventy, an inch or two taller than Dom, who stood about five-feet-eight. "My wife's in the bathroom. We'll be on our way in just a minute.

"Maybe you didn't hear me! Move that piece of shit before I get my shotgun and put a hole in it!" He then walked over to the old-timer, placed his nose about five inches from his face, and grimaced, "or maybe I'll just kick your ass!" The old guy smiled, took a step backward, and planted his right fist squarely on Dom's nose, putting the skinny Italian flat on his back, where he remained, asleep for a full minute.

Dom did have a few redeeming qualities. Not many, but a few. He was meticulous about the quality of urchins that were harvested on his boat. The *Francesca* consistently delivered top-grade product that brought the highest prices.

He was a tough negotiator, too. Every evening he called the processor whom he was currently selling to.

"Hey, this is Dom."

"Oh, hello Dom." The voice brought on a cringe.

"I was looking at some of the other loads on the dock last night. Those guys are bringing you a bunch of crap. My urchins from yesterday are beautiful."

"You always bring me the best, Dom." (Everyone knew not to disagree with him—it would only make the conversation last longer.)

"I heard you paid the *Pack Rat* twenty cents for one of their loads last month. I only got eighteen. Why are you screwing me?"

"You're my top boat, Dom, my favorite. You know I take good care of you." The processor spoke delicately. "I have another call, Dom. I have to go."

"Goddamnit, don't hang up on me! You owe me two cents a pound for that load on the twentieth of June."

"All right, you'll get it. Good night." It was a relief to hear the click on the other end.

Putting up with him was a chore, but well worth it. Even the buyers in Tokyo knew the reputation of the *Francesca*. For the processor, Dom was a gold mine.

Only one time did I see Dom fire the shotgun—but it wasn't at a human.

Sea otters, the cute, furry mammals that float on their backs while eating abalone, lobster, and of course, sea urchins, were expanding their range from their home in Monterey. We'd heard reports of sightings at Cojo Bay, near Point Conception, and there were rumors of a sighting at San Miguel Island.

On a glassy day, after turning the corner at the east end of San Miguel, Dom spoke for the first time in over an hour. "Those motherfuckers on the *Hard On* better not be in my kelp bed—they spotted us there yesterday."

I had by now taken on the role of therapist. "They had a good pile yesterday, Dom," I said soothingly, as I noticed the familiar veins in his neck beginning to stick out. "I'm sure they'll be on their same spot."

He sneered. "Yeah, well—Holy Shit!" He threw the shifter into neutral, then slammed it into reverse, quickly bringing the *Francesca* to a stop.

"What the hell!" I shouted, after being shoved into the forward bulkhead.

Then I saw it. Twenty yards off our starboard bow, an otter floated on its back, pounding on an abalone shell with a rock.

I was mesmerized by the sight—it was the first otter I had ever seen. I stared at it, transfixed, and watched as it rolled over and over in the calm water, splashing and tapping on the abalone shell. It had long whiskers, and black beads for eyes. It was oblivious to us as it expertly held the rock and continued tapping.

BLAM! The peaceful quiet was interrupted by Dom's shotgun. BLAM! Another blast. "Got him!" Dom screamed gleefully. "You won't be getting any of my urchins, you motherfucker!"

The otter was gone. I wasn't sure if Dom had actually hit him or not, but he was nowhere to be seen.

"Jesus, Dom. What'd you do that for?"

"You dumb shit!" He screamed. He was sweating and shaking, the smoking shotgun still in his hands. "If those motherfuckers start a colony here, we're screwed! They'll put us out of business!"

I kept quiet. Even that night on the dock when he was bragging about his kill, I stayed on the boat.

Sea otters eat a lot, there's no doubt about that. In fact, since they have no blubber layer, it's necessary for them to consume a full 25 percent of their body weight daily. But for me, it was a tough call. Dom wasn't the only person I had heard talking of the dangers of otters wiping out local shellfish populations. But I don't think I would kill one.

The spineless Italian was hard to get along with and I only lasted a few months with him before quitting and moving on. He was also a blatant spot jumper and an asshole. My time on the *Francesca* was beneficial though—I became familiar with the East-Coast lobster boats. They're nice—stable and roomy. But the mid-engine setup is noisy, and they were too expensive.

The *Pisagna* (pronounced piss on ya), was the second of three boats built by Matt Chapin. The twenty-six-foot hull was constructed at the Wilson yard to his custom specifications. A lighter grade of fiberglass cloth, with fewer laminations was used. The sides of the boat were lowered three inches. Matt was weight conscious and proud that his boat only weighed three thousand four hundred and forty-two pounds, including fuel and gear. A custom built Chevy motor with thru-hull exhaust easily put the boat up on plane with four thousand pounds aboard.

Matt was a loner, always working by himself. No tender, just him. He was sneaky, too. We all did whatever we could not to bring attention to ourselves—it might keep our spot from being found. Unlike the polished yachts with lots of chrome, urchin boats avoided having anything shiny aboard that might reflect sunlight, so as to keep from being seen by the competition. The paint on our boats was allowed to fade for the same reason. The *Pisagna* was flat black and blended well against the islands, making her difficult to spot.

Coming in at night, the running lights of the *Pisagna* were kept off. The boats he passed up could not see what direction he was coming from, so nobody knew which island he was diving. The *Pisagna* was fast, and stealthy.

Matt would pull out at dawn, with a lunch consisting of a root beer and an Eskimo pie, beat everyone to the harbor that night, and kick all our asses.

Six foot six, tall and skinny, he was born and raised in Santa Barbara. His long blonde hair gave him the appearance of a typical California surfer, which he was.

Unlike most of the other divers and fishermen, Matt neither smoked nor drank. He did have some idiosyncrasies though. His blue Volkswagen sported a Coupe De Ville insignia he had removed from a Cadillac.

A natural tendency for inventing, along with a playful sense of humor, were his hallmarks. He built a stainless steel slingshot with a three-foot-long handle that slipped into a sleeve on the stern corner of the *Pisagna*. From underwater spear gun bands and a leather purse he fashioned a weapon that could launch a projectile over a hundred yards. Next, he fabricated a nozzle that he welded onto his cooling system. This device could fill a water balloon in three seconds.

After a few days of practice, and several hundred water balloons, he could hit another boat from a football field away. But, in the interest of safety, he always gave fair warning by giving a couple of blasts on a hand-held air horn before he commenced firing. Nobody ever got hurt by the powerful weapon, but he did put out the window of the *Wet Willie*, who jumped his spot.

After breaking down one night in the middle of the shipping lanes, his distress call came over the radio loud and clear. "Coast Guard, Santa Barbara, piss on ya. I'm adrift mid channel and requesting assistance. Coast Guard, Santa Barbara, piss on ya.

Twenty-six-foot Wilson—very custom, very nice.

The *Snubnose* was old, slow, and stinky. It was a former Navy transport that Barry McNellis had converted into a dive boat, and the motor (an old Detroit diesel), had more hours on it than my dad. Oil spewed from all points, and the engine room had no insulation, making it unbearably loud.

The *Snubber*, as it was called, only made about seven knots. The propeller was bent, creating a constant vibration that shimmied throughout the boat, and her long, narrow hull made for a constant rocking motion, so seasickness was a common occurrence.

Besides the dreadful things described above, the *Snubnose* was ugly. A dark navy gray, it had not seen a new coat of paint for decades.

The engine room was a disaster area. Electrical wires wandered aimlessly about, some connected to something, some lying in the oily bilge. Rust and oil were everywhere, and the fact that it ran at all was remarkable.

Barry was tall and lanky, with red hair and a beard. A twang in his voice alerted people to his upbringing in Houston, Texas. He wound up in Santa Barbara while working as a crewmember on a yacht that had pulled into town for a brief visit. After a couple of weeks, when the owner wanted to shove off, Barry jumped ship, making Santa Barbara his home.

If you could use one word to describe Barry, it would be exuberant. Smiling came easy. He used to say "Why be miserable? Happiness is a better option!" Life excited the tall, easygoing Texan who had many friends.

He was a collector. Old derelict cars, motorcycles, lawnmowers, you name it. He had an uncanny way of getting things for free, or for next to nothing, then selling them for a huge profit.

The *Snubnose* was Barry's home, but within a year he had somehow managed to buy a small house in an exclusive area of town. A few months later there was a baby blue Jaguar parked in the garage. He had bought the car, which did not run at the time, for $500. Three months later he sold it for $5,000.

The perpetually happy Texan with holes in his jeans had the ugliest boat in the harbor, but he was one of the nicest people you could ever hope to meet. His boat, however, was a disaster—I knew a Navy hull would not be in my future.

The decision was made. A twenty-six-foot Wilson hull sat in our front yard, waiting to be outfitted. It was brown and tan, with an enclosed steering station. Two large holds, capable of carrying 500 pounds each had been built into the deck. These holds had become standard for any new urchin boat being built, for they lowered the center of gravity, making the boat more stable with a load. They also provided more room for urchins and provided a storage area below decks.

Buying the engine package separately, wiring up the lights, and installing a mast and boom myself, I hoped to save about ten thousand dollars. I did save money, but the work took several months, so the logic was questionable.

Finally, in December 1981, she was ready; all we needed was a name. This was a most important decision, not to be taken lightly.

A boat name tells something about its owner. It can announce love for mother, father, wife, or loved one. Or it can send a message, like tough guy Mark Evanoff and the *Defiance*, or the two-man partnership, *Joint Venture*. A college educated diver (there weren't many of us), named his boat the *Gray Matter*.

Boat names have a habit of being shamefully distorted by the other divers. The guy who had the *Gravy Train* kept a messy boat. It became the *Gravy Stain*. The lazy owner of the *Pack Rat* earned the title, *Slack Rat*. The *Phillip Lloyd*, which was named after the owner's father, rolled over from overloading. When the boat reappeared a year later, it was cruelly called the *Flip Lloyd*. The *Sea Cow*, owned by the fattest diver on the coast, required no change. Nor did the aptly named *Hard On*.

Even a person's name was subject to conversion. John Colgate, when he was new in the business, followed other boats in order to find their spots (we all did). His nickname became Tailgate. There was Filthy Phil, Poacher Pete, and of course, speedy Steve Hagen—Hydroplane.

We racked our brains for days, but could not come up with a name. Then it finally came.

A Dalmatian puppy had come into our lives a few months before—it was always getting under our feet, so we had named him Tripper.

"How about Tripper?" Debbie offered.

"Or Trippin', after the surf song?" I countered.

"You like naming things after songs, right? The boat is set up for one day trips, right? How about the Beatles song, 'Day Tripper'?"

"Perfect!"

We named our boat after the dog. Debbie and I both liked it, and I thought it would be immune from an embarrassing mutation, but I was wrong. Several months later, after encroaching on another diver's spot, my boat, to my dismay, was dubbed the *Day Jumper*.

### Launch Day

"Moan back, moan back," John Holcomb was hollering. A good-natured diver pal, John was somewhat of a hillbilly. As I was backing his truck and trailer down the ramp, he was telling me to "C'mon back."

The last two weeks had been a frenzy of nonstop work, but it was finally launch day for the *Day Tripper*. We were broke now, just squeaking by on Debbie's piano money.

John was nice enough to give a hand with his truck and trailer, and as I drove the truck, he coaxed me down the ramp. "Moan back, Tom, moan back."

I was filled with pride, making a big production out of the launching. Our neighbors, who had been extremely tolerant having to look at the boat for months, came down. My parents showed up of course, and some other friends.

Just before the *Day Tripper* went into the water, Debbie broke a bottle of tequila on the bow. Everybody cheered—it was great.

"Moan back," John guided me down the ramp. A cheer went up from the small crowd of onlookers as the boat slipped smoothly off the trailer. She was floating! A brand new boat hitting the water for the first time is a beautiful sight. It really is.

I pulled the trailer out of the water as John tied the boat to the dock. After parking the truck, I stood at the top of the ramp basking in accolades and receiving several pats on the back. Meanwhile, John opened the engine hatch. "Hey, somthin' ain't right here," he shouted. "There's water comin' in."

Tearing away from my family and friends, I hopped on the boat, where, from inside the engine room, came the distinct sound of running water. My boat was leaking! If we didn't get the trailer back under her, she was going to sink!

160

John scratched his head as he watched the waterfall in the engine room, the guests gazed at the boat with curiosity, and I ran back to the parking lot to get the truck. It turned out to be a minor leak around the transom plate, and after we got her out of the water it only took a couple of hours to fix. My face was red for a few days though, when word got around the harbor that my new boat almost sank on launch day.

The *Day Tripper* was first-rate. She jumped up on plane, cruising at twenty-three knots. Filtered air was supplied by a compressor system built by Crazy Harold, and the aluminum mast and boom from Waterfront Fabricators was light and strong. Brown and tan were good colors for the boat, for she could not be easily seen by the competition, and even though she was only two feet longer than the Coyote, she had the feel of a much bigger boat. The two fish holds held 1,000 pounds below decks, and now all the nets and gear could be stored below, instead of cluttering up the main deck. An overhead roof with side walls afforded protection from the sea spray, and swept back tinted windows gave her a sleek, somewhat mysterious profile. Raytheon had recently come out with small digital radar, which fit perfectly on the dash. I had myself a fine boat.

## 100% Cotton

Lenny bought the *Little Wing* from Hydroplane Hagen, so I was on the lookout for a diver.

Jim Cotton, who worked at Waterfront Fabricators and had built my boom system, was also an urchin diver. He accepted my job offer and became the first crewmember of the *Day Tripper*.

Cotton's favorite color was green. His shirts were green. His bag lines on the boat were green. He even found green netting for his urchin bags. When asked why he liked green so much, a broad smile came over his face. "Because it's the fastest color!"

In order to understand this happy, creative, and downright different man, some of his background needs to be known.

Cotton was a Santa Barbara local. The ocean had been a big part of his life since he was a kid learning how to sail. One of his passions was windsurfing, and he owned several sailboards, all of them green.

Five-foot-ten, tan and balding, Cotton could best be described as "Burly." He was not overly fat nor was he in top athletic condition. This was partly due to another of his passions—chips, guacamole, and cervezas at the Brophy Brothers restaurant, overlooking the Santa Barbara harbor.

Cotton's mind did not work like mine. I studied a kelp bed, looking for signs of a potential harvesting area. He pointed out the beauty of the sunlight reflecting off of the kelp leaves.

He was an artist, a metal fabricator, a creator. He had a strange sense of humor that kept everyone around him off guard.

The main ingredient of this man's good humor and twisted outlook on life can be traced back to the days he spent in captivity.

Cotton was also a smuggler. In the late seventies, while on his way to pick up a load of weed from Southeast Asia, his boat was confiscated by Vietnamese authorities. He was arrested and put into a small bamboo "Monkey Cage," where he lived for over a year, undergoing interrogation. Periodically, he was forced to stand up in the corner of his cage, his captors forbidding him the luxury of sitting down. Eventually, he collapsed in tears, to the delight of the soldiers, who apparently suspected the tan, longhaired westerner of being a CIA spy.

A guard was stationed near his cage. One day, he began whittling on some bamboo, making several long, thin shoots. His perpetual smile made my friend nervous. Jim figured these items would be inserted underneath his fingernails and used for torture.

As the guard approached him one day with the bamboo stalks, Cotton cringed. He sank into the corner of his cage, preparing to defend himself, figuring that this could quite possibly be the end.

Reaching his hand through the bars, the guard shoved the stalks toward him. Practically in tears, Cotton made ready for the final fight.

As he pulled a stalk from the bundle, the guard demonstrated its use to the prisoner. He placed one end into his mouth, and began cleaning his teeth. He had been making toothpicks! Cotton eagerly grabbed at his gifts, thanking the soldier in broken Vietnamese.

Back home, his parents had contacted the American Embassy, trying in vain to discover any information regarding their son. All of his friends had given him up for dead.

After eleven months of living in the cage, Cotton was released. He had lost thirty pounds, was weak and frail, but happy to be free.

Friends in Santa Barbara were taken by surprise. Cotton had returned from the dead!

A party was thrown in his honor at the boatyard. "Where the hell have you been?" he was asked by one of the divers.

"I was taking a Vietnamese immersion language course, but I'm back." He was obviously feeble, but the smile was still there." Hope the conditions are good. I'm ready for some windsurfing!"

Cotton was a joy to have on the boat; he was a hard worker with a good attitude. We elected not to use a tender, so his percentage was to be 60 percent of his catch. In no time at all, the overdue bills were paid, and the bank account was growing.

## Mexico

It was around this time that I got a phone call from Lenny, who had recently returned from a surfing trip to northern Baja.

"Meet me at the Minnow in thirty minutes! Bring Cotton if you can find him!"

Cotton was in the shop, welding up a mast and boom system, but tore himself away and joined me. When we arrived at the Minnow, Lenny was at one of the outdoor tables with three styrofoam coffee cups in front of him. Cotton and I exchanged suspicious glances, as neither of us had ever known Lenny to spring for coffee.

"How was the surf?" I asked the traveler. His skin was peeling, an even darker brown than usual.

"Really good, I wound up about a hundred and fifty kilometers below the border. The guy who was with me bailed, but I stayed an extra week, and it's a good thing I did."

Cotton was looking at his fingers, wishing he was back in the shop. He'd promised his client that the job would be finished by tomorrow. "So, good waves, huh? That's great, Lenny." He was planning his escape. We both knew that once our friend started a story, it was difficult to get away.

"Yeah, yeah, excellent waves. But that's not why I called you guys. I'm gonna tell you something, but first, you gotta swear to keep it a secret."

After securing our vows of silence, he continued.

"I wound up in the Punta Cabras area. A local family took me in. They gave me a hammock and kept me stuffed with fish tacos for several days."

"So, I'm surfing one morning, and I look out in the kelp bed, a couple of hundred yards outside of me. What do you think I see?"

"A whale!" I chuckled.

"A naked girl swimming!" Cotton snickered.

"No. I saw a little skiff, and guess what they were doing?"

"C'mon, Lenny, just tell us! I gotta get back to work." Cotton was losing his patience, his free cup of coffee having been drained.

"Okay, okay. They were diving urchins! I paddled out to the boat, and started up a conversation. Turns out he's the brother of the guy whose house I'm staying at."

"So, we chat for awhile, I tell 'em I'm an urchin diver in California. He gets interested, says he heard we make up to twenty cents a pound. He says they get, like, eight to ten cents. I say, yeah, we get around twenty cents, right? He tells me the whole area is loaded, but there are only two boats, him and his cousin. Plus, they have these little tiny compressors that only get them down to thirty or forty feet. They've never even checked out the deeper beds." Cotton and I leaned forward. We were now interested.

"The two cousins come over to the house that night and we have a barbeque with my new family. Turns out, my landlord is like the mayor of the little pueblito. He owns about twenty hectares of tomatoes, and a bunch of empty beachfront land. He's either the father or uncle to the whole village.

"Now comes the good part. I say, how about if I bring a couple of friends down from Santa Barbara, and train some of the locals. We'll provide nice air systems, and get them checked out on safe diving techniques. Then, we'll have a truck come down to take the urchins to our California processor. I'll guarantee the divers seventeen cents a pound. They all look at each other and say, "Si, como no? Sure, why not?"

I interrupted. "But we're getting thirty cents, Lenny."

"Bingo!" He smiles, obviously pleased with himself. "They have another boat in the next town over, and know other guys who want to dive. After we get these guys trained, they'll be able to bring in about ten thousand pounds a day between them. We can pay them seventeen cents a pound, which'll make them happier than clams, so we'll net ten cents, or a thousand bucks per load, maybe two loads per week. And that's just the beginning—just think if we can help them to put a little fleet together, say five or six boats. We can do a truckload every day! We rotate, so one of us is always down there, and split the profit three ways. That's three or four hundred a day each, and we're not even getting wet, except to go surfing. Chew on that, amigos!

Cotton and I looked at each other, our heads were spinning.

Cotton spoke first. "We can't tell a soul."

Lenny continued. "Listen, this'll be a lot of work, and we need to spend some money. For starters, I told them I'd be down in a couple of weeks with two nice air systems. Tom, you spend a lot of time over at Crazy's. See what he'd charge us for two compressor rigs, with mounting stands and small volume tanks. Cotton, you're Ocean Princess's favorite diver. Everybody knows that Mitsiko has a crush on you. Do you think she'd guarantee us thirty cents a pound for a steady supply from Mexico?" (Mitsiko's plant now employed over a hundred workers. Rumor had it that she and Cotton had a "special" relationship.)

"Are you kidding? She's expanding, moving her operations to a new, bigger location. She's dying for more product! I can talk to her tomorrow, but I know she'll jump on it. She's even got two new trucks on order!"

"Are we all in?" Lenny stuck his hand out. Cotton and I placed our hands atop our pal's. "We need a name!" I shouted. After much discussion on this important topic, Lenny finalized it.

"This is our dream, being at a place where we can surf and make money. It's a lovely little village, but poor.

Who knows, maybe someday we can help them—maybe build them a soccer field, or a basketball court. Let's call it Sueña Nuestra, Our Dream."

Debbie was skeptical, but she could see how excited I was, so she reluctantly agreed. When I got into a frenzy like this, it was useless to argue. She knew I would eventually wear her down.

Crazy Harold had a boat in his driveway he was working on, but he agreed to put a rush on the air systems. "Gitchyer dumb ass over here in a week and bring hundreds," he told me.

Two months later, after spending close to two thousand dollars for the air rigs and some dive gear for our Mexican recruits, we were up and rolling. As expected, Ocean Princess took care of the trucking, and thanks to Cotton, Mitsiko agreed to pay us thirty-two cents a pound. She wanted to renegotiate every ninety days, which made us a little nervous, but we had the product she wanted, and besides, we trusted her. Sort of.

Our Mexican compadres had two fiberglass pangas, which we dubbed the Mexican Radons. They were twenty feet long, with high bows and open cockpits. The boats were nice, the only downside being that they had no radios and were powered by old, tired Mercury outboard motors. The third boat was a thirty-foot wooden scow with no motor, but since the diving beds were only a couple of miles away from the little beach at Punta Cabras, they could just tow it out there.

It was a lot more work than we thought. There was no hoist or pier for the urchins to be offloaded. As the boats came in each afternoon, they were driven right up on to the beach. Then the bags, which weighed about a hundred pounds each, were unloaded by hand, and stacked in waiting pickup trucks. The trucks, which were four-wheel drive, drove up the beach and into the village where the urchins were loaded, again by hand, into the waiting Ocean Princess trucks.

We hadn't realized the operation would be so labor intensive—it took almost the whole town to load the trucks, but the people were excited, and did not want any pay. They were all related, and knew that the gringo surfers were bringing prosperity to the little village. We felt guilty, and insisted that they allow us to pay them, but our offers were refused.

Within a few weeks, things were going smoothly. It was so good in fact, that whoever was down there was able to go surfing in the morning, then meet the boats in the afternoon and oversee the truck loading. By late September 1985, we were delivering two trucks per week, each one carrying between eight and twelve thousand pounds—plus Mitsiko was taking care of the trucking costs.

Sueña Nuestra was a smashing success. For three months.

"No puedes trabajar aqui." A fat man in a rumpled white shirt stood beside his new Ford Explorer. Lenny, who was our man on the spot, understood enough Spanish to know that there was a complication. The three young soldiers with machine guns were further evidence of a problem.

Mexican fishing operations are run by cooperatives, local organizations that oversee certain areas of the coast. This man was the head of the local *cooperativa*, which was located about thirty miles south of Cabras. Apparently, word had gotten around of some gringos taking their sea urchins to Los Angeles.

"Lo siento, amigo." I'm sorry, my friend. The mayor carried much weight in the town, but this was over his head, and he was powerless to help.

It all happened very quickly. Lenny was escorted to the border by the three gun-toting teenagers but was not allowed to bring any of our gear or air compressors back to the States.

He noticed however, that the Ocean Princess trucks were permitted to stay.

"We got burned, amigos." Cotton and I sat at the Minnow, sipping coffee, listening to Lenny. "They were watching us the whole time. As soon as we got things going, they went straight to Ocean Princess and made a deal. Mitsiko's hands were tied 'cause they had the government behind them—now she's getting the urchins and we got screwed."

We made some money on the Mexico venture, but not nearly enough to make it worth the hassle. Ocean Princess benefited greatly, though, and she remained grateful to us for opening up a new supply for her.

For the three of us it was a learning experience. We went in naively, didn't go through the proper channels, and paid for our ignorance.

"Yeah, we got burned. But you know what?" Cotton stirred his coffee. He was scanning the horizon with squinted eyes, a faraway look on his face. "Those villagers are some of the nicest people I've ever met. They were constantly helping us out, not expecting anything in return. All those lobsters and fish tacos they fed us, not to mention the whole damn town coming down and lugging those urchin bags from the boats. Punta Cabras will always have a special place in my heart. I'm going to make it a point to visit there at least once a year for a couple of weeks—maybe take the kids a few bags of clothes from the Goodwill." Lenny and I nodded our heads in agreement.

We'd all fallen in love with the little pueblito—the people we met, and the small community had become a part of us. We had been exposed to the beauty of Mexico and her people, and the simplicity of life down there. All of the houses had dirt floors. There was no indoor plumbing, no television, no radio. The kids were shoeless, their toys were sticks and rocks. We had never known anybody so poor, or so happy. In fact, none of us had ever known so many people with such natural good will and generosity.

So it came to be that in the course of failing miserably at our endeavor, we gained something more valuable than we ever could have imagined. We discovered people who did not measure happiness in dollars. Making do with what you have, and helping out your fellow man are worthy goals in life.

That morning at the Minnow Café the three founding members of Sueña Nuestra made a solemn commitment to try to be more like the inhabitants of Punta Cabras, and to visit them often.

By 1985, competition from other parts of the world was beginning to make it tougher on us. Urchins were being harvested in Mexico and Canada. A small fleet was getting started in Washington, and there was talk about Alaska. The green sea urchin, a smaller variety, had been discovered off the coast of Maine. Our immediate concern though, was Chile, where the divers were working for pennies.

Since the supply was on the increase, the Japanese could afford to be pickier. There was now a large spread in price, depending on things like roe color, yield of A grade, freshness, and firmness. One boat might get paid twenty cents a pound, and another would get sixty cents.

I once made an overnighter by myself to Talcott Shoals. The urchins stayed on deck in the sun on a hot day, which softened the roe. My check was for two cents a pound.

If a boat consistently brought in an inferior product, the processor would fire him. We had to become quality conscious to survive.

The technological advances that were a part of this decade contributed to the boating industry. Raytheon, a leader in marine electronics came out with a digital radar that could fit into the smaller boats. LORAN, a navigational system using land based triangulation, also became available. We could now pinpoint our location, and by entering a position on the unit, we could return to the area, placing the boat within fifty feet of our spot. Subtle skills, such as lining up landmarks on the islands, and "reading" the kelp beds, were replaced by the skill of operating your LORAN unit.

The old fathometers sent a Doppler signal from the boat to the bottom, giving a number indicating the depth. Now, however, we had color Fish Finders, which drew a picture of the reefs below. No longer were we swimming down to the bottom, only to find sand.

Wrist-mounted dive computers that calculate the maximum allowable bottom time were being used so the diver knew exactly how long he could safely stay on the bottom without fear of decompression sickness.

Boats were faster, more reliable, and carried more weight. Urchin beds at the islands were thinning out, and the days of pulling up to a random kelp bed, tossing the anchor, and loading up were gone. Some boats began running three divers to get their load.

The fishery was still wide open, with new people getting in every year. It didn't happen all at once, but changes were in the air, and we all knew it.

# PART II

# The North Coast

*When you come to a fork
in the road, take it.*
    —*Yogi Berra*

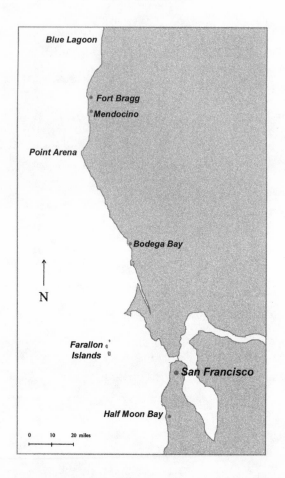

## Pioneers

I'm telling you guys, we can make a killing. I've got it all planned out—trucks, buyers, everything."

George Tomlinson had brought a select group of urchin divers together for a meeting in his house across from Oak Grove Park in Santa Barbara.

"The Mendocino coast is loaded with uni. I negotiated a base price of twenty-five cents a pound with The Spaniard. Now, I know it's not as much as we're getting for our

Channel Islands product, but consider this—we'll only travel two miles or less to the urchin beds, and the picking is unlimited. I spent two days surveying last month. It's all virgin territory!"

George was an ex-Navy SEAL, who had commanded a platoon of men in Vietnam. His exploits, even in that elite group, were widely known. A regimen of physical conditioning drilled into him from the military kept his forty-year-old body lean and hard.

He was a serious man, looking at each day as a mission to be completed. In the competitive business of sea urchin harvesting, George was a front runner.

Tomlinson was not a tall person, and did not stand out in a crowd—until you saw his eyes. They were light blue, with a piercing quality that seemed to look right through you. When he was talking, his eyes captured your attention.

Hydroplane Hagen, Jim Robinson and Mike Kitihara listened. They were under his spell, each of them silently calculating.

"Where are we gonna stay?"

"I've got a place in escrow up on the Navarro Ridge. It's a thirty-minute drive from the cove at Point Arena, where there's a pier with a fish hoist. There's no marina though, so our boats need to stay on moorings—we'll have to row out to them in dinghies.

"The coastline up there is incredibly beautiful, and the bottom is untouched. We need four boats to fill the truck. You're the guys I want, and I hope you join me. But if you decide to stay here, I'll find somebody else."

After a fourteen-hour drive in September 1986, the caravan of trucks, trailers, and boats arrived at George's property on the Navarro Ridge, Mendocino County.

The four men got out and stretched under the light of a full moon.

"I'm ready to crash. Lead me to my bed." Mike Kitihara spoke for the three recruits. All they could see were trees.

George fixed his eyes on the group, pointing to a small clearing. "We'll camp here. After some of these trees are cleared, this is where I'm going to build my house."

Steve, Weener, and Mike were aghast. "There's no fucking house! We just towed our boats five hundred miles, and we're sleeping on the ground!" Hydroplane was dumfounded.

"Calm down you guys. I knew if I told you there was no house, you wouldn't have come. Right now we need to get some sleep, then we'll get the boats in the water tomorrow. A truck will be on the pier at Point Arena in two days, and we're gonna have twenty thousand pounds of urchins waiting for it. After that first load, we can relax for a few days, and if you want, you can find a place to rent. But I'm staying here."

They knew they'd been snookered but were too tired to argue. Sleeping bags were unloaded from the trucks and soon the grumbling and cursing subsided. The four adventurers lay under the redwood trees and snored atop the moist earth of northern California.

Although they did not know it at the time, the small band of fortune seekers was spearheading a boom, the likes of which had not been seen since the days of the gold rush. Within two years, over a hundred boats were harvesting urchins in the waters from Bodega Bay to Fort Bragg, and beyond.

Logging and commercial fishing, the two primary industries in the area, had been on the decline for years, but the large influx of divers brought demand for businesses of all types. Local families learned how to make urchin bags, baskets, and rakes. Welders had a new supply of customers needing parts repaired and manufactured. Boat mechanics no longer sat idle in their shops, wishing for a customer.

Hotels, rental properties, and of course bar owners were now busily taking care of the newcomers from central and southern California.

Real estate sales, which had been in a slump since the severe winter of 1983, were now on the rise. Attendance in the grade schools grew as divers relocated their families. A young local entrepreneur, Bob Juntz, opened up a processing plant, and within a year, Ocean Fresh Seafoods, located on the dock in Fort Bragg was employing fifty workers.

Truck drivers, dock workers, teachers, even local doctors were busy. Medical specialists quickly learned how to carefully remove the brittle sea urchin spines from deep inside a hand or foot.

In 1985, less than one million pounds of urchins were harvested from the waters off Mendocino and Sonoma counties. Two years later, in 1987, over thirty-five million pounds were landed. In the ten year period beginning in 1986, North Coast divers were paid over one hundred million dollars.

The four pioneers worked together for that first season, filling the trucks that Andreas sent them. As new processors moved in however, and the boom got under way, the friends parted company.

Mike Kitihara bought a place in the town of Albion, and began working out of the small harbor there. His children grew up on the North Coast, where the Kitiharas have made their home.

Steve Hagen settled in Philo, several miles inland, away from the coastal fog. After eight years of diving on the North Coast, his enterprising spirit took him to Norway, where he was instrumental in creating a new sea urchin fishery.

After two seasons on the North Coast, Weener returned to Santa Barbara, and his beloved San Miguel Island.

George Tomlinson bought two more boats, at one time running a crew of eight divers. He built his house on Navarro Ridge, complete with imported Australian Rosewood furniture, and a well-stocked library.

Our paths were not to cross for two more years, in other waters.

## Road Trip

A combination of El Niño conditions along with two winters of big surf had wiped out the kelp beds at the Channel Islands. The urchins were not eating, making the roe skinny and of poor quality. A tremendous amount of pressure had been put on the Santa Barbara urchin beds in the last few years. Our loads were smaller now, and prices had dropped.

By now, the winter of 1986, we'd heard of some boats heading up north. Word had trickled down that they were doing good—big loads and short trips.

We were struggling, but Debbie was pregnant, so we weren't going anywhere.

Donovan James Kendrick was born on December 15, 1986. He was huge, dwarfing the other babies in the nursery ward. Both of our families came to Goleta Valley Hospital to see our ten-pound-three-ounce baby. My Dad brought a football, Debbie's Mom joked that the floor underneath his crib needed reinforcing. We were parents!

Cotton and I attacked the islands with renewed vigor. I had a family to support now. Debbie was taking time off from her piano teaching, which made me feel even more dedicated to my task. But after a few more weeks of slim pickings and low prices, I'd had enough.

I was itching to check out the North Coast, so when Donovan was six weeks old, we packed up our 1977 Oldsmobile and burned rubber. Just before leaving the house, the phone rang. It was Cotton.

"You goin' up north to check it out?"

"Yep."

"Well, if you decide to take the *Day Tripper* up there, count me in."

"Roger that, amigo."

It's about a twelve-hour drive from Santa Barbara to Mendocino, but we took three days, stopping at relatives along the way to show off the baby.

We stayed at a motel one night. After I brought our bags in, Debbie gave me a funny look. "Did you forget anything?"

"Nope." I answered, glancing around the room. "I got both bags, honey."

"You forgot the baby!" I slapped myself, then retrieved Donovan from his car seat.

The next day we arrived at the North Coast. Coming off of Highway 128, seeing Big River, and looking down at Albion Bay, we were awestruck, and overcome with emotion. The beauty and wildness of the coastline was so powerful that we pulled the car over and sat for a time without speaking.

Santa Barbara is a beautiful coastline, but houses and sidewalks line the bluffs overlooking the sea. Here, thick green forests came to an abrupt end at the ocean, which crashed onto high barren cliffs and huge offshore rocks. From our perch high above, on the Albion Bridge, we could see the small boat basin, the tranquil Albion Bay, and on out to the open sea. We were amazed and overwhelmed by the splendor and magnitude of the North Coast.

Fort Bragg was our next stop, and after driving the windy roads through Elk, Little River, and Mendocino, we checked into the Reef Motel. Then I made a beeline for the harbor to find a boat to work on the next day.

It didn't take long to line something up. Gilbert Mercado, a Santa Barbara transplant, offered me a spot on his boat, the *Nichole Marie*, which sat in a slip in Noyo Harbor.

The *Nichole Marie* was a thirty-five-foot Radon clone. She was painted a horrendous green, and stuck out like a sore thumb. Cotton later told me that by the time he had finished building the boat, Gilbert was flat broke, and didn't have money for the final color coat. When one of the guys at the boatyard offered to give him the green gelcoat for free, he gratefully accepted. It became known by the fleet as the Sea Pickle.

Gilbert and I got an early start. This was the first time I had ever seen ice on the deck of a boat—the January air was cold, but like many of the other North Coast boats, the *Nichole Marie* had been rigged with a hot water hose for getting into your wetsuit and raising your body temperature between dives.

We soon found what I'd been hearing about. Urchins, urchins, and more urchins.

By four o'clock I was back in the motel room.

"It looks good, honey."

"So, you want to move up here, I suppose."

"Can you put your students on hold for six weeks or so? Steve and Lori are up here, it might be fun!"

"Six weeks?"

"Six weeks."

"Are you turning into a capitalist?"

"An adventure capitalist! How much time do you need to notify your students?"

She laughed. "I told them two weeks ago."

I picked up the phone and called Cotton.

"Start packing pal."

## Changes in Latitudes

Bring her down, buddy." Cotton worked the chain hoist, lowering the new engine into the 1978 Ford truck as I eased it onto the mounting brackets.

"The wind's howling, all my sailboard buddies are up at Jalama, and here I am, playing auto mechanic," he grumbled as we set the motor in place.

"Don't worry, I hear Bodega Bay has some of the best windsurfing conditions in the world. Besides, you're gonna be rich!" I'd been trying for months to turn him into a capitalist, with no success.

It took longer than I had figured. Two months alone for the truck—new brakes, u-joints, tires, engine, everything. Cotton talked a friend into selling me his rusty boat trailer. It needed sandblasting, paint and brakes. When the weather was good we dove, but we were both anxious to get up north.

On July 8, 1987, Debbie and I locked up the house, said goodbye to Santa Barbara, and hit the road. Cotton drove his truck, I towed the boat, and Debbie followed with Donovan in the Oldsmobile.

Two days later the *Day Tripper* floated in tiny Albion harbor. Cotton took a picture from the bridge as I drove the boat out of the narrow inlet—the image of that first excursion out into the gray, calm ocean of the North Coast hangs on my wall today, and is one of my finest treasures.

We rented a little house in Irish Beach, a small development fifteen minutes up the road from Point Arena. Cotton camped in our front yard in his truck.

It was July—foggy, flat, and beautiful.

Everything here was different. There was no dock to walk down to step onto the boats. They sat on moorings in the cove at Point Arena. Small skiffs, tied to the pier pilings, or dragged up on to the rocky beach, were used to access the boats.

The underwater visibility on this coast was dramatically dirtier than we were used to at the Channel Islands. The bottom was mostly sand channels with smooth reefs. Some areas had long, deep rock canyons. The bland, brown reefs were downright ugly compared to the spectacular diving areas we had come to know in Santa Barbara.

There were two redeeming factors, though. One, instead of the twenty-five mile open water crossing, the dive spots here were five minutes away. Two, there were more urchins than we had ever seen. A typical survey of the bottom would last about thirty seconds before finding a place to throw the anchor. In short, it was urchin diver heaven.

Point Arena is forty miles south of Fort Bragg and sixty miles north of Bodega Bay. These are not freeway miles, the roads are winding and driving on this coastline is slow and dangerous.

At first glance, a city dweller from San Francisco or Santa Barbara might think he has stepped back in time fifty years. The town of Point Arena, two miles inland of the cove, is small, with a population of about 500. There is one main street with no stoplights. A dry goods store and a real estate office occupy this area, along with two small eateries and a gas station. The buildings are old and in disrepair. The sidewalks are uneven too, but even so, the small, three block area has a disarming charm about it.

The Seashell Motel was built in the fifties. The floors slant a little, and the building leans to starboard, but for fifty dollars a clean room can be had for your stay in beautiful downtown Point Arena. The refurbished movie theatre is the one notable exception to this otherwise nondescript street.

As in many small towns all across the country, the residents wave and smile at one another, offering a friendly daily greeting. Strangers however, are generally ignored.

The cove is large, able to accommodate up to forty boats. It offers protection from the fierce northerly winds, but not from the large winter ocean swells, sometimes up to twenty feet, that assault the North Coast every year.

Early names by the seagoing Spaniards were Barra De Arena and Punta De Arena (Sand Point). Prior to 1866, when the first wharf was built, schooners were loaded with lumber by using chutes. Several wharfs were destroyed over the years by storms, but after the severe winter storm of 1983, the Army Corps of Engineers constructed a concrete pier, complete with two fish hoists, a boat hoist, a piermaster's office, and hot showers.

Surfers, exploring the North Coast in the seventies, discovered good waves in this lonely, desolate area. The hardy band of waveriders who live there today are a rugged bunch, protective of their coastline, and sometimes unfriendly to visitors.

I was clearing eight hundred bucks a day, Cotton was clearing three fifty. We were home by three, working seven days a week. I loved it. Debbie was busy with the baby, making her new nest, and learning how to chop wood for the stove.

The move up north proved to be therapeutic for Tripper, our dog. Ever since he was a little puppy, he was shy and timid. I think it was because when he used to get under foot, we'd always trip over him, inadvertently kicking him. He got kicked around the house so much, he developed some sort of dog neurosis, and as he got older, his manly instincts never quite developed. Now I'm no dog shrink, but it just seemed like he was afraid of everybody and everything, even little kids.

The move to Irish Beach changed all that—he discovered the one thing on the planet that was more docile than him, and that he could bother and boss around and beat up.

Soon after he discovered the sheep pasture nearby, his whole dog persona changed—he became a macho hunter, a stud. He was proud, and began walking with a strut. Never before had he barked at visitors—he'd always run and hide for fear of getting kicked. Now, though, if anybody set foot on the property, he'd snarl and bare his teeth and try to work up a little foam in his mouth to display to them. Before, when I'd take him down to the harbor, he'd always try to hide between my legs, which, of course only caused him to get kicked more, and worsen his mental state. Now, after a few short weeks, when he came down to the cove at Point Arena, he walked in front of me, proud and tall, leading the way and protecting me. I was so proud of him.

Eventually we had to put a stop to his carousing. I found a note from the sheep owner on the windshield of my truck one day, essentially telling Tripper that he was pretty close to getting himself shot, and that he better cool it. But even after he had to be tied up to a tree and could no longer go terrorize the sheep, he retained his virile, confident demeanor, and he continued to strut and be protective of his family, like all normal, well-balanced dogs should. This unexpected and welcome cure to his previous condition was further justification that we had made the right decision in our northward migration.

"When are we going back to Santa Barbara?" After a month of no television or radio, my wife was getting bored. The novelty of the trees and remote surroundings had worn off. Her home no longer had the sound of piano students practicing their scales. She wanted to go home.

"Let's rent the house out, and live up here for a year or two." I loved the easy diving, not to mention we were putting plenty of money in the bank.

"What! I've got forty students I put on hold. What about them?"

"Honey, we can live up here for two years and tuck away a bundle of money. When we go home we'll be rich!"

She hit the roof. We locked horns, and for the next several days we glared at each other, neither of us willing to budge.

One night, after arguing about our future, and having a good cry, she called her Dad. After patiently listening to his daughter lay out her predicament, the old Texan gave his advice. "He's your husband. Do as he tells you." After another week of arguing, she finally gave in.

We drove down to Santa Barbara the next month, packed up a U-Haul truck, rented out the house, and returned to the North Coast to begin a new life. Although we did not know it at the time, it was to be our final farewell to the town where we had met, fallen in love, and started our life together.

In late October 1987, the weather at Point Arena took a turn. The *Day Tripper* was anchored up at Mote Creek, a few miles south of the cove—we were trying to get up the ambition to put our suits on. The water was a filthy brown. We knew the visibility was going to be terrible on the bottom. And a northwest wind was howling at twenty-five knots, yanking the *Day Tripper* around like a cork.

"I'm sick of this crap." The dirty water of the last few weeks was wearing me down. I'd never worked in such miserable conditions. There were urchins down there, but we could hardly see them, the viz was so crappy. My motivation factor was zero.

"Gravy!" Cotton had a strange habit of saying words not pertinent to the topic.

"Huh?" My irritation showed.

"It's all gravy, buddy." I was now treated to Jim Cotton's philosophy of life.

"A year in the Monkey Cage, thinking my life was over, changed my outlook on things. Every day is a good day. There are no bad days. Life is good. It's all gravy, man."

Jim Cotton, master of attitude.

## A Harsh Welcome

When the first swell of the season hit Point Arena, I did an immediate U-turn, speeding back to Irish Beach to get my board. Upon returning to the parking lot at the cove I witnessed an amazing sight—George Tomlinson was flying off the top of a wind blown twelve-foot wave on his surf ski. He sat on top of the strange Australian-made device with his feet strapped in front of him, and a kayak paddle clenched in his fists as he twisted high in the spraying sea air. To my amazement, the ski was deftly brought straight back into the face of the monstrous wave, where upon reentry, the shaggy haired wild man carved a long, sweeping bottom turn, then gracefully exited over the wave shoulder.

I was stunned, not only from the high caliber performance that I had witnessed, but at the exceptional quality of the waves that were entering the cove in long, evenly spaced lines.

After quickly suiting up and negotiating the rocky trail up the beach, I scrambled into the numbingly cold water to begin the long paddle out to the lineup.

Tomlinson passed me by on his way in.

"Nice wave!" I shouted. He splashed me with his paddle as we met.

"I was wondering when you'd show up." His fiery blue eyes issued both greeting and warning, for although we were friends, we were also competitors.

During the long paddle out, I was further impressed by the large magnificent waves as well as by the remarkable abilities of the local surfers who casually teased the liquid boomers with graceful turns and slashing cutbacks.

Upon reaching the lineup, I was met with an unfriendly silence and piercing stares from the six local surfers who were huddled together waiting for the next set.

Following a time-honored protocol, I took my place further in from the main peak and closer to the wave shoulder than the others. An established pecking order was in place here, and it was obvious from the vibes being cast my way where I stood.

After letting several waves pass, and ensuring that all six of the local pack had caught one, I slowly moved into position, being careful not to place myself at the outside peak, which was a reserved area.

Three more waves passed. But now, a large swell loomed, and two quick strokes put me in the slot. My gaze locked onto the fellow next to me, but as our eyes met, he gave me a short nod. It was my turn.

The outgoing tide had created a sucking action, causing the waves to jump up quickly as they hit the reef, making for steep, near vertical wave faces. The thick lips violently pitched out over the shallows, breaking hard, with a deafening noise, followed by an impact vibration through the water.

I glanced into the thundering barrel during my take-off. That moment of hesitation was all it took as the stiff offshore wind held me at the top of the wave, not allowing me into it. Even as I jumped to my feet, I knew it was too late. The lip of the wave threw out, holding me firmly in its grasp. I was flung like a rock from a slingshot, out, and over. Looking down, I was now resigned to my fate, and after a long, weightless free fall, I hit the concrete hard water with a painful splat.

The small volume of air that remained in my lungs was needed, for this wave, my first at Point Arena, was not yet finished with me. All was dark now, and I was afforded a split second of quiet calm under the water. But I knew what was coming, as once more I was sucked up into the massive machine, thrown over the falls, and slammed to the bottom, taking the full force of the breaking wave as it rippled through my body. After being scraped over the reef and getting my face sliced by the sharp leaves of bottom-lurking palm kelp, I reached the surface where a much needed breath of air was stifled by a thick layer of foam.

The wipeout had taken up only about fifty feet of space, and fortunately was the last wave of the set, for if it had been the first, my beating would have continued.

Grateful that my board was still in one piece, as well as my body, I paddled back into the lineup, where I was greeted with more silence from the surly Point Arena surfers. Finally, one of them, an older guy with long gray hair halfway down his back, looked over at me. "That looked like fun." A slight grin escaped, creasing his weather beaten face.

My next wave was a disaster as well. I got lazy on my bottom turn, was swallowed, and again mauled. I finally made one though, an insider that hollowed out and screamed by the shallow rock fingers. After two more clean rides, my confidence grew, and a wonderful three hour session ensued as the stiff wind backed off for the afternoon.

After my obligatory thrashing, it seemed as though the Point Arena waves had accepted me. I was now permitted to enjoy their smooth, exhilarating power without fear of further punishment.

And although few words passed between us, I was grudgingly accepted by my wave-riding peers who had witnessed my pounding, as well as my observance of surfing convention.

And so I was welcomed by water and by flesh, and it was documented in my log that for one October day in 1987, my dues on the North Coast had been paid.

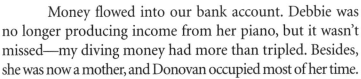

Money flowed into our bank account. Debbie was no longer producing income from her piano, but it wasn't missed—my diving money had more than tripled. Besides, she was now a mother, and Donovan occupied most of her time.

Everything was clicking—the boat was running well, a healthy market prevailed, and the weather, up to now, had cooperated.

Santa Rosa, a metropolitan city twenty-five miles east of Bodega Bay seemed like a good place to invest our savings. After a few phone calls to realtors in the area, we drove over Highway 128 to Cloverdale, down 101 into Santa Rosa, and in one day, found a reasonably priced home in a nice neighborhood, and bought it as an investment property.

Our estate was growing, and I was filled with pride. We now owned title to two homes. My hard work was paying off and the money continued to roll in.

The future looked bright indeed.

### North Coast Family

"Throw the line, honey!" Ben Hakes floated on the calm surface next to his full bag of urchins. His wife, Susan, was up on the boat, tending.

"Here you go, sweetie!" The bag line flew through the air, the brass snap splashing two feet from her diver husband.

"Not bad! You're finally getting the hang of it!"

"Shut up, you! I've been handling boat lines since I was a kid."

He swam lazily over to the boat and climbed aboard. "How long has Mike been down?"

"He should be up any minute." She yelled over the noise of the compressor motor.

"Good, I'm hungry. We won't need to move the boat. There's plenty here to finish off the day. We'll have lunch, then get two more bags each and head home."

The young couple had met at Fort Bragg High School, where Ben played varsity football. That was five years ago, but his body had changed little since the days when he was the starting split end. A steady regimen of jogging was keeping him in good shape, and his red hair was a familiar sight as he trotted around town in the early mornings.

Susan's father owned one of the commercial fishing boats in Noyo Harbor, the heart of Fort Bragg. According to Susan, some of her earliest memories were of being on her dad's boat, the *Phyliss J*. Like her peers, boats were a part of her life, and by the time she was ten, the decks of the *Phyliss J*. were as familiar to her as her home on Second Street.

Susan blossomed late. She had few friends in high school, due mostly to her quiet nature. By her senior year though, she had filled out, as young women do, and the heads began to turn. The short brown hair that she had worn all her life grew long, softening the appearance of the former tomboy.

Two years after graduating from high school they were married. Ben had a steady job at the auto parts store in town, but every Saturday he fished with Susan's dad. Sunday's were reserved for watching football and snuggling on the couch with cold beers.

When the urchin fleet arrived from Santa Barbara, Ben hustled down to the dive shop to begin working toward his diving certificate. There was money to be made diving. Big money. He had heard of divers making anywhere from two to five hundred dollars per day, and the boat owners were bringing in up to a thousand per day.

Ben was ambitious. Within two months he was a proficient diver, and he landed a job on one of the boats. Six months later he was harvesting an average of two thousand pounds per day, bringing home five hundred dollars per trip.

Susan started a savings account. The money she was socking away would be for their future. Although she loved her home and family, she had never traveled farther than Crescent City, two hours north of Fort Bragg. In her secret heart, she wanted to see the beaches of Mexico.

In the fall of 1987, the two decided to buy a boat. Ben had been diving for a year, and he felt confident in his abilities.

A thirty-foot Chris-Craft was for sale, and although it was an old cabin-cruiser, not meant for rough ocean waters, Ben knew he could make it work. After some bargaining with an anxious seller, the twenty-five year old boat was purchased for three thousand dollars.

Ben and Susan worked feverishly, day and night. The V-8 gas motor ran well, but the rear deck of the boat was rotten. Within two weeks, the soft wood had been replaced with strong fiberglass. A small fish hold was built, with enough room to store five hundred pounds of urchins below decks. A new anchor was needed, as well as chain and line.

Steve Carson owned the welding shop in town. He was backed up with work from other dive boats, but Susan's dad was a good friend, so it only took three days to have a hoist built and installed.

Reliable but expensive air systems put together by Crazy Harold sat on the sleek Radons and Wilsons from Santa Barbara. After studying them, Ben decided he could save time and money by rigging up his own system. He bought a small compressor and gas motor at the hardware store and attached them to a steel stand that Steve Carson built for him. The unit was mounted on the deck, directly behind the cabin, on the port side. This placement gave the system protection from the salty spray and wind. A muffler directed the exhaust outboard, off the side of the boat, and away from the air intake of the compressor.

The previous owner had named the boat *Annie,* after his wife. But over a six pack of beer on a Sunday afternoon, the new owners renamed it the *Bottom Bandit.*

Most of their savings was gone, but the *Bottom Bandit* was ready to work. Surprisingly, it had taken them less than a month.

The Chris-Craft was never meant to be a commercial fishing boat. It was an old wooden yacht from a bygone era. The huge windows would have disintegrated on their first encounter with a white buffalo, but for the short runs out of Noyo, the *Bottom Bandit* worked perfectly.

Susan and Ben made a good team. They worked hard, and within a few months Ben's fish tickets showed he was keeping up with most of the long-time divers from out of town.

Bob Juntz, the owner of Ocean Fresh Seafoods, was a friend of the family. Having known Ben for years, he proudly watched the young man's rapid progress in the diving business.

When Ben approached the urchin processor to ask if Ocean Fresh would buy his product, Bob smiled. "This is your home, Ben. I'll see to it that none of your urchins are ever trucked down to Los Angeles. They'll be processed right here, and you'll get a fair price. Make sure you bring me good stuff though!" he chuckled. Ben had already established a reputation for harvesting high quality urchins.

Mike Stanson was a member of Ben's graduating class, and the two had been friends since grade school. Mike was one of the first local urchin divers, and held a good job on the *Kelp Monster*, a boat I recognized from Santa Barbara.

He was short and stocky—he wore his dark hair long and always had a pinch of tobacco under his lower lip, creating a large lump. When Ben offered him a spot on the *Bottom Bandit*, Mike quickly accepted. They had played football together; now they were teammates once again.

"Okay, he's up. Shut the popper off." Ben peeled his wetsuit top off. His wife hit the switch, quieting the compressor motor, as Mike climbed aboard.

"These urchins are beautiful! You think we'll keep getting our twenty-eight cents a pound this week?" Mike's carefree attitude was infectious. On this unusually warm afternoon the three of them sat on the back deck, sunburned and happy, enjoying the life they were living.

Small ripples slapped the hull of the *Bottom Bandit*. Gulls swooped down, snatching the crumbs being tossed overboard. The high cliffs of the land were only a quarter of a mile away, and looking through the binoculars, Ben watched a man mowing his lawn.

"Come on, you guys. It's only thirty feet here, so there's no need for decompressing. Get back in the water!"

"Okay, okay. Jees, Ben. You married a slave driver."

"You got that right." Ben winked, and gave his wife a grin.

The divers pulled their wetsuit tops on. Susan yanked the starter cord on the compressor motor.

She watched the bubbles. Her husband was twenty feet directly behind the boat, and Mike was forward, near the anchor. They usually averaged about thirty minutes per bag—Susan expected them to surface at any time.

Being on her father's boat as a child had given Susan valuable experience, so becoming an expert tender had come quickly for her. She efficiently loaded the bags, and kept the *Bottom Bandit* spotless.

Both men had been down for over thirty minutes. A slight breeze came up from the north, creating a small chop on the surface. The boat began to roll some, but Susan knew they were only four miles from the harbor. There was nothing to worry about.

At the forty minute mark, she decided to give Ben's hose a tug. The bubbles were no longer visible, due to the wind chop on the water. Pulling the slack from his hose, she gave two big tugs, the signal to come up. He didn't come to the surface right away, but it could be he didn't feel her pulling. She gave three more tugs, pulling harder than before. "I know he felt that," she said to herself.

Ben would be up in a minute, so she went forward and tugged on Mike's hose. It was getting windier now. The bow began to buck into the chop. She wanted to head for the harbor.

Neither diver came up. It had been fifty minutes. Susan's heart was pounding as she pulled on Ben's hose. It had some resistance, but not too much. "He's swimming up. I'll just pull him up slowly."

Ben came to the surface, face down.

"Ben!" She screamed, letting go of the hose. He began to sink as she ran into the cabin. She grabbed the radio transmitter, dropped it, then picked it up and shrieked. "Mayday! Mayday! Mayday! This is the *Bottom Bandit!* Mayday! Mayday!"

Two boats were close by. They sped to Ben and Susan's boat to help out.

But they were too late.

Susan lay sobbing on the deck as the two bodies were pulled aboard.

The news spread fast, bringing the close knit community of Fort Bragg to a standstill. Ben and Mike had grown up there, everyone knew them. Over five hundred people attended the dual memorial service for the long-time friends.

Ben Hakes and Mike Stanson died that day from sudden carbon monoxide poisoning, brought about by a series of mistakes in the design and placement of the air system. The air compressor on the *Bottom Bandit* was small—in order to provide enough air for two divers, it had been necessary to run it at a high speed. Excessive vibration, caused by not using vibration dampeners during installation, loosened the muffler, allowing exhaust fumes to escape from the muffler joint, which was ten inches from the air intake. Even this dangerous situation would not have caused the tragedy if the unit had been mounted further aft, out in the wind. But by being mounted in the protected area behind the cabin, the exhaust fumes bounced off of the cabin bulkhead, directly into the intake. Within minutes after the muffler vibrated loose, carbon monoxide fumes reached the two divers, quickly killing them.

Ocean Fresh Seafoods notified buyers in Japan that they were shutting down operations for one week. Boats from Noyo to Bodega Bay remained in port out of respect for their fallen comrades.

Ten days later a fog bank rolled in, enveloping the entire North Coast. A storm from Alaska arrived the next week, and twenty-foot seas were accompanied by ten inches of rain and gale force winds. River mouths spit logs into the sea by the dozens. The ocean turned dark brown for a month.

I turned out the bedroom light.

"How long do you plan to keep diving?" Debbie asked.

"I don't know, I never thought about it. I like it and we make good money. I'm thirty-seven, in pretty good shape. I guess till I'm forty-five. Why?"

"I just keep thinking about those guys on the *Bottom Bandit*. They were so young."

"I know, I do too honey. But I have a good air system, and a good boat."

"Did you know them?"

"Not well. I chatted with Ben on the dock once. He seemed like a good guy."

"It's a dangerous way to make a living."

"I'll be careful."

"Promise?"

"Promise."

"I love you."

"I love you too, honey."

## Noyo

The large winter swells that hit the North Coast turn the cove at Point Arena into a fool's harbor—by early November boats either sit on a trailer, or move to safety for the winter. The harbor at Fort Bragg, where the Noyo River feeds into the Pacific, would be the *Day Tripper's* next home.

I called The Spaniard to notify him of our impending move.

"No prolem. I already kaf a trok peeking op een Fart Bedagg."

Winding through Mendocino County, the Noyo River passes through Hopland and Willits. The terrain is thickly populated with redwood and fir trees, and very few humans. Tributaries feed into the river, widening it as it nears the coast, where it spills out and meets the ocean at Fort Bragg.

High above, the Noyo Bridge spans the river, looking down at the harbor basin below. The view is spectacular, as you can see the river on your right, winding up into the boat basin, the harbor entrance on your left, and the open ocean beyond.

Noyo Harbor is pleasant and inviting. Large, long docks stretch for hundreds of feet on the left side of the deep green river. Two-story fish houses are set back from the docks, which are filled with hoists, fork lifts, and all the gear necessary for fish receiving operations. Pier pilings, oozing with tar, provide temporary space to boats that are unloading fish, or getting supplies.

A narrow dirt road lined with small eateries, a couple of fishing supply stores, and a scattering of small houses winds its way behind the fish houses. An old rusty, abandoned boat trailer sits on flat tires, providing a home for weeds.

A few hundred feet down the road, which hugs the river, is a small graveyard. The cemetery does not hold human remains. The skeletons that rest here are those of old wooden boats, long ago left for dead. The decaying hulks lie on their keels, or on their sides. Their ribs are broken, and their decks are rotten.

In a time forgotten by most, each of them floated proudly in the nearby harbor, only a stone's throw away. With newly painted hulls, fresh linseed oil on their decks, and immaculate machinery, they waited patiently for the next trip out to sea. Now, though, their dignity was gone, as they sat rotting in their final resting place.

On the south side of the river, a long, narrow dock floats, seemingly untethered to the land. It's a small dock, in constant motion from the movement of the river. Eight or ten boats tie up here, but the dock lines need to be checked constantly due to continual river action.

Just past the docks and fish houses is the main boat basin. The wide bend has slips for over a hundred boats of all shapes and sizes. Salmon trollers, purse seiners, and the big crabbers—it is a commercial harbor. A few sailboats and cabin cruisers dot the basin, but not many.

Half a mile farther up river is Dolphin Isle—a small marina built back in the fifties. The water is not deep here, allowing only shallow draft boats to venture this far back. The docks are old, and in disrepair. Here, in this cut of the Noyo, the water does not flow well, and is foul. Cigarette butts and empty beer cans gather in the nooks and crannies of the ancient marina, moving back and forth only when a boat passes by. But the beauty in this tranquil section of the river, away from the bustle of the main harbor, is inviting. Dolphin Isle marina was to be the *Day Tripper's* home for almost two years.

The thirty-mile run from Point Arena to Fort Bragg was cushioned by three thousand pounds of urchins that we harvested on the way up, but the ride was terrible—we were bucking into an oncoming sea the entire way. Seven miles south of Noyo it came on strong, and within minutes steep waves were breaking over the cabin, forcing us to throttle down to a crawl.

Four miles out we were barely making five knots. Then the bottoms started dropping out. We'd fall ten feet into the trough, and plow through green water. A feeling of being underwater and a terrifying silence would ensue for a few seconds, then the boat would pop up, and the cycle would start over again.

"The hatches caved in!" Cotton screamed. Both fish hold covers were broken in half from two thousand pounds of urchins being lifted up, becoming weightless, and crashing down on them. Seawater now poured into the hold.

"Turn on the pump!"

I hit the switch and looked over my right shoulder to see the powerful stream of water shooting out the side of the boat from the high volume pump. Capable of moving two thousand gallons per hour, it couldn't keep up with the water that was now flooding the hold. But it helped to keep us from sinking as we slogged the final two miles and wallowed into the mild waters of Noyo.

"That was close." A weak smile cracked Cotton's face. A cold November wind was blowing, but we were bathed in sweat.

"That was close," I agreed.

A surreal feeling overtook us as we transitioned from trying to survive an onslaught of raging white buffaloes, to the still, calm waters of the harbor. In a matter of seconds, the loud crashing waves hitting the *Day Tripper* were replaced by the sounds of people talking on the docks.

Suddenly we were overcome with a most agreeable smell. The Thanksgiving Coffee Company borders the south side of Noyo, across from the big fish houses, and the wondrous aroma filled our nostrils, welcoming Cotton and me to Fort Bragg.

"You're late, dinner's cold."

"Sorry, honey."

"Everything go okay?"

"Uh huh."

"Where's the boat?"

"In Dolphin Isle marina—wait'll you see it. The whole area is incredibly beautiful—you'll love it."

"How was the ride up?"

"A little bumpy."

"Lori Hagen, Karen Tomlinson, and I are going to lunch tomorrow—do you want to join us?"

"I have a fiberglass project on the boat."

## The Good and the Evil

Noyo was alive with the excitement and commotion of the sea urchin boom. A fleet of forty boats, most of them from down south, harvested the nearby reefs of Whiskey Gulch, Van Damm Bay, and the Mendocino Headlands. About once every couple of weeks a new boat and crew showed up, rabidly gearing up for their first dive trip and a piece of the North Coast pie. One local resident, who had lived there for his entire life, said he had never seen anything like it—the harbor had never been so busy.

Mark Evanoff, a fellow transplant from southern waters, owned the *Defiance*, a forty-two foot Bruno and Stillman. The East Coast lobster boat was one of the sharpest in Noyo Harbor, and the pride of the urchin fleet. Her decks were immaculate, not an urchin spine in sight. The engine room housed a gleaming Detroit Diesel motor with a spotless bilge underneath. A neat and orderly forward cabin slept four people, and the fully-stocked galley held drawers, cabinets, and shelves for storage. Cooking and warmth was provided by a small diesel stove that stayed on all day during winter dive trips, keeping the cabin warm and cozy. She was beamy too—her fourteen-foot width provided stability in rough seas.

Two leather captain's chairs were bolted to the floor of the steering station, which was equipped with state of the art electronics and navigation equipment. The radar, digital plotter, color bottom finder, and marine radio were all made by Furuno. For long runs, the autopilot, which interfaced with the plotter, automatically kept the boat on course to its intended destination.

In the high production days of the mid-eighties, Mark used three divers and a tender. Most of the guys never lasted more than a few months with the scowling slave driver before they moved on. No one could keep up with him. His nickname fit perfectly—"Never off."

The prominent feature you first noticed when looking at Mark was his square chin, which protrudes from his ruggedly handsome, chiseled face. A stickler for grooming, his heavy beard needed shaving sometimes twice per day. The thick, dark head of hair was kept neatly trimmed and combed, even when he was out at sea. An abuser of tooth brushes, he scrubbed his teeth ferociously until they matched the bleached white decks of his boat.

A scowl was etched into his features, incorrectly telegraphing a sour mood. Looking at Mark, a new acquaintance would think he was angry, but this was not the case, as it was his normal expression.

While I was assessing the damage to the hatches of the *Day Tripper* from our nightmarish journey the previous day, the *Defiance* idled by, her white hull gleaming in the morning sun. After spotting my boat, Mark tossed a line and hopped aboard for a visit, one captain to another. After our initial greetings and obligatory lies about our prices, the *Defiance* gently floated in the calm river water and Mark told me the story of the Good and the Evil.

A diver who'd been working on the *Defiance* for a few weeks seemed to have a split personality. One day he'd be cheerful, clean shaven, work hard, and have a good attitude. On the next trip, he was grumpy, unshaven, and lazy. Even underwater he was different, for sometimes he spent countless hours on the bottom, periodically out-picking the skipper. Then, other days, he was an underwater sloth—always the last one to hit the water, and the first one to get out.

It was common for him to stay at the dock to give the tender a hand with cleanup—he was sometimes a nice, helpful guy. Other days though, he was gone as soon as the bow reached the slip, jumping off without so much as a goodbye.

Mark said he couldn't believe the change the guy would undergo. It was like being with two different people.

My friend said that after putting up with this Jekyll and Hyde personality for a month, he began suspecting that the guy was on drugs. Fishermen have always been a "colorful" bunch. It's a tough life, and alcohol and drug abuse is sometimes a problem. It had gotten to a point where it was driving Mark nuts. He finally had a talk with the guy about his attitude, but nothing changed. One day he was an asshole, and the next day he was the nicest guy in the world.

"I'm going bananas!" Mark was on the dock, talking to a friend. "You had Mike on your boat for a while, didn't you?"

"Yeah, he's a good guy and a hard worker too. I hated having to let him go, but I promised my wife that I'd hire my stupid brother-in-law." The other skipper continued: "It's funny though, he has a twin brother who looks exactly like him, but the guy's a prick. He's lazy, never bathes, and most people can't stand him. It's hard to believe two brothers can be so different."

Immediately things clicked—only one of the brothers owned an urchin permit, and they'd been taking turns making dive trips on the *Defiance*.

Mark hit the roof, and fired both of them—the Good, and the Evil.

### Duag

With winter rapidly approaching, it was nice having the *Day Tripper* safely tied up in a slip. The hatch covers were both broken cleanly, so with fiberglass cloth and resin purchased from Fort Bragg Marine, it only took a day to fix them.

"It's been a great run buddy, but I'm outta here." Cotton had an electric grinder in his hand, feathering the edges of the newly glassed hatches.

"Sure you won't change your mind? I'm hearing rumors of forty cents a pound from The Spaniard." My feeble attempt at coaxing him to stay fell flat.

"My wallet's fat, dude. I need warm sunshine and some windsurfing. And after that pounding we took on the way up from Arena—well, I've had enough of this place."

Cotton and I discovered the North Coast together—including our time in Santa Barbara, we had worked together for over a year. It was a pleasure having the amiable smuggler on the boat, and I learned a lot from him.

After we said our goodbyes, and gave each other a manly hug, I watched with sadness as his truck rambled away. I knew I'd miss the old pirate.

I worked alone for a while but was used to having another diver aboard, so I went down to the local dive shop and put a note up, advertising for an experienced urchin diver.

A rusty brown Ford truck drove up the driveway of our newly rented house across the bay from the town of Mendocino.

Duct tape held the frames of the black horn rimmed glasses together, but they remained as helplessly bent as the nose they were perched on. Squinted eyes looked at me through dirty lenses, which were thick, and resembled magnifying glasses. Confused blonde hair made me question the last time it had been combed, and two long arms hung alongside a narrow waist that attached to short, bowed legs. His blue jeans, plaid shirt, and tennis shoes all looked like they had been scavenged from the bottom of a dumpster behind the local grocery store.

"I'm Doug," he jabbered. "I've had my urchin permit for three years, but haven't hardly dove at all since my back got tweaked a year and a half ago. I'd like to give it a try though. It feels pretty good. Plus, I'm broke. I really need the money."

My first thought was to send him packing. Especially after hearing Mark Evanoff's story of the good and the evil twins.

He looked like a short scrawny invalid, and it was hard to imagine him being much of a threat to the sea urchin population. He was my only prospect though, so I told him to be on the boat at seven the next morning.

By the time I stepped on the *Day Tripper*, Doug had his hose on the engine lid, neatly coiled next to mine. I considered this to be a good sign as we took off south toward the Mendocino Headlands, about seven miles south of Noyo.

That first day I had twenty-three hundred pounds, Doug had four hundred. The second day I had nineteen hundred, he had twelve hundred.

Doug and I wound up diving together on my boat for eight years, making over six hundred dive trips together. Since those first two days, I never out-picked him once.

We also became surf buddies, and in years to come we would travel thousands of miles together in our search for waves. The small, bespectacled son of a dairy farmer became my closest friend, and a familiar sight around our house.

I've known plenty of dockworkers over the years, and have made a few observations about this unique crew. For the most part they are honest, friendly, hard-working men, with a good work ethic, and a sense of humor.

The young man who unloaded us at the Noyo Dock was all of the above, but he couldn't have had much more than a sixth grade education. He was a good worker and responsible, but the guy could barely read or write. When we were handed our fish tickets that first day, he'd spelled Doug's name DUAG. Ever since that day, Doug has been called Duag by me and my family.

## The Blue Lagoon

Most of my dive buddies feel the same as me. We are blessed to have found a way to make a living that is exciting, enjoyable, and challenging.

We work on the ocean, which can be calm and peaceful, but sometimes incredibly frightening. Diving in murky water with only two or three feet visibility, thirty-knot winds on the surface, and a boat flopping around up above can be terrifying. Falling into the water fully clothed, or worse, falling onto a bag of urchins is an eventuality—both have happened to all of us.

Urchin diving can, at times, be extremely dangerous. Powerful swells can slam you into underwater rocks. Vicious currents sometimes sweep you down a reef channel, in between rock walls. The carburetor, or venturi effect created by this water action, renders you helpless—all you can do is go for the ride and hope for the best. Then your dive hose gets hung up on a rock and you desperately cling to your bag of urchins as the underwater windstorm tries to rip the mask off your face. As further insult, all the urchins fly out of the bag, negating your last thirty minutes of harvesting.

Being a few feet under a bouncing boat in rough seas can be a nightmare. More than one melon has been split open by a boat hull, or worse, an outdrive.

Sometimes the diving is relatively boring—crawling along a flat bottom putting urchins in a bag one at a time can get monotonous.

I was once interviewed for a newspaper article.

"What's going through your mind when you're out to sea, under the waves, harvesting the urchins?" The writer asked.

"Put the urchin in the bag, put the urchin in the bag, put the urchin in the bag …."

Often times, however, the water is clear and calm. There are unusual creatures and magnificent underwater formations to see. Glittery rays of early morning sunlight penetrating the surface and dancing around the swaying strands of kelp put on a spectacular show.

Swimming thirty feet into a cave, then seeing it open up into an underwater room bathed in a kaleidoscope of light and color is an awesome and wonderful experience. You look up at your bubbles, which are being trapped on the ceiling of the cave, forming one huge, growing bubble. I call these giant bubbles, which few people in the world have ever seen, underwater amoebas. You just never get tired of these unique experiences.

In my entire career, the Blue Lagoon is the most extraordinary spot I have ever worked. It's a place that Doug and I discovered and, before the *Day Tripper*, I would bet that no boat had ever been there.

About twelve miles north of Noyo, near the small town of Westport, we were employing the interesting, fun, and dangerous technique of "live boat" surveying, in about fifteen to twenty feet of water. This is where one person drives the boat, while the diver is surveying underwater. It's only done on relatively mild days, because of the obvious dangers involved with a spinning propeller, a diver, and his hose in the water. Only the most experienced seaman can be trusted to drive the boat, while keeping a careful eye on his diver, and minding the hose.

I was in the water, Doug was driving the boat. We were fairly tight to the rocks, about twenty feet, when I noticed a strong current trying to suck me into a channel. I surfaced to have a look around, and noticed a narrow inlet with breaking waves, and frothy whitewater. About twenty yards beyond, however, there was a small bay that a boat could possibly fit into.

"Move the boat out from the rocks and toss the hook! I wanna check out this little bay!" I floated in the water next to the boat, looking up at Doug. "And couple your hose to mine too—it looks like it goes back a ways."

After the anchor was down I swam under the breaking waves, and into the hidden cove for a survey, where I saw a patch of virgin reef the size of a football field. I almost choked in my regulator.

"How's it look?" Doug asked as I was climbing on to the boat.

"No problem. The opening is fifteen feet deep. Once you get inside it drops to thirty, and it's like a mill pond in there. And it's holding, dude."

"How 'bout the entrance?"

"It's narrow and sloppy—it's gonna be dicey, but I think we can pull it off."

After positioning the boat about two hundred feet from the entrance, I gave it plenty of throttle and charged for the small opening. With the breaking waves, whitewater, and powerful surge, a slow speed entry was impossible—we needed to use the power of the boat to overcome the sloppy seas. It was full commitment, and with five feet on either side of us at the inlet, it wouldn't take much of a miscalculation to wind up with a crunched boat.

Our hearts were in our throats as we shot through the narrow gap in the rocks, but it worked like a charm. Instantly, the *Day Tripper* was calmly floating in the serene bay that we would come to call The Blue Lagoon.

"Piece a cake!" Doug whooped as we both exhaled. Now we looked down into the clear water and saw a field of polka dots on the bottom.

"Look!" I pointed back out to the open sea. My partner saw it too. The large rocks we had negotiated blocked the view to the outside.

"Nobody can see us!" He shouted. "We're invisible!" It was true. Unless a boat was within fifteen feet of the shoreline, the opening could not be seen. And even if someone was that close, we could tuck back a little further into our pond, and remain unseen.

Within minutes of entering the water to begin our work day, we realized what a truly special place we had stumbled onto. Not only was there a huge flat reef covered with thousands of pounds of urchins, there were also deep canyons whose walls were black with spines. There were caves too—some burrowing so deep they turned to blackness. Huge abalone were stacked three high on top of each other. Others had climbed up stalks of palm kelp, where they had eaten off all the leaves. They looked like three-foot-tall mushrooms.

An astounding variety of sea-life filled the Blue Lagoon. Vermillion, a large dark red fish with delicious white meat roamed the reef top, while ling cod, some three feet long, lay in the deep cracks of the rock valleys. Pole spears carried on the boat kept our refrigerators well stocked with plunder from our private reserve.

One wall of the lagoon was completely barren of urchins. Instead, it was blanketed with giant sea anemones—all of them white. It looked like a fifty-foot bed sheet.

Never in one place had I seen so many octopi—the place was littered with the strange, eight legged creatures, some of them obscenely huge. Periodically, we would inadvertently disturb one, and be treated to a face full of dark ink. Doug, my pal, came up from behind me one day while we were on a shallow fifteen foot reef top. He reached around and stuck an octopus on my mask. As he expected, it quickly glommed onto my head, dislodged my mask, and caused me to start gagging. Being so shallow, I was never in danger (not much anyway), and within a few seconds I was on the surface, choking, and trying to pry the thing off. I wound up having to climb up on to the boat with a multilegged creature stuck to my head, and work at it for awhile before finally getting free, which wasn't easy (picture prying two legs full of suction cups off your face, while six more are wrapping around you). Not sure that's what they mean when they say use the buddy system while diving. It was a beauty though—we took it to the Meredith fish dock, where they pickled it for us, putting it in two jars. We chewed on it for weeks.

For a month solid we worked the Lagoon, and after the first few trips, the nerve rattling job of shooting the rocky gap to get inside became routine. It wasn't long before we could make a ninety degree turn while cruising at twenty knots, and blaze on into the secret cove.

Word quickly spread among the Noyo fleet that we were delivering big loads of superior quality urchins. Some of the boats tried to find us, but we were well hidden in our urchin paradise.

An old dirt road wound its way down to the water on the southern edge of the lagoon from the coast road. Debbie and I took a drive one day, and after going down several dead ends, we found a way to drive to within fifty feet of the lagoon. After some careful planning, we picked our day, and she drove to the lagoon with our lunch. Doug and I swam about thirty feet from the boat, climbed up the rocks, and we had a picnic!

Our secret spot was accessible by land and by sea, but nobody could find us. And although we harvested seventy-five thousand pounds of legal urchins from the Blue Lagoon in April of 1988, thousands of "shorts" were left behind, and would be ready for harvest by October.

## A Fine Group

The sea urchin fleet is comprised of "citizens" and "non-citizens". For purposes of this discussion we are talking about men, for although there are a few female urchin divers, they are all citizens.

In order to be a citizen, three of the four following conditions must be met:

1. Must live in a house or an apartment. Not in a car.

2. Must have a telephone and must know his telephone number.

3. Does not need to own a car, but if he does, he must know where it is at least seventy-five percent of the time.

4. Does not need to be married, but must need to know the name of the last person he slept with.

As you can see, the criterion for citizenry is quite lenient. This is due to the fact that even the most upstanding and law abiding urchin divers lurk on the fringes of lunacy (even to be in this line of work necessitates a certain amount of mental imbalance).

I married into a family of mega citizens. My father-in-law was a high level manager at General Electric, overseeing hundreds of employees and a team of mid-level managers. All the people he worked with were college educated with post-graduate degrees.

I have three brothers-in-law. One owns a high production metal fabrication shop with fifty employees who work shifts around the clock. Another is a nuclear engineer, whose peers all have master's degrees. My third brother-in-law is a PhD. He teaches university classes and heads up a research laboratory dealing in laser ablation theory, among other things. His colleagues are other PhD's, think-tank scientists, and Nobel Prize winners.

All of my in-laws' peers are of the same class; that is, highly educated men and women, citizens all. So, I can say with no small amount of pride that my group comes from all walks—a diverse collection including thieves, murderers, alcoholics, drug addicts, liars, high school dropouts, and parking violators. It's nice to live in a country that has a niche for everyone.

During family gatherings, usually at holiday time, we men sometimes find ourselves together, alone, in the same room. Discussions revolve around politics, global warming, and nuclear reactor fueling schedules. I usually remain silent during these meetings, but as always, my in-laws, who are very considerate of my feelings, attempt to include me in the dialogue.

"So, Tom! How's business?"

"Oh, things are goin' pretty good. I got a spine in my thumb last week."

"Hmmm. So … all the machinery on the boat is working well?"

"Yeah. Oh, well, the popper was acting up, you know, sputtering and missing. So I took the spark plug out and cleaned it, which did the trick for a week or so. Then it started acting up again, so, you know, I had to go to the auto parts store over on Milpas Street and get a new one. Of course, when you buy just one instead of a whole box, it costs more, so I had to pay three dollars for the goddamn thing, but oh well, it fixed the problem, and the pieceacrap's runnin' okay now."

For the next minute or two, enthusiastic heads bob and nod in agreement, after which a long, uncomfortable period of silence follows. The conversation then returns to geopolitical problems and solutions to world hunger.

…

I never knew anybody who decided when they were ten years old they wanted to be an urchin diver, and there's not a school on earth that can prepare you for it. For many of us, urchin diving, like some other forms of commercial fishing, is not something you aspire to —it's someplace you end up. For some of us it's the bottom of the barrel, the last house on the block. The lucrative job provides an avenue for former scoundrels to rise from the gutter to become "citizens", while others prefer to remain societal slugs, cashing their paychecks and quickly hitting the bars, or calling their connections.

One guy was found in the cabin of his boat, dead from a heroin overdose. He was a damn good diver, and a hell of a surfer, too. Another diver was a Vietnam vet who fought at Khe San, during the Tet offensive of 1968. He was quiet, and kept to himself. But his eyes were always wide open and unblinking, with a crazed look of perpetual fear in them. He rarely talked at all, and he never talked of his time in Vietnam. Nobody ever messed with him.

Some of us are just plain nuts. As a dramatic suicide attempt, one of the divers shot himself in the mouth with a flare gun. He was unsuccessful in killing himself, but the results to his face put an end to any thoughts of a Hollywood career.

Some of us shaved periodically, some did away with that pretense of civility long ago. Some of us had families— wives and kids who loved us in spite of who we were. Others had families that no longer wanted anything to do with them. And some of us had no families at all.

On the beach we were nobody. Just smelly commercial fishermen wearing blue jeans that should have been thrown in a dumpster years ago. But once we cleared the breakwater, and left the land behind, nobody could touch us. Not wives, families, creditors, cops, nobody. At sea, there were no more bosses, other than the skipper, who was usually on the same wave length. Nobody called the shots but us. There were no more rules—they were back in the harbor. Nobody could tell us when to dive, how to dive, or even to dive at all. And certainly nobody could tell us where to dive—although they tried.

Certain areas of the California coast are closed to commercial urchin harvest. Sometimes they are in an area designated for scientific study. Some areas are federally-mandated reserves, closed to all fishing or diving. We would never go into any of these areas. Particularly the Point Cabrillo reserve. Or Gerstle Cove. Or the entrance to Tomales Bay. We never went into any of these areas. It was illegal. Unless of course it was foggy. That's different. Fog is God's way of saying "Its okay now. If you can find 'em, pick 'em."

The California coast is crawling with Department of Fish and Game boats looking for bad guys. They are merciless and unforgiving. Their job is to either issue citations to, or arrest violators of, sport and commercial fishing regulations. When the sun is shining, they are out in full force, wreaking havoc on the criminals of the sea.

When the fog rolls in however, they are nowhere to be seen. And that's when the rumors begin. For years, rumors have circulated about nefarious deeds committed by divers. Rumors of diving in illegal waters. Rumors of smuggling contraband. And rumors of poaching.

Radar and GPS (global positioning system) plotters, which use satellite triangulation, put the unscrupulous villain where he wants to be—right in the middle of the closed area, where a boatload of urchins can be snatched in a few hours. For the less adventuresome pirate, the boat is carefully anchored on the edge of the virgin reserve. Next, extra dive hoses are coupled together—sometimes two or three, adding another eight hundred feet of diving range. It takes more swimming, but the skipper justifies it by knowing that his boat is anchored in legal waters.

Rumor has it that the small, speedy urchin boats are perfect for smuggling contraband of all types from an offshore mother ship to the mainland. The operation can be done quickly at night, and when the boat returns to port the next day, it's rarely ever suspected of anything. It's just coming back in after a routine diving trip. These midnight runs have allegedly proven lucrative for more than one of us.

The most consistently profitable, and riskiest illegal activity of sea urchin divers though, is abalone poaching on the North Coast (the meat of the mollusk is tender, and is an expensive item in restaurants). And although relatively few of the divers engage in this dastardly practice, we all shoulder the blame. In fact, on the North Coast, when someone finds out you are an urchin diver, they always ask two questions: "Ever seen a shark?" and "How many abalones have you poached?" (And not necessarily in that order.) Several of us have often said to ourselves, "Shit, I might as well start poachin' the damn things—I'm gettin' blamed for it anyway."

One of my acquaintances, it is rumored, financed a forty-foot sailboat on illegal abalone money—but he's dead, so that's that. Another had a false floor built into the bottom of his boat, and it has been suggested that he poached thousands of abalone. But it's kind of funny how these things work out— his beautiful young wife had a roving eye. It literally drove him crazy trying to keep her away from other men. He wound up in the hospital, and eventually in the mental ward due to his fretting over her philandering ways. Now she's remarried to a vineyard owner, and he's still doing the thorazine shuffle.

Another piece of scandalous gossip has it that one of the finest resorts on the Mendocino coast was built on illegal abalone. But it's all rumor. Most of us are fine citizens.

## We Get Regulated

Canada, Alaska, Oregon, even Mexico had strict seasons and regulations in place by the time California got into the act.

Up to now the urchin business was wide open. Our coastline had been harvested steadily for over a decade by a fleet of boats that now numbered over two hundred, and was still growing. The constant pressure on the kelp beds and reefs by the unrelenting divers was taking its toll.

The California Department of Fish and Game (CDFG) is the regulating body overseeing all commercial and sport fishing in the state, including the harvest of sea urchins. Like everyone else, they've had some good ideas, and some bad ones.

In the late sixties, prior to there being an urchin fishery, scientists were concerned about the damaging effects of urchins to the kelp beds of southern California. Under the direction of Wheeler J. North, noted kelp expert, divers wielding ball peen hammers were sent down with orders to kill as many urchins as possible. In a related program, lime was dispersed on urchin dominated reefs, killing everything it came in contact with.

In the mid-eighties, the Sea Urchin Harvesters Advisory Committee was formed. SUHAC, as it was called, had meetings, and began discussing the future of the business with CDFG. Scientists at the Department expressed concern over the volume of urchins being harvested, and were studying methods of reducing the poundage. The processing companies, which now numbered over twenty in the state, also formed a group, and hired consultants to protect their interests.

In an effort to bring poundage down to a sustainable number, these regulations were implemented:

1985: A special sea urchin harvesting permit was required to be purchased, in addition to the standard commercial fishing license.

Seasons: April through October became partial months. Divers could only work on specified days—Monday through Thursday. In addition, a ten-day closure would take place every month. The potential work days decreased from thirty to twelve.

1987: In order to reduce the number of permit holders from over 900, to the target number of 300, a limited entry system was devised. The fishery was closed to new entrants. For every four permits that were not renewed in a calendar year, one permit would become available, and would be sold on a lottery.

1989: Size limits implemented. Divers were now required to carry gauges and not take any under-sized urchins. Any urchin with a shell size less than three and a quarter inches in southern California, and three and a half inches in northern California, could not be taken.

Log books: Boat owners were supplied with books by the UDFG, and were required to keep records of diving areas, number of divers on the boat, average depth, and pounds harvested.

We all thought it was the end of the world. The measuring would slow us down to a crawl, and the limited number of work days would severely cut into our profits.

It was difficult to learn how to use the measuring tools, and they slowed us down considerably. Our income sufferered approximately a 30 percent reduction, which none of us were happy about. But after a couple of years we could see results, and most of us were pleased with the changes.

Debbie's favorite regulation was the forced down time in the spring and summer. She could now plan things like little weekend jaunts, or trips to see family. Before the seasonal rules, every plan she made was contingent on the weather.

As it turned out, the new regulations were a good thing, and they eventually accomplished their stated goals. The greatest benefit was to the ocean enviornment. There is no doubt in my mind that although every rule was beneficial, the size limit alone created an immeasurable source of protection to the reefs and urchin populations. In my opinion, the implementation of a size limit was a godsend to our harvesting beds, and it created a sustainable sea urchin fishery.

## A Clandestine Operation

The weather had been funky for three weeks—a big northwest swell with twenty knots of wind kept all the boats in. Nobody was getting out. We were all hungry for work.

The phone rang. "Hey, buddy. You'll never guess what's down here at the Ocean Fresh plant." Doug's voice sounded more excited than normal. He must have had a fourth cup of coffee this morning, I thought.

"Talk to me, Duag."

"A rental truck just pulled up with ten thousand pounds of uni on it. The workers are crackin' 'em now, and they look primo."

"Where'd they come from? The whole North Coast is shut down."

"Nobody's sayin'. Even Bob's tight lipped."

"Any suggestions?" I asked. But we were both thinking the same thing.

"Yeah, let's follow the truck."

We lurked around the harbor, waiting for the workers to finish unloading—a meal at Captain Jacks was followed by more hiding behind buildings with periodic checks on the truck. Finally, at four-thirty, the driver climbed in, started his motor, and headed down Highway One.

Doug kept his distance from the large stakebed truck as we tailed him out Highway 128, past Santa Rosa, Petaluma, Marin, and through San Francisco.

"How far are we gonna follow this guy?" Doug asked. "For all we know he might be going to San Diego!"

"Those urchins were fresh—they just can't be that far away."

A short while later, the driver exited on the coast road, heading toward Pacifica and Santa Cruz.

It was after dark when the truck driver, unaware that he had been followed, pulled into foggy Pillar Point Harbor, Half Moon Bay—our brown Ford truck was a few car-lengths behind. We parked, still unseen by the driver, and slinked toward the public hoist, where his truck sat.

Tied to the pilings under the hoist was the *Tsunami*, George Tomlinson's new boat. It was an aluminum rig, thirty-eight feet, with tilt-forward storm windows and a fully enclosed cabin and steering station. A huge pile of urchins covered the aft deck.

A dark figure, partially obscured by the fog, puffed on a pipe while he fed quarters into the coin operated hoist.

After skulking back to Doug's truck without being spotted, we turned on the cab light and pulled out the large chart book. "Where's he finding 'em?" I asked. "The swell is fifteen feet—there can't be more than six inches visibility anywhere!"

Doug's finger moved slowly across the chart, offshore. "Right here, partner. The Farallon Islands."

# The Farallones

*For believe me: the secret for harvesting
from existence the greatest fruitfulness and greatest
enjoyment is to live dangerously.*

—Fredrich Nietzsche

## Virgin Reef

There was no time to waste. A week's worth of food, along with a change of clothes, was carried down to the boat. Debbie was a little put out—she'd made it clear that after a year and a half, she was tired of the damp, chilly Mendocino coast, and now I was leaving her for a week. She made me promise that when I got back home, we would start thinking about moving.

The downhill run from Noyo to our launching point, Bodega Bay, was easy. The swells were big, and a stiff wind was blowing, but the *Day Tripper*, with her raised bow, was good in a following sea—we were just part of the herd of white buffaloes on the five-hour run down the coast. The ride was exciting in our little boat, but she handled it well, and after rounding "The Head" and negotiating Seal Rock, we entered Bodega Bay. A slip in the Spud Point Marina was rented for the night, after which we walked across the bay to the Sandpiper restaurant for a bite to eat.

After a night of fitful sleep on the boat, the fuel tank was topped off for the thirty-eight mile run to the Farallon Islands. Trucking arrangements with The Spaniard had already been made, so after a quick bowl of oatmeal on the boat, we were off.

Bright sunshine greeted us as we negotiated the inner channel, and cleared the breakwall. A brisk northwest wind welcomed us back to the ocean for the second leg of our journey to the Farallones, which we calculated would take us less than two hours to reach.

"Turn on the radar, boss. We're headed into a wall of fog."

My mind was elsewhere, but as we passed by the lighthouse at Point Reyes, halfway to our destination, I snapped out of it. Doug was right. A thick fogbank lay just ahead.

We were on a big time adventure, and our hearts pounded as we crossed the open sea of the San Francisco Channel. Visibility was less than a quarter of a mile, but the rough wind chop that had accompanied us was beginning to die down. Following the radar the entire way, we never saw a thing until the island loomed dead ahead. It was eerie.

The Farallon Islands lie due west of the Golden Gate Bridge, and are comprised of four islands: Southeast, North Island, Noonday, and Middle Farallon (affectionately known by local fishermen as "The Pimple").

Southeast is the largest, roughly one mile across by a half a mile, and has the most diving area. It is twenty-five miles from the Golden Gate Bridge, twenty-seven miles from Half Moon Bay, and thirty-eight miles from Bodega Bay.

The terrain is rough and barren, with no trees and little vegetation. Birds however, cover the island. There is a large population of harbor seals, elephant seals, California sea lions, and Stellar sea lions.

The Farallones are also a feeding ground for the great white shark.

The south side of the island, as we had hoped, was protected from the northerly winds.

"Drop it!" I shouted. Doug let the anchor go in the shallows near Mussel Flat.

"Good news," he said, as he ducked back into the cabin area. "The anchor's on the bottom at twenty feet, and I can see it perfectly."

He was right. The last time I had seen water this clear was at San Miguel Island, almost two years ago.

We took in our surroundings. The boat gently bobbed about three hundred feet from the island, which looked like a series of huge boulders and rubble. There was no color, but for a nondescript tan, with a small amount of vegetation scattered about. Rising straight up from the island was a large hill with an old lighthouse on it.

Birds were everywhere, and they were loud. The pungent smell of their droppings permeated the air. In fact there was so much bird crap, the rocks looked like they had snow on them.

The winch groaned as we brought up the first bag. "Man, these things are heavy!" Doug was grinning.

"Yeah, I cracked a few to check the roe. It's fat, and the shells are thick—these suckers'r dinosaurs."

The bottom was beautiful. A thick blanket of eel grass and short, lettuce-like vegetation covered the solid reef bottom, where the urchins clung to the crevices in long, thick rows, ripe for the picking.

The shallow water we were diving in allowed the rays of sunlight to reach the bottom, putting on a show as they hit the leaves of bottom growth. Unlike the thick beds of macrocystis kelp in Santa Barbara, or the long strands of bullwhip kelp on the North Coast, the Farallon Islands have no kelp. Urchins there feed on bottom growing algae, shallow eelgrass, and waterborne nutrients.

"We have company." The fog had lifted. Doug pointed to a boat three hundred yards east of us. It was the *Tsunami*—George Tomlinson stood on deck, his binoculars trained on us.

Our week diving at the Farallones had been nothing short of incredible. On the third day the sea flattened out, allowing us to take several survey dives around the island. And although the waters of Mendocino still had reasonably good picking, we were now in virgin reef. It was loaded beyond our wildest dreams, with no other boats in sight, except for the *Tsunami*.

The run into Half Moon Bay was easy too. It was a little like the crossing from Santa Barbara to the front side of Santa Cruz Island, but not as rough.

The *Day Tripper* stayed in a slip at the Pillar Point marina while we rode a bus back to Mendocino.

Debbie knew I was only going to be home for a few days. "I missed you." She gave me a warm kiss, but I could tell she wasn't happy.

"I missed you too, honey."

"How was the trip?" The question was curt. Her eyes gazed blankly out the window, toward the bay.

"Good. We filled the boat every day, six days in a row. It was easy."

"That's nice. I'm glad you did well. We need to talk." She had spoken the words all husbands dread.

"I'm leaving tomorrow. My sister is meeting me in Santa Rosa. It's been a long time since we've seen each other." Her eyes continued looking at the bay. "I should be back in a few days."

She had never left me before! I had always been the one to leave! I had to think fast.

"Do you want some company?" I probed.

Her head turned slightly toward me. "I thought you were hot to get back to Half Moon Bay."

"We had a good run. The urchins down there aren't going anywhere. It would be fun to get away for a few days." I was dying, not believing the words that had escaped from my mouth.

She turned and looked at me. "Sure. Judy would love to see you. Maybe we could look at some houses in the area." She was anxious to get away from the cold, foggy Mendocino coast, even if it meant living in Santa Rosa, twenty-five miles from the ocean.

"Sounds great," I gagged, trying to sound sincere.

"You're what?" Doug was astounded. "The bank's open, man!"

"I'll be back in a few days, then we'll charge."

"Okay," he grumbled.

The visit with Debbie's sister was nice. She had driven up from San Jose with her four kids. Spending a day with that crew made our house seem like a library, but it was a fun two days, and my wife was happier.

We drove around the western part of Sonoma County, ending up in Sebastopol. Debbie took an immediate liking to the small town of seven thousand.

"This might be a nice place to raise our son. Karen Tomlinson said the schools here are good."

My mind was racing. If we sold the *Day Tripper* and moved up to a bigger boat, I could access the Farallones from Bodega Bay, only a fifteen minute drive from Sebastopol.

"Sounds good, honey."

We'd made the decision to get a bigger boat, which I ordered from H&F Custom Boats in Bandon, Oregon. Harold Montgomery, a retired abalone diver, had acquired the thirty-two-foot Radon mold from Don Radon, who was experimenting with a new twenty-nine footer.

The boat was scheduled for completion in April of 1989, only three months away. As things worked out, she was delivered to Bodega Bay the same day we closed escrow on our house in Sebastopol.

One of the urchin divers who had grown up in Fort Bragg had expressed an interest in the *Day Tripper*. The fellow had been diving for a year, and had recently married. He was twenty-two years old and ready to move up in the business.

Letting go of the *Day Tripper* was tough—she was a good boat, and we'd covered a lot of territory in our eight years together. She was easy to handle, reliable, and stable. My future, however, lay thirty-eight miles from Bodega Bay, out in the ocean. We needed something bigger.

By April 20, the *Debbie K.* was ready for her maiden voyage.

The new, bigger boat was a sweetheart. Twin Mercruiser V-8s pushed her along at twenty-four knots, and she wasn't even breathing hard. With two powerful motors, we could plane an eight thousand pound load at eighteen knots.

The steering area was fully enclosed, with a clear lexan sliding door and tilt forward windows. An electric heater with a fan kept the cabin warm—it was the first thing to be turned on every morning after starting the engines. A compact water heater provided hot showers on the back deck, with a hundred gallon fresh water tank and soap dispenser. Two fish holds with a capacity of a thousand pounds each were covered by lightweight hatches.

She had a dark gray hull, a light gray cabin, and maroon trim. A mast and boom rig had a radar platform attached to it, and she had a full compliment of electronics, including a new satellite GPS plotter, with a coastal chart interface. This state of the art device displayed a detailed image of the coast and all offshore islands. Now, instead of punching in a series of latitudinal and longitudinal numbers on the land based LORAN unit, we simply moved the rollerball cursor with our thumb to a spot on the chart display, and clicked on it.

The nicest feature of the new boat, however, was the hydraulic anchor winch. After ten years of pulling the hook by hand, I now had a "Back Saver."

Bodega Bay is 68 miles north of San Francisco, and 25 miles west of Santa Rosa. The strong prevailing northwesterlies that howl through the marinas have given rise to the nickname, "Blowdega Bay."

The large natural bay has two marinas, Spud Point and Porto Bodega.

Porto Bodega (nicknamed Porta Potty) was built in the fifties. The old narrow wooden docks that squeak and bob remind me of the 1970s docks in Santa Barbara. The only bathroom is up in the harbor office, which is housed in a building that serves as the marina office. The floors slant, and the entire building is a little cockeyed.

There are no dock boxes for the slips, and the parking lot is dirt. Several old house-trailers that have been there for forty years serve as quarters for dock and restaurant workers. A large dumpster, usually overflowing, sits in the parking lot. A short walk from the old marina will take you to the Sandpiper restaurant, and although the food is excellent and the service first-class, some low-life urchin diver renamed it the Sandpooper and, unfortunately, the name stuck.

On the other side of the bay is Spud Point marina, a state of the art facility with wide concrete docks, boxes and hose bibs for every slip. The fuel dock can accommodate several boats, and a nearby building has restrooms, laundry facilities, and a shower. Each dock is kept locked, and boat owners are issued keys. It's like being on the other side of the tracks.

A few miles up the road toward Sebastopol is the tiny town of Bodega, made famous in 1963 as the filming location of Alfred Hithcock's movie, *The Birds*.

By 1991, urchin divers had been harvesting the areas around the bay for almost five years. The visibility in this area of the coast is generally poor, so if a diver can see twelve feet here he is happy. Timber Cove, Stillwater, and Salt Point are popular locations to the north. Tomales Bay, Bird Rock, and Elephant Rock, south of Bodega Bay, have inferior urchins, and for the most part are avoided.

Surfers are plentiful on this coast, chasing the waves at Salmon Creek, Jenner, and Dillon Beach.

## Dangerous Times

Things could not have been better at home. Debbie was getting acquainted with our neighbors in Sebastopol, happy to be living in the small community. Donovan was three, just starting nursery school.

Doug rented a small house a stone's throw from Spud Point marina, where the *Debbie K.* was berthed. The Farallon Islands became our main diving area for the next three years. Demand was strong due to a booming Japanese economy and during this time we saw prices range from fifty cents to a dollar twenty per pound, depending on roe quality and time of year. We worked out of Bodega Bay, San Francisco, and Half Moon Bay.

The Farallones lie in the heart of the "Red Triangle," the area encompassing Bodega Bay to Monterey. Marine biologists stationed on the island have been studying the Great White Shark for years. Some have been tagged with tracking devices in order to monitor their migration patterns. Predatory attacks on sea lions (Mr. GW's favorite meal), are monitored by the scientists as well.

Multiple attacks on humans have occurred there over the years, including my pal John Holcomb, who had helped me launch the *Day Tripper.* John was fortunate, but still has several scars on his body after being bitten and dragged through the water.

"Did you guys see the shark today?" Doug and I were tied up near the hoist at Pillar Point, waiting in line behind the *Tsunami.* George Tomlinson had finally come to grips with the fact that he was going to have to share the island with another boat. The normally reclusive former Naval officer and commando had accepted us, and we periodically had breakfast together when the weather forced us into Half Moon.

"Nope, we've made about twenty trips out there so far. Haven't seen a one." Doug was usually on the quiet side, but this night we were all in a good mood. It was December 1989. Urchin prices were at an all-time high, and I had just paid him two thousand dollars for one day of work.

George smoked a pipe. As he puffed and directed the unloading of his boat, his blue eyes bored into me. "It was a fifteen footer, less than a hundred yards off my port bow. He was a third of the way out of the water, with a seal in his mouth, wagging it around." He seemed nonchalant. "Don't worry, you'll see one."

I respected George but we weren't close. There was a powerful intensity about him. He was a serious man, not one who smiled or laughed often. Whether surfing on his wave ski, diving urchins, or overseeing business deals, George was a dominator, and always a step or two ahead of the rest of the fleet. He kept to himself mostly, and while many unproven stories circulated about his alleged nefarious deeds, it was well known that he was not one to be trifled with. Everyone knew the rumor of what had happened the year before.

Stepping aboard the *Tsunami* on a cold morning in Fort Bragg, Tomlinson surprised a thief. Two weight belts were strapped around the burglar's waist, a bag of dive gear hung from his arm.

Two minutes later, the unfortunate bandit found himself locked in the cabin, heading out the mouth of Noyo, and nursing a growing bruise on his left cheekbone.

Before long, the *Tsunami* drifted a half mile offshore with the robber lying on the deck, whimpering. His eyes were open wide. His hands and feet were tied, and he was wrapped head to toe with twenty feet of chain. Tears rolled down his puffy face and he shivered with fear as he looked into the steely blue eyes of the former Vietnam warrior.

When George figured he'd made his point, he headed the boat back to the harbor and released his captive. He didn't call the authorities, nor did he further threaten the would-be robber. It wasn't necessary.

Our second child, Tammi Sue, was born in the spring of 1990. She was a perfect baby, sleeping through the night, and crying very little. Even when she was unhappy, her cries were soft and delicate. Donovan had a little sister, and Debbie was in heaven. She was busy though, and needed my help. The *Debbie K.* stayed tied up in Bodega Bay for most of the spring and summer, mostly due to lousy weather and shrinking prices.

Doug had a steady girl, and was just closing a deal on a fifty-foot steel fishing boat. His lifelong dream of running his own boat was becoming a reality. But money poured out of his bank account. For months he worked nonstop on his new boat, the *Olinka*. A master welder and fabricator, most of his days were spent wearing a leather apron, with sparks flying. Next summer, when the albacore season came around, the *Olinka* would be a thousand miles offshore. Right now though, my pal was almost broke.

It was not yet light when I called.

"You ready for some diving?" We'd been off for months. It was early October.

"You bet. I was just looking at the weather. The buoys are three feet at eleven seconds, wind is southeast at four knots."

Our computers, and the internet, were our forecasters these days. Precise weather conditions anywhere in the world could be checked in a matter of seconds.

"Yeah, it looks good. I'll see you on the boat at six."

"Roger that."

Maintop Bay, Southeast Farallon Island, was as calm as a mill pond. A large contingent of sea lions obnoxiously barked a loud welcome from their perch on the rocks before diving in the water to inspect the visitors. From an overcast sky a continuous damp drizzle fell. But being October the air wasn't cold yet, and as we climbed into our wetsuits we could see urchins clearly visible on the bottom. It promised to be a lucrative day. We were anchored in fifteen feet. The water was crystal clear.

With the *Debbie K.*, bigger bags were possible. We now used large baskets to fill bags weighing from six to nine hundred pounds.

My first bag of the day was half full within fifteen minutes. Doug's bubbles formed a steady stream, rising to the surface forty feet away from me.

The left pectoral fin of the Great White was the first thing I saw. He must have come up from behind, and then turned at the last second. The massive gray beast passed within two feet of me, his entire body clearly visible. I watched, paralyzed, as the tail slowly swayed from side to side. He continued a gradual, sweeping turn to his right. It was then that I had my best view of the entire animal. It was fifteen feet long, with a huge girth, and white underbelly. His eye was black with a vacant stare, the large mouth was slightly open.

The deliberate turn continued. He was approaching me again. Positioning my body behind the partially full urchin bag, I watched, mesmerized. He swam right at me.

Ten feet away from me he turned, and slowly departed. I watched him disappear, the long tail gently guiding him back to deep water. I remained motionless.

Doug was on the boat with his wetsuit top off. His face was pale. He had been "buzzed" as well.

"I hope we're going home," he said.

"We are."

Our usual chatter was missing on the ride home, both of us silently reliving the episode in our own minds.

We unloaded quickly that night, tied the boat up, and gave it a fast, inadequate cleaning. I was anxious to get home to my family, so we mumbled our goodbyes in the parking lot, got in our trucks, and left.

When people find out they are talking to a diver, they always ask the same questions. "Have you ever seen a shark?" Upon hearing the reply, the next question is, "Was it scary?"

I always give the same answer. "It goes beyond fear."

Just the thought of being in the water with a man-eating shark is terrifying. There is simply nothing you can do, and nowhere to go, other than try to find a crack or crevice to burrow into. Even then, you know that if he wants you, he's going to dig you out, just like we pry urchins from their cracks.

In an effort to gain the upper hand, Doug bought a pneumatic spear gun, with a "powerhead" containing a forty-four caliber slug. The weapon, which is manufactured by the Mares Company, is capable of blowing the head clean off of a forty-inch ling cod.

He made a sheath for his gun out of a PVC tube, which he attached to his picking basket, and after a bit of practice, he was able to pull it out in a matter of one or two seconds. I never bothered getting one myself, for a couple of reasons. One, it seemed that the only time I ever saw a shark was when he had come from behind me, and was turning away, already having decided I wasn't what he had in mind for his meal. I figured that even if I did have a weapon, I'd probably be inside his mouth before I knew he was even there. Secondly, although the gun had a safety on it, it was not beyond the realm of possibility that the switch could inadvertently be disengaged, and a diver could accidentally blow his leg off. I just figured I'd take my chances unprotected, rather than trying to pull a gun out of its holster while being devoured.

As frightening as it sounds, our encounters with these monsters became almost, well, routine. We spotted them about once every ten or twelve trips, and after the first few sightings, a new plan was put into place.

Instead of ending a potentially profitable day (and I'm talking several thousand dollars), any encounter with "Mr. GW" simply meant it was time for a lunch break, after which we would move the boat a few hundred yards, or to the other side of the small island (as if we could hide from them). This brilliant idea, concocted by our brains, which are about the size of a pea, would, in theory, insure our safety and keep us on the road to riches.

As other boats ventured farther up the coast, we heard more stories, equally as horrifying as any of ours. This little gem was related to Doug and me by Dave Abernathy and Joey Lara, fellow North Coast urchin divers.

We listened with mouths agape as the two divers told their story in between mouthfuls of pancakes at the Sandpiper restaurant.

December 4, 1991. The three-man crew of the *Oomoo* took advantage of a ten-day calm stretch to survey the previously untouched reefs near Shelter Cove, north of Fort Bragg. In the middle of a protected bay, Dave Abernathy located a virgin reef while liveboating—Joey Lara drove the boat while Gerald Vickers tended the dive hose.

"I was surveying with about five or six foot viz, which actually isn't too bad for that area," Dave spoke rapidly. "I found a wall that was covered—it looked like at least a couple thousand pounds, so I came up to tell the boys to drop the hook."

Joey spoke up. "Dave had just reached the surface, when a huge shark swam up right behind him with his mouth wide open! Gerald and I just froze!"

"I had my regulator out of my mouth to holler at them to drop the hook, but they were just staring with big eyes and open mouths. Suddenly, I felt something hit me hard in the small of my back—I guess I instinctively curled my legs up under me."

"We saw the shark chomp down on Dave, but he missed. He hit him and shoved him across the top of the water. But he got the dive hose caught in his mouth. Then he took off, dragging Dave with him."

"At first I thought it was a Stellar sea lion. I turned around to hit him with my rake, but I was looking down the back of the shark. It was a monster, and it had me."

"The fuckin' thing was huge! I mean the boat is twenty-five feet, and he was at least two thirds as big—at least! So he's twisting and turning, trying to bite Dave, but he can't cause he's slinging him around by his hose."

"Every time he'd yank me around, I'd wind up on his back. By now I knew a shark had me—I knew I was dead."

"He swam right by the boat, looking at us, dragging Dave. There was only about a foot or two of hose between them. He twisted his head almost all the way around to his tail, but Dave was thrown over onto his back again. Then he swam away from the boat."

"I went limp—I figured I'd just play dead. That's about all I could do."

"Then he took Dave underwater. They both disappeared—we couldn't do anything. I mean we were paralyzed!"

"He took me down, maybe eight or ten feet. I pretty much gave up at that point. I knew my life was over. Then, suddenly, I was free! I popped up to the surface and started screaming—Come get me! I'm alive! But they just stood there—they couldn't move."

"He was screaming at us, but it was like a dream. Then he yelled my name, and I guess I snapped out of it. By now he was about fifty feet away. I ran to the helm and gunned the boat toward him. All the hose was floating in the water, but there wasn't time to get it on the boat."

"They were coming to get me and I thought I might make it. Then, Joey veered the boat and went around me— I couldn't figure out what the hell he was doing!"

"I saw the damn thing coming for him again—I just gave the boat full throttle and maneuvered it between them, trying to save my diver."

"They went around me instead of coming to get me—what were they doing?"

"Dave was next to the boat. I yelled, Get on! He's coming! But all he could do was lift his arms up—he was helpless. The shark swam under the boat, but missed Dave. We both ran to the rail and hauled him up just as a huge swirl of water hit the surface."

"I was on the boat! I was whole! I was crying—we all were! Crying and shaking and hugging each other. I kept shouting, I'm whole! I'm alive!"

In the mad dash to retrieve the diver, a mass of floating dive hose had become fouled in the prop, killing the motor. Now the boat was adrift, dead, in the calm, gray water. The three men looked at each other. They were all thinking the same thing—sharks have been known to attack boats.

"We huddled in the middle of the deck," Joey said. "I mean the *Oomoo* is a pretty small boat. But after floating around for five or six minutes without seeing him, we figured he was gone. Now we had another problem. One of us was going to have to get down in the water to cut the damn hose from the prop."

"The outdrive came up okay, so it was mostly out of the water, but when Joey had his face down, hanging off the stern, all we could picture was that shark, jumping up and biting his head off."

"Yeah, that was a little nerve-racking, cutting that stupid hose from the prop. Anyway, the only injuries were a few cuts and bruises to Dave, and a chewed up hose."

Doug spoke first. "Jesus, I thought we'd had some close calls."

"Yeah, well that was three weeks ago." Joey munched on his pancake. "My nerves finally settled down, and I'm back at it."

"How 'bout you, Dave?" I asked. "Have you been back in the water yet?"

His answer was priceless. "Are you kidding? Shit, I'm afraid of my bathtub!"

## Mr. Farallon Islands

Doug and I were picking between three and four thousand pounds each per day at the Farallones. We'd been together for over a year now, and we got along well (being cooped up in a thirty-two-foot space day after day, month after month, will test even the best friendships.)

But the *Debbie K.* could hold a lot more than we were putting on her, so I approached my pal about hiring another diver.

"Only if it's the right guy," he told me. "I like our method of you being on your side of the boat, and me on my side."

"I know, I like it too. Just think about it, that's all I ask. We'll only bring somebody aboard if he'll play by our rules." I could tell he wasn't thrilled by the idea, but he gave me a grudging nod.

It wasn't more than a week later when Ron Elliott, a longtime uni diver approached me at the Spud Point Boatyard, where I had the boat hauled out for maintenance. He'd just sold his twenty-four-footer, the *Carol Ann* and was looking for a ride.

Good people are hard to find—I didn't hesitate. "I'll pay you sixty percent to start. If the three of us get along, I'll take it up to sixty-five after three months." It was a good offer. He shook my greasy hand and became the third man on the *Debbie K.*

Ron was fairly short, with dark, close-cropped hair, and mysterious, squinting eyes. Although we had gotten into the business at about the same time, we didn't know each other well. During our South Coast days, he worked out of Channel Islands Harbor, near Oxnard, so our paths rarely crossed. He had a reputation, though, as a hard worker and a family man, plus he was a nondrinker and a nonsmoker.

Our first three or four trips were uneventful. He was quiet, worked hard, and fit well with our operation. But it was later, after a month or two of being on the boat, that his true nature began to appear. There's just no easy way to say it—the guy was fuckin' nuts. Not unusual, not quirky—he was over-the-top crazy.

The next few paragraphs will be a feeble attempt to explain the absolute psychosis of Ron Elliott:

Doug and I learned that the fairly quiet and well-mannered diver could, on occasion, become moody. His face would darken, and his short fuse periodically went off. And although we were just getting acquainted with Ron's twisted ways, many of the other guys knew about the dark-haired dynamo who was rumored to sometimes simply go berserk.

I had gotten into a mild squabble at the fuel dock one morning while we were gassing up. The other fellow and I both claimed that the spot in question (up the coast, near Salt Point) was our turf. Unfriendly banter quickly escalated into a shouting match, and it was beginning to get ugly. We edged closer and closer to each other, eyeball to eyeball, neither of us backing down. A crooked finger was stuck in my face. "I'm gonna come down here some night and sink your fuckin' boat!" he screamed. At that precise moment, Ron came out of the cabin. "You better not." He said with a quiet glare. "My gear's on this boat."

"Oh, hi Ron! How's it going? I didn't know you were diving on this boat! How's the family? Well, see you later—I gotta run! Good seeing you, say hi to the wife!"

I was amazed at the sudden retreat as he back-pedaled away from us. This guy, I said to myself, knows something I don't know. Later, after I related the strange tale to Doug, my friend spoke these words of wisdom; "Sometimes it pays to have a psychopath on your boat."

Besides being a well mannered, likeable nutcase, Ron had the oddest sense of humor of anyone I've ever known. His pranks and mischievous ways would have put Jerome to shame.

Seal bombs, a high-powered firecracker equivalent to a small stick of dynamite, are a legal weapon salmon fishermen use to scare seals away from their catch. Ron brought some out on the boat one day for a few laughs. At first I thought it was a good idea—toss a bomb into the water prior to jumping in, just in case Mr. GW was lurking about. That changed in a hurry when, a few seconds after surfacing next to the boat, a bomb went off just above my head. It about knocked me out. When my eyes cleared and I could see again, there was Ron, hopping around on deck, cackling like an old witch.

"No more seal bombs on the boat, Ron." I said on the way home that evening.

"Oh, come on, Tom! I won't throw them at you anymore—I promise!" I was so mad I couldn't even look at him.

"No more bombs on my boat, Ron." He became dark and sullen, and didn't speak for over an hour, except to emit a high-pitched snicker now and then.

After the seal bomb episode, I gave great thought to firing Ron, but I didn't. For one thing, the guy was an incredible urchin harvester, out-picking Doug and me on a regular basis. He was fearless, always wanting to charge, no matter how rough the weather was. And, he loved the mysterious Farallones. In a short time, he became the prime motivator aboard the *Debbie K*. Plus, he was making me tons of money.

But the real reason I kept him on was because of his insane unpredictability. I just couldn't wait to see what he was going to do next! He tied our hoses around the outdrive multiple times. He'd sneak up behind us underwater, take a breath, then remove the regulator from his mouth and let out a primal scream as loud as he could, right into our ear. As long as I didn't have a heart attack, it was funny as hell. Every day it was something new—Doug and I went back and forth, being so pissed off we could kill him, to absolute, uncontrollable laughter.

Then, on a dank November day, Ron pulled the ultimate prank. To this day, I wake up at night thinking about it.

Visibility at the Farallones can be incredible—sometimes forty or fifty feet. But like anywhere else, it can get murky. We hated diving out there when the viz was at its worst, six to eight feet or so. Some people use the term *sharky*. I've never cared much for the word, nor do I use it, but I guess when your vision is restricted, and you're diving in arguably the most dangerous place in the world, it's a pretty good word.

If I could get inside Ron's head (God knows what's in there), this might be how the story would be told:

"Man, the viz sucks—I'm sure glad I found this nice patch up here by the anchor. Looks like I'm gonna kick their asses again today. Ha! But shit, I haven't pulled a prank on those fuckers all week—they're overdue. I gotta think of somethin'. "

On poor visibility days like this, we'd pull about fifty feet of hose off the boat, then tie it to our bag (so as not to lose it), and take off with our picking baskets, which held about a hundred pounds. After filling the basket, we'd follow our hose back to the main bag, dump our urchins, and take off again.

As he crept along the murky bottom with his basket, Ron came upon Doug's bag. His hose was tied to it and was heading off into the darkness. Once again, we'll enter into the demented one's head:

"Oops, there's Doug's bag—guess I'll do a U-turn.

Don't wanna crowd him. Better mind my manners and give him plenty of room."

He turned away from the bag, but had only swam about ten feet from it. "Hey, what's this? By golly, it's a sea lion, and he's missing his head! And there's fresh blood coming out of it! Wow!"

After pondering the five-foot-long prize for a few seconds, Ron smiled. "I think I'll give Doug a present! After all, it's almost Christmas, it's the least I can do!" With that, the deranged diver picked up the still-bleeding headless corpse, tucked it under his arm, lugged it over to Doug's bag, dropped it in, and went back to work.

I will not attempt to enter Doug's head at the time of his gruesome discovery. Nor will I repeat his oratory on the way home that night, other than to say it was loud, angry, and nonstop. I will, however, say that Doug, who is a very sanitary man and never pees in his suit, had the unmistakable scent of urine about him.

Ron only lasted six months with us—we just couldn't take it anymore. He became a loner. He built a beautiful twenty-six-foot aluminum rig that he named (of course) the *GW*, and continues to this day, diving the Farallones, alone.

Besides the one hundred odd trips he made out there on the *Debbie K.*, he has logged another three hundred plus on the *GW*. His stories, among the divers of the North Coast, are legend, and they are all true. If I could bestow a title on the friendly, unstable lunatic, it would be, "Mr. Farallon Islands."

Ron and I don't see each other much these days, but I consider him a good friend and I have a world of respect for him. He is polite, intelligent, and a good provider for his family. I would, however, caution anyone who does not know Ron Elliott to humor him, and give him wide berth.

There is a surf spot at the Farallones. A right break-ing wave peels off the point at Indian Head, on the western side of Southeast Island. It needs a pretty hefty ground swell to make it work, at least eight feet, and it can't tolerate any wind, other than a light southeasterly.

I had the seven-fifties pinned to my face as Doug climbed up the outdrive onto the rocking boat. "What do you see, Captain?" he asked, yelling over the noise of the popper. I walked over and shut it off. It was quieter now, but not much, due to the hundreds of birds squawking their disapproval to the invaders.

"Check out the wave peeling off the point. You could take off next to that wash rock."

He peeled off his wetsuit top and peed off the port side of the boat, so as not to offend the birds. "Lemme see the binocs." After we watched a few sets roll by, he spoke up. "Looks like the first and second waves of the set are the best—the next two are bumpy."

"Yeah, but the second one is bigger. That one's mine. You get the first one."

"Sounds good, let's suit up."

"Okay, after you, amigo."

"You first."

There is surf at the Farallones, and it's not crowded. If you want some empty waves, go ahead. Dangle your legs in Mr. GW's feeding grounds.

Within a two-year period beginning in 1989, our prices more than doubled. We were making money hand over fist. We were making so much money we couldn't keep up with it. A flat stretch turned into a blur of diving, unloading, a few hours of sleep, then up early, fueling up, and more diving. We had sacks of money, we had bags of money, we had barrels of money. Every day a new check was in our mailbox. Forty cents a pound, then sixty, then eighty. The Spaniard was paying out over fifty grand a day to his boats. At the peak of the market in December 1990, we were paid a buck fifty for an 8,000 pound load. Twelve thousand dollars, the record payday for my urchin career.

Times were good. Times were really good.

But it was about to get bad. Really bad.

# Hitting Bottom

*A friend may well be reckoned the masterpiece of nature.*

—*Ralph Waldo Emerson*

## We Lose Our Heart

For many years I considered myself a hard charger, and always strove to be a highliner. I set big goals, and anybody diving on my boat worked hard and made good money. Bad weather and big swells meant higher prices. Some of us preferred the weather a little rough—it reduced the amount of product hitting the dock, helping to keep the prices high.

By no means was I at the top of the heap though. On the North Coast in the eighties, the same names always came up. Steve Kuphal on the *Melinda K.*, Mark Evanoff on the *Defiance*, and the man who set the pace: George Tomlinson.

The ex-Navy SEAL soon established a reputation as a hard worker, and a man not to be taken lightly. George was always a step ahead of the rest of us. By the time I made it up to Mendocino, he was getting his license for the fledgling Oregon urchin fishery, building an incredible house on the pristine Navarro Ridge, and buying real estate in Fiji. Within two years the house was completed, and he had two more boats. He used to station his boats in three different locations on the West Coast, and move them around, so you never knew where they were. He hired crews for his two boats, and expected them to keep up with him on the third. Of course it was an impossible task, but he always seemed to keep the boats running, and with good crews. It was well known that if you were working with George, you didn't crawl out of the water until the sun was down.

On April 30, 1991, we got a phone call from a tearful Lori Hagen, Steve's wife.

"George died of a heart attack while he was diving yesterday up in Depot Bay, Oregon." She was clearly distraught, but was making the necessary calls.

The entire northern fleet was stunned. We headed for George's house to say goodbye.

The memorial service at the Tomlinson property was incredibly moving, and beautiful. It was one of the most emotional days of my life. I have no doubt that all who were in attendance that day feel the same.

A cold, gray mist lingered over the Navarro Ridge. The damp fog cast an eerie hue over the entire coast, and even though we were well over a mile inland, the sun would not appear on this day. Even the majestic redwoods, whose branches usually swayed in the breeze, providing kaleidoscopes of light and shadow, were still. They hung limp, under the heavy weight of the morning dew.

In the middle of a field was a huge pyre, with a cord of split oak nearby. The gathering of family and friends, over a hundred people, formed a large circle and held hands. One by one we stepped forward and told stories about George. Some were sad, many were exciting, and some were hilariously funny. A couple of people broke down in tears, and could not complete their stories. Then, the pyre was lit. A line formed and we all came forward, one at a time, to throw a log onto the massive fire. To me, the huge fire was representative of the man—so intense, so hot, so bright, you couldn't get close to it. It burned on into the night with an intensity that could only be matched by George's eyes.

After the ceremony, his wife, Karen, opened the house to all, and we wandered around looking at pictures, perusing his library, and admiring the furnishings, many of which had been imported from exotic lands.

George packed more living into his forty-four years than any person I have ever known. His accomplishments were unparalleled, and the house still stands as a testament to his drive and focus. A rosewood table that he imported from Australia found its way into our living room, and serves as a daily reminder of a man with vision, and limitless energy. George Tomlinson, the man who set a pace that not even he could keep up with.

## Trapped

I never planned on becoming financially successful. All I really ever wanted was to make a little money and have time to surf. In the past, keeping track of wave conditions was just as important, if not more so, as knowing the dive conditions. Now, days of big, perfect surf meant a day for working on the boat. Money had taken over as the motivating factor. In the beginning I was satisfied making a hundred dollars a day. Now, two thousand was my minimum goal. Even after a ten thousand dollar week, I couldn't sleep at night for fear of someone finding my spot and getting my urchins. My priorities had changed. I was involved in a serious business, taking serious risks, making serious money.

My marriage began to suffer. Withholding information from Debbie about the day's events, or simply lying, was now routine. I told myself it was because I didn't want her to worry, but in the back of my mind I knew the real reason. She wasn't stupid. We were making forty mile crossings in the rapidly changing seas of northern California, diving in shark-infested waters. We were pushing to be highliners in every area—the best price, biggest loads, and working in questionable weather conditions. I simply wanted the *Debbie K.* to be known as a pacesetter. I craved the prestige of being the top dog in the fleet, the one to beat.

Dinnertime conversations were quieter. She tried to keep me up on events around the house, and our children's daily accomplishments. But my mind was somewhere else. Boat maintenance, market conditions, weather, and product price now consumed my thoughts. I had little or no interest in the mundane world of my household. We began to have little spats. Eventually I tuned her out, not paying attention to the unspoken message of a door being slammed in another part of the house, or her long periods of silence.

For twelve years we had kissed each other good night, but when that ritual disappeared, I didn't even notice it was gone.

Surfing, the driving force since childhood, was all but forgotten. My boards sat up in the garage rafters collecting dust.

We had a core group of divers on the North Coast that got together about once a month for breakfast at the Sandpiper restaurant in Bodega Bay. Prices were discussed, or our competition from other parts of the world. We talked about our boats—how to diagnose overheating problems, or combating the ever present corrosion from the sea air. If someone tried out a new style winch, we learned about it. We talked about our families, and those of us with children bragged about them.

Two members of the group were surfers, and talk of perfect waves, or someone's new board always found its way into the conversation.

A feeling of confidence and self reliance had become part of my mindset. I was doing everything right. Doug and I were looked at as leading forces in the business, and other boat skippers admired not only the poundage being hauled by the *Debbie K.*, but how constant maintenance kept her in top condition.

But even with this close-knit group of friends I became secretive, not wanting to share information with my peers. I felt they had nothing to offer me. I quit attending the breakfasts.

Doug, my closest friend, noticed the change.

"The Head was good yesterday—eight-to-ten foot sets. I thought I might see you in the lineup."

"I had to change the oil. Plus the starboard riser was a little warm, so I pulled it off and flushed it out. Replaced the winch line too."

"Well, you missed it. The wind never came up. It stayed glassy all day."

"Yeah. It's just tough with the prices right now. I want to be ready."

"Right. So I was talking with the crew at breakfast the other day. Your name came up."

"Yeah?"

"Somebody said you've been a bit on the arrogant side lately."

"Hmmm."

"Somebody else said you're aloof. Think you're pretty hot stuff."

"What do you think?"

"I think you're gettin' to be an asshole."

Tom Kendrick

## We Lose Our Soul

Doug's words stung. But he was right. I'd become single-minded, with few friends and a crumbling marriage. I was now consumed by two thoughts only—urchins and money. The slide had begun.

The sea urchin market is tied to the yen, and therefore to the Japanese economy. All through the eighties, while our country was in a recession, Japan was booming. They were buying up real estate in Hawaii and California, and were snatching up big companies that were American icons. They even bought Pebble Beach. The Japanese were ordering lots of uni, and we were supplying it.

The nineties brought a slowdown in Japan, and more competition from other parts of the world. Chile was now supplying large quantities, and their divers were working for a fraction of our prices. A couple of our processors even packed up and moved down there. Canada and Mexico were in full swing. Alaska and Russia were being explored. The picking was getting slimmer, and big paydays were coming around less and less.

By the end of 1994, things had been going downhill for awhile, but the urchins were only part of the problem. We were coming off a couple of bad winters, and I was getting tired. After fifteen years of full-time diving, my motivation had dwindled. Even when the weather was good, I had to drag myself down to the boat.

Doug's many months of work on the *Olinka* were finally paying off. More and more of his time was spent fishing offshore, and he was only with me about four months a year now.

Debbie understood, but she saw the writing on the wall, and quietly began advertising for more piano students. She rarely brought up the subject of my quitting diving anymore. We'd been over it many times, and I had begun snapping at her. I was having periods of depression, and wondering how long I could keep diving.

But all this was nothing compared to what happened next.

From Cuyler Harbor, on the front side of San Miguel Island, it's about a thirty minute run to Castle Rock, a large outcropping two miles off the west end of the island. As the *Florentia Marie* motored out of the anchorage on the second day of an overnighter, she was met by a fifteen knot northwest breeze and a sloppy two-foot wind chop. The December air had a bite to it, the gray sky thick, with a gloomy overcast. It was their fourth turnaround trip in a row—just a cold, crappy day.

Ward Motyer was a longtime friend of his skipper, Jim (Weener) Robinson, and had been diving on the *Florentia* for over five years. But on their eighth consecutive day of diving, his frustration showed. "We've been working this spot for two months, man. I'm sick of it. I don't know how you think we're gonna scratch another day outta there."

Steve Stickney tried to keep his coffee in his cup as they made their way past Harris Point, and into the brunt of the weather. After tending on the *Florentia* for two years, he knew his job well. He also knew that choosing dive spots wasn't his area. He kept his mouth shut and concentrated on his coffee.

As skipper and boat owner, Weener's thoughts were split into different areas. His ear subconsciously tuned to the rumble of the Caterpillar diesel, which sounded fine, but was due for an oil change. The boat had hit a log (or something) in the middle of the night the week before, and now a slight vibration could be felt through the steering wheel. It wasn't bad, but he knew the prop needed to come off and get rebalanced. Several bags had holes that needed patching. "I'll ask Steve to take care of that when we get some time off," he said to himself.

Based on the weather, which was bad, but not terrible, he figured there were probably ten boats working this day, so they would not be flooding the market. The three thousand pounds of uni below decks was fresh after being kept in the cold water of Cuylers overnight, and December was traditionally a month of high prices due to the upcoming New Year's celebration in Japan. "We might see a buck fifty for these from The Spaniard, if we're lucky," he silently calculated.

Now he thought about the spot. "Ward's right. We've been milking this area for too long. We had a couple of weeks of decent picking at forty and fifty feet, but we're off the edge of the reef now, in sixty to seventy feet, not to mention the drop-offs to a hundred and twenty."

"Yeah, okay, you're right Wardy. Let's finish up that edge we were on yesterday, see if we can make a day of it, and then move on. Maybe we'll check our old spot at Sandy Point—we haven't been there for a while."

Castle Rock now loomed five hundred yards off their port bow. "Take it, Wardy. I'm gonna suit up." He joined Steve on deck and while the tender made hoses and bags ready for the day, Weener coated his arms and legs with a thin layer of hair conditioner and slipped into his wetsuit.

Ward could read the plotter as well, if not better, than Weener, and now as he steered the boat, closing in on the numbers he had punched in the day before, his thoughts echoed his feelings. "I'm burned out on this fuckin' spot. We're out in the middle of nowhere, not a blade of kelp anywhere. It just creeps me out." He shifted the motor into neutral, gave his diver the thumbs up, and glanced out the window just in time to see Weener disappear under the water.

"Diver killed in shark attack off San Miguel" read the huge headline of the *Santa Barbara News Press*.

But the newspaper only told a small part of the story.

Within hours, the news of the tragedy aboard the *Florentia Marie* traveled up and down the coast, sending the urchin diving community into shock. From San Diego to Fort Bragg, divers tied up their boats and headed to Santa Barbara. Network news journalists from Los Angeles came in their white vans with satellite dishes, interviewing anyone who could talk.

At four o'clock in the afternoon, Ward Motyer and Steve Stickney arrived at the dock. The captainless crew that unloaded the *Florentia Marie* was drained and emotionless. They ignored the news microphones and went home.

Four days later, on December 13, Weener's memorial was held at the Free Methodist Church on Cliff Drive. Hundreds of mourners attended, many having to stand outside. Tributes were given, stories were told, and some of his favorite music was played, including Tom Waits's emotional ballad, "On the Nickel." One of the mourners recited the Walt Whitman poem "Oh Captain, My Captain," an unending stream of tears flowing down his face.

After the service, fifty boats headed slowly out of the harbor to scatter Weener's ashes where they belonged, in the waters off Santa Barbara. Prayers were said, tequila flowed, and several people stripped and jumped off their boats to swim with Weener one last time.

In a way, we all died that day. Weener, to many of the divers, was more than just another friend—to some he was a mentor, to some a father figure. And to some of us he was a hero, someone to pattern our life after.

But on that one terrible December day, all of us, every single diver on the coast, became instantly aware of our mortality, of our frailness. Up to now, like Weener, we were invincible, we were indestructible, we were bulletproof. But not anymore. What would happen to us? Our hero, our champion! He was gone.

Weener *was* the urchin business. Like me, Dewey, Jerome, Lenny, Cotton, and others, Weener had caught the wave early on. And he rode it like no other. For almost his entire career, he managed to stay in virgin territory, delivering the biggest loads, and commanding the highest prices. It was a game! A dangerous, exciting, lucrative game full of odd characters, ruthless processors, friends, enemies, villains. Good times, lean times, happy times, and sad times.

But it was coming to a close, for Weener's death was like a signal—the beginning of the end for the business as we knew it. Oh sure, the urchin business would survive, just like we would. But also, like us, it was changed. There would be no more nights of laying out the coastal charts, looking for the next Point Arena, the next Blue Lagoon, the next

Farallon Islands. No more jumping off the side of the boat with reckless abandon, smiles on our faces, and no thought for the future.

The glory days were gone—along with our exuberance and bright smiles— along with our carefree lifestyle and youthful innocence— along with Weener.

Both of our faces were wet with tears. We were driving home from Santa Barbara. We hadn't spoken for a long time. There were just no words.

"He always called us TK and DK," she said.

"Yeah."

"I loved listening to him play the piano—that time he came to Sebastopol, remember?"

"He sprung for dinner for everybody."

"He was so good with the kids—when we stopped by his house in Goleta on our way to Mexico?"

"He played with 'em all afternoon."

We drove for another hour in silence, both of us deep in our own thoughts. After crossing the Golden Gate Bridge and winding our way through the Porsches and BMW's of Marin, the green rolling hills of Sonoma County came into view. Long shadows fell across the empty countryside.

"I want you to quit diving."

"And do what?"

"I don't know, and I don't care."

"Okay, honey, we'll figure something out."

"Promise?"

"I promise."

# At the End
# of My Hose

*Don't cry because it's over.*
*Smile because it happened.*

*—Dr. Suess*

### Back to the Beginning

For years I couldn't wait to get down to the harbor. Everything about my job was a rush. The calm ocean in the morning, the smell of the salt air. I even loved the smell of the urchins.

Unloading at night was the social hour. Sipping hot coffee while telling stories of the day's misadventures, and inflating our estimates of how many urchins we had on board. Some of us had a big pile on deck, and we would tie our boats up where everybody could see. Others, who had a lousy day, would sneak in, unload, and go home with their tails between their legs. I loved it all.

The year was 1995. Things were going stale. I'd lost my nerve out at the Farallones, and the cold dirty water of the North Coast had gotten old. I was finding reasons not to go to work, and on the few days that I did, it felt like I was just going through the motions. I was forty-four years old. It had been eight years since we moved north.

"I'd like to take the *Debbie K.* down south for a few weeks." We were at the dinner table. Donovan, now nine years old, had been out on the boat many times. "Can I go, Dad?"

"You can't miss school, honey. Besides, you have a soccer game Saturday." Debbie's life was full. Tammi was six. Her swim coach seemed to think there was great potential for her in competitive swimming. The youngster was already keeping up with kids much older than she.

Besides taxiing the kids to school and their activities, Debbie now had thirty-five piano students. "Are you going down to Half Moon?"

"I've never worked the southern islands. It might be my last chance—Duag wants to go too. We thought we might take the boat to San Clemente Island for a couple of weeks, see what it's like down there."

"Go watch television, kids. Your father and I need to talk."

She was quiet for a long time.

"So, will you trailer her down?"

"I thought we might run her down, maybe stop at The Ranch and surf for a day or two if the waves are good."

Again she was quiet.

"Look, honey. I know Jim's death had a terrible effect on you. It did me, too—I think about him all the time, even though it's been months. But at some point, you're going to have to get back to your life. I've been holding back saying anything, but I want my husband back. Do you know the back yard hasn't been mowed in two months?

"Our kids are at a tender age, and they need their father. Have you been giving any thought to what we talked about?" The idea of selling the boat had come up again a couple of weeks ago. She'd worried some about the diving over the years, but Weener's death gave her a new sense of urgency. She wanted me to sell the boat and get out of diving.

"I want to go dive San Miguel, unload at the dock, see Wes, and some of the guys. And I want to dive Clemente. I want to go somewhere I've never been before."

"Why are you doing this?"

"It's just that I ... I miss it down there. I miss it all." I looked away. "I miss ..."

"I know you do, honey." Her fingers rubbed my neck as I wiped my eyes. "How long will you be gone?"

"No more than three weeks. I promise. Then, we'll talk about selling the boat."

"Isn't San Clemente Island off San Diego somewhere?"

"Yeah, but we'll be delivering into San Pedro Harbor."

"Three weeks. No more."

"I'm a lucky guy to have you."

"Yes, you are." She gave me a long kiss.

In August 1995, after loading the *Debbie K.* with clothes, food, and surfboards, Doug and I headed out of the mouth of Bodega Bay, on our way to the land of the Chumash. After overnight stops at Santa Cruz and Morro Bay, we rounded Point Conception, where we were pleasantly surprised—a large southern hemisphere ground swell was pounding the central coast.

"Western Gate" was the name given by the Chumash Indians to an area of land near Point Conception. The eight mile stretch of pristine coastline was considered sacred. It was thought to be a part of the passage to the next life.

Colonel William Hollister acquired the land, then known as "Rancho Nuestra Señora del Refugio" in 1869, and for the next hundred years it was a working cattle ranch.

Surfing at "The Ranch" as it is now called, began in the early sixties. Bob Perko, Bobby Hazard, and Reynolds Yater formed the Santa Barbara Surf Club, and for nearly ten years these surf pioneers were the sole guardians of the flawless, uncrowded waves.

Currently, The Ranch is owned by a group of individuals that make up the Hollister Ranch Owners Association. It has remained relatively unspoiled over the years, and is truly one of California's finest treasures.

This day, as we dropped our anchor at Little Drakes, a slight offshore breeze was helping to shape perfect six-foot waves, and the crowd was light. Within minutes, we had our boards unpacked, and were paddling into the lineup.

The sun, which was low in the sky, could be seen through the sculpted waves as they approached the shoreline, creating a green, translucent effect. Empty, rolling hills behind the shoreline revealed the loneliness of this sparsely populated jewel that is the Hollister Ranch.

Three hours later the sun dropped below the horizon. We climbed onto the boat and collapsed, our bodies spent.

"Epic," Doug sighed. This was his first time at The Ranch.

"I concur, amigo. If the boat breaks down, and we don't get a single urchin, this day alone has made the trip worth it."

We stayed on the boat and surfed for three days, then took off straight to San Miguel Island, a twenty one mile crossing from The Ranch, for some clear water diving.

What a feeling, pulling into the Santa Barbara harbor after so many years! As we waited our turn to offload, I introduced Doug to Wes, who was back from Costa Rica, and once again pushing the hoist button.

"I told Doug about the mummy," I said, while shaking his hand.

"Well, bring him over, I'll show it to him!"

"Say, where's The Spaniard? Are you guys sharing the dock?"

Wes looked out toward the islands. "Weener's death pretty much did him in. You know, it took the wind out of all our sails, but Andreas just never recovered. It's like he lost his reason for living. Anyway, the Josefina Fish Company folded and he went bankrupt."

After unloading and a little socializing, a group of us walked up and invaded Brophy Brothers restaurant for dinner and drinks.

"Did you hear about Crazy Harold and the dog?" Bill Hooten had our ear. He was yelling in order to be heard over the usual high decibel level of Brophy's. When Doug and I indicated we had not, Bill rubbed his hands together and began his story.

"A gang of elementary age school kids had been riding their bikes around Harold's neighborhood. They were a little on the loud side, you know, normal kids. One of the neighbors hated them. He was always yelling, trying to get the little hooligans to quiet down. He had a dog that he would turn loose and it would chase 'em down the street, barking and nipping at their feet as they rode by.

"Crazy Harold figured the kids had a right to ride their bikes down the street without being harassed by animals, so he pays his neighbor a friendly visit. *Why don't you keep your fucking dog on your own property? Those goddamn kids aren't hurting anybody.*

"I guess they'd been neighbors for years, and never did like each other. I mean, jees, its Crazy Harold, what's not to like?

"Anyway, about a week later, when the runts cruised by, the dog ran out and bit one of 'em on his calf. It wasn't bad, but it did break the skin.

"So the next day the guy goes out to get his morning paper. He finds his dog lying on the front lawn, dead, with an underwater spear gun arrow through it.

"The guy flips out. He knows Crazy did it, and he calls the cops.

"I was in his garage picking up a regulator when the cops showed up.

*Mornin' Harold,* says one of the cops.

"Now you gotta understand. Everybody knows Crazy, and everybody knows he's fuckin' nuts.

"So Crazy keeps sweeping. *Ya! Did you kill your neighbor's dog, Harold?* asks the cop. *What dog? Being a diver, you must have a spear gun. Not a fish eater. I like hamburgers. Mind if we have a look in your garage? Mind if I see your fucking warrant?"* Bill's eyes were wide. "He just kept sweeping, his eyes never left the floor!"

A few more Crazy Harold stories were told, along with dive stories of years gone by. But we were now talking about Weener, and a melancholy mood, fueled by tequila and emotion, overtook the crowd.

Everyone had a Weener story, some hilarious, some terrifying. Kenny Ludwig told of the time he was on the *Florentia* as she free fell fifteen feet off of a wave, breaking everything in the cabin, including two windows. Mark Brubaker remembered the time he and a friend were surfing at a secret spot out at the islands, when Weener swam into the lineup, buck naked. "Weener didn't have a board with him, he just wanted to get out in the surf!"

"Okay, here's a story, I swear this is true." Jimmy Marshall's eyes were big and bloodshot. Dinner had been finished hours before, but the tequila still flowed.

"A few days after the memorial, I was up at The Ranch with Hillary. I'd been moping around the house; the boat was tied up in the slip. Thinking some surf might help get me out of my gloom, she dragged me up there.

"The waves were good, and Hillary was right, I felt much better.

"After a two hour session, it was time to catch one in and head home. But within a few minutes, the sky turned gray, and a light south wind picked up, putting a funky chop on the face of the waves. I waited and waited, but it seemed like the pump had been turned off. Everyone else had either caught a wave, or had paddled in, so I was alone, with a darkening sky, and getting cold.

"Finally, in desperation, I looked up to the heavens, and whispered, *Send me a wave, Weener, just send me one wave.* Sure enough, a minute later, a set loomed on the horizon. I picked out the biggest one, caught it, and rode it all the way in to the beach."

Hillary Hauser interrupted him, laughing, tears rolling down her face.

"He came running up with his board under his arm, screaming at the top of his lungs, *He's a Saint! Weener's a Saint! It's Saint Weener!*"

The entire table erupted with laughter. Jimmy's drink splashed to the floor. The yacht crowd, over in the corner, gave the loud smelly mob a disapproving stare.

Under our table at Brophy's was a large wet spot. Most of it was tequila. But some of it was tears for our missing friend.

## Deep Diver

Spike Wagner climbed out of the water, onto his boat, the *Sea Slug*. One of the old wooden boats from the fifties, it had been appropriately named. She only made eight knots. Spike had owned the boat for twelve years. He had grown up in San Diego, so when the urchin diving started there, he was already familiar with the kelp beds near La Jolla. But that was twenty years ago. Now the *Sea Slug* worked out of San Pedro Harbor, making three and four-day trips to San Clemente Island.

"You did it, Boss. I'll get this bag on, and we'll head home." Tim Clancy had been Spike's tender for eight years. Unlike most of the other boats that went fast and used two or three divers, Spike and Tim worked the old way, one diver, with one tender.

The *Sea Slug* was slow, the trip to Pedro would take them over seven hours. But she was roomy and comfortable, and autopilot steered the boat, while the two-man crew napped and watched videos.

"I'm glad that day is over. That last bag took forever. Hurry up and get us headed home, will you?" Spike sometimes was grumpy after diving, but Tim had come to know his skipper well. The tender kept quiet, going about his business.

The hot water felt good. Spike was out of his suit, showering on the deck of the *Sea Slug*. Feeling a dizzy spell coming on, he reached for the cabin door to steady himself. The familiar headache and "tunnel vision" he sometimes experienced after diving was happening. "Shit," he muttered to himself. "Not again."

"Tim, get me four Advils, will you?" Spike had been "bent" several times over the years, and had made two trips to the "chamber" for recompression treatments.

An old enemy was coming back to visit him again.

This time was different, though. He was having trouble speaking, his words were garbled. His legs felt heavy.

"You okay, Boss?" They had another fifteen miles to go. Tim sat at the helm; Spike was in his bunk, below. "I guess those Advils helped, he's sound asleep," the tender thought. He had seen his diver experience similar symptoms in previous years, always taking a handful of Advil and "toughing it out."

"Okay, Skipper. It's my turn to crash. You've been sleeping for four hours." Tim had been generous, allowing Spike extra bunk time. "Wake up, sleeping beauty."

But he did not move.

"Hey, Spike, wake up! I'm not gonna drive forever!" Tim was shaking his foot, but the diver did not respond.

In the mid-1800s, early divers sometimes experienced unusual symptoms after returning to the surface. Dizzy spells, fainting, and an inability to bend their joints was fairly common, but the causes for the "bends" as they were called, were unknown.

At depths over 33 feet, the diver is subjected to pressure. A portion of the compressed air the diver breathes (mostly nitrogen) is absorbed into his body tissues. Amount of time on the bottom, coupled with depth, determine the amount of nitrogen that is retained in his tissue.

As the diver ascends, the nitrogen undergoes a change. Bubbles form, similar to the bubbles seen in a glass of carbonated water.

"Dive tables" are schedules of allowable times the diver may spend at certain depths without fear of experiencing decompression sickness. For example, dive tables allow 130 minutes at 40 feet, 80 minutes at fifty feet, and 55 minutes at 60 feet. Other factors are the residual nitrogen retention in the body when making repetitive dives, age, and the physical condition of the diver.

Problems occur if the diver ascends too quickly, not allowing the bubbles to properly dissipate into the tissue. The bubbles can lodge in a joint, usually an arm or a leg, and can block blood flow. Musculoskeletal, or Type One decompression sickness, is indicated by pain, moderate to severe, in a joint, most commonly an arm or leg. Type Two, or central nervous system decompression sickness is more severe—blood supply to the brain, spinal cord, or heart occurs, causing paralysis, or sometimes death.

Decompression sickness can be alleviated by having the afflicted diver treated in a decompression chamber. Sometimes, multiple treatments are necessary. The more time that elapses after symptoms occur, the less effective the treatment is. Hyperbaric medicine is the field of medicine involved in the study and treatment of decompression sickness.

Spike was awake, but groggy. His speech was slurred and he was unable to get up from his bunk.

"Boss, I'm gonna call the Coast Guard!" Spike shook his head. "I'll be okay. If I'm still hurtin' when we get to Pedro, I'll call the hospital. They have a chamber if I need it. I been through this before."

Tim drove the entire seven hours. When the *Sea Slug* arrived at the dock, Spike was too weak to stand. He was fading in and out of consciousness.

Spike was transported to the hospital by ambulance, where he was put into the chamber. It had been more than nine hours since his last dive. He had suffered a severe Type Two "hit," his spinal cord and brain had been affected, and although after thirteen recompression treatments he regained his speech and brain function, blood flow had been restricted to his spinal cord for too long. Spike Wagner was permanently paralyzed from the waist down.

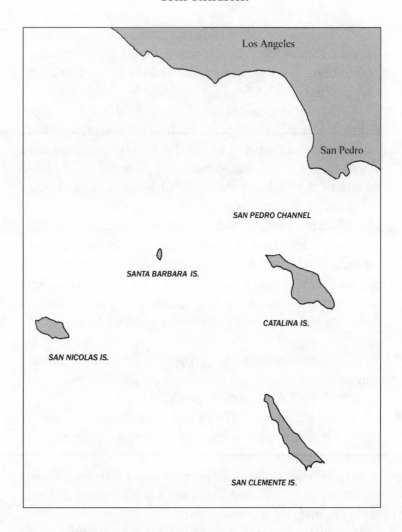

## Clemente

The diving at San Clemente Island is some of the prettiest I've ever seen. It's common to be on the bottom at seventy feet, and look up the anchor line to see the boat. Giant kelp stalks sway lazily back and forth, and sea life abounds.

Working along the top edge of a sixty-foot under-water cliff, I would sometimes look down and see a patch of urchins far below, at around a hundred feet. With picking basket in hand, I'd launch off the cliff, disregarding the dangers of depth and pressure. My body would pay for those deep jumps, but there's nothing like floating down through that dark blue, liquid space, like a wetsuit clad, slow-motion Olympic diver.

Occasionally, a black sea bass, which is a federally protected species, swam up to inspect us. The huge, docile fish are an inquisitive bunch. They'll come right up to you, with their frown-like mouth and look at you with big, blank eyes that seem to be saying, "What are you doing here? This is my spot!" These awesome animals are a member of the grouper family, and can weigh up to five hundred pounds.

The magnificent purple coral is plentiful in the deep waters of San Clemente, and giant underwater fans gently wave in the underwater breeze. The diving at this island can be spellbinding, making it difficult to concentrate on the task at hand. We felt like tourists!

San Clemente Island lies a hundred miles south of Santa Barbara and sixty-five miles south by southwest of San Pedro Harbor, where we would offload after making trips ranging from two to four days. Since the weather was warm, at the end of each day we'd find a protected cove, place our bags in the water, sink them to the bottom, and buoy them off, thereby helping to keep the roe healthy and fresh. On our way home, we'd retrieve our product from the natural "cold storage."

Our typical routine would be to go to Santa Catalina (about twenty-two miles from Pedro) on the first day, get groceries, and continue on.

Avalon Harbor, on the front side of Catalina, is a party town. Sometimes we stayed on a mooring, took the water taxi in to shore, ate at a nice restaurant, and hit the Chi Chi or the Marlin Club. When the occasional guilt pangs hit me as I thought about my wife taking care of the kids at home, it became necessary to remind myself that I was down there providing for them. While lounging on the boat in Avalon on a warm day and watching the bikinis frolicking on the yacht next to us, it was sometimes difficult to keep the guilt feelings away. Difficult, but not impossible.

Unlike Catalina, which is privately owned, San Clemente is owned and operated by the U.S. government, and the Navy conducts regular exercises there. While anchored in Northwest Harbor as the sun came up, we sipped our coffee as Navy SEAL trainees swam past our boat in full combat gear, carrying rifles over their heads.

The most exciting thing by far was when the destroyers were having target practice down toward the south end of the island, near China Cove. Radio transmissions went out on channel sixteen, notifying boats that a certain area would be "hot," and that all vessels were required to head to the north end. We would all scamper up the backside to a safe area and listen to the fireworks. About every five minutes, a series of shells would hit the island, and besides hearing a big boom, everything would shake, rattle, and roll. Boats, water, even the island would shake. Often times, we could feel the concussion underwater.

There is a runway near Northwest Harbor, and during flight drills, fighter jets were landing and taking off every thirty seconds. When they hit the after burners and climbed straight up, it was an awesome sight, but by eleven o'clock at night, it got old.

Calico bass, also called kelp bass, or kelpies, are plentiful in the thick beds at Clemente. We found them perfect for our lunchtime fish tacos. Small polespears were lashed to our picking baskets, and on our last dive before lunch, we would each get a kelpie, fry them in butter and garlic, and fold the fillet into a tortilla with a little salsa. Anchored up on the backside of Clemente in the early fall, with eighty degree air temperature, a light Santa Ana breeze blowing, and a tummy full of fish tacos is good therapy for any North Coast urchin diver.

The island is also loaded with lobsters, and although it's illegal for anyone other than commercial lobstermen, or licensed sport divers to take them, we consumed a little contraband now and then. Doug is a great cook and loves to experiment. He makes a mean meatloaf, and so it seemed natural to try his recipe using lobster. It was a smashing success. He called it "lob loaf."

A rumbling in the distance disturbed my dreams. I rolled over in my bunk and opened one eye—it was already light outside. Then the unmistakable crack of a hard breaking wave brought me out of my sleep, back to the *Debbie K* and the anchorage at Northwest Harbor. I sprang from my bunk and went out on deck, where Doug was standing, gazing through the seven-fifties. "There's a guy out!" he shouted.

"Gimme those," I said. But he wouldn't let go of them.

"There's two guys out! Those waves are double overhead!" But I was already back in the cabin, digging out my surf suit.

"Good morning, sir!" The two short-haired young men greeted us after our long paddle from the boat.

"How'd you guys get out here?" I asked. The only boat around was mine.

"We're Navy SEAL instructors, sir—we keep surfboards here on the island, and we surf on our days off."

I laughed. "So, these are my tax dollars at work?"

"Yes sir, we gotta stay in shape. It's part of the job."
They wore wide grins.

"Say, does the name George Tomlinson ring any bells?"

"Yes sir. Our CO served with a Lt. George Tomlinson in Vietnam. He talks about him all the time. I think he still holds one of the obstacle course records."

"Not to change the subject," Doug interrupted, "but is this the only surf spot on the island?"

"Oh, no sir—there's Helmet's, it's a nice right peeler about five miles from here, and China Cove down at the east end. But the best spot..."

"No!" His buddy cut him off. "Sorry, sir, we can't tell you about that one."

"Yeah," I said, "I heard about a spot over by Wilson Cove that holds up to triple overhead, and it's protected from the northwesterlies."

Doug chimed in, "Come on you guys—you know it's not gonna stay a secret forever."

"Well, I guess we could tell you. And we could take you there for a surf. But unfortunately, after that we'd have to kill you." More grins.

"Okay, okay."

We had to make do surfing the outer reef at Northwest anchorage. It was perfect—a solid eight feet and glassy, with only the four of us out.

But I've always wondered about that other spot.

### End of An Era

$T$wo factors caused the California sea urchin business to take a sudden downturn in the mid-nineties. The oceanic weather phenomenon called El Niño brought unusually warm water to the California coastal region. Kelp beds, which thrive on cooler water temperatures, were decimated. This lack of food supply caused the urchin roe to shrink, making for an inferior product. The second reason was that the California product, which had dominated the Japanese market for years, was now on the decline, and our prices plummeted as foreign markets became firmly established. The Kuril Islands of Russia were now delivering a large supply as were Korea, Canada, Mexico and Chile. Prices fell to levels not seen for ten years.

In a two-year period, over half the divers in the fleet quit and got out of diving altogether. Of the 300 or so remaining divers, a full two-thirds became part-timers as they scrambled to support their families.

The final blow for me came on that fall trip in 1995 while making repetitive jumps to ninety feet on the backside of beautiful San Clemente Island. On the first day of our third turnaround trip, Doug and I were up on deck, tending bags. He had a knife, and was hacking kelp leaves off of a bag as it came up out of the water. I had the control button in my hand, lifting the bag up onto the deck. Suddenly, I felt a stabbing, knifelike pain in my shoulder. My hand went numb and I dropped the button. It fell to the deck.

"C'mon, bring it up!" Doug shouted. The heavy bag was half out of the water, the boat was leaning. I just stood there, looking down at my hand, which was asleep.

"I can't feel my hand," I said. Doug let go of the bag, picked up the button, and lowered the urchins back down into the water.

"Any pain?"

"I gotta knife in my shoulder."

"You're bent. I'm gonna fire up the popper. We gotta get you back down on the bottom to relieve that bubble."

A few minutes later, I sat on the rail of the boat, my right arm dangling at my side. Doug yelled over the noise of the compressor motor. "Stay on the bottom for a half a minute or so, then come up real slow—hang off at ten feet for a few minutes too," I fell off the boat and began kicking downward into the deep, blue water. At eighty feet my arm felt better, and after pinning myself to the bottom for a short time, I began my slow ascent. But at forty feet from the surface, the pain returned, and by the time I was back on the boat, it was no better. Again, I went down to the bottom, with the same result.

After three trips to the bottom, the searing pain in my shoulder remained.

"We gotta get you to a chamber, buddy."

I was lucky. After three treatments in the Long Beach recompression chamber, my pain, for the most part, went away, and I regained feeling in my hand. X-rays showed slight bone damage in my shoulder, but it was thought to be from years of harvesting urchins rather than from necrosis, or bone death. In less than a week, all the numbness was gone, and I quickly regained full use of my arm.

Being healthy once again was a great relief, but just as important to me was that during my hospital stay I had time to think about my life, my family, and the future. I'd enjoyed a relatively injury-free career in a business that had claimed the lives of two of my friends, and crippled another. My wife and kids wanted and deserved a husband and father who was a participant in their lives, not someone who was always gone, or somewhere else mentally.

These things had been in the back of my mind for the last couple of years, but I just told myself, This is my job. This is what I do. Any thoughts of a life after diving had always been postponed.

Looking back, I'm thankful for the injury. It forced me to reevaluate, and it sped up the decision-making process, which had started with Weener's death. During my time in the hospital I made the commitment to quit diving, and sell the boat. Sure, I could have stretched it out for several more years, but eight thousand hours on the bottom was enough for me. It was time to call it quits.

"Don't do it." My old pal Jerome sat across from me at a table outside the Minnow Cafe. He'd seen the For Sale sign on my boat. "You'll be sorry you sold her and within a year you'll have a boat again. After being a diver and a boat skipper for so long, it gets in your blood. You won't be able to work for somebody else. I've seen it time and time again. Hey, we've all been bent—it comes with the territory. Just slow down on the deep stuff, and take it easy. Heck, I rarely go deeper than thirty feet, I limit my bottom time to three hours a day, and I'm still makin' a decent living."

I'd been hearing the same story from others, and was plenty nervous, especially when I thought of what was going to come next. I had no trade to fall back on like some of the other guys. I never finished college. Plus I had no clue as to what I wanted to do.

Lenny, whom I had made my first island surf trip with, suggested I put an ad in the newspaper: Former sea urchin diver looking for employment. Able to work ten days per month. Prefer salary of one thousand dollars per day, minimum.

A curator for an aquarium near pier 39 in San Francisco was on the dock in Santa Barbara looking over the boat and expressed an interest in her. She said it would be perfect for collecting sea life for the aquarium. After several phone calls to the main office and a couple of days of negotiating, we struck a deal.

Debbie and I had been talking on the phone every day—of course she was thrilled. She kept trying to boost my confidence. "Don't worry, honey, we're in it together. You'll find something."

Damn the torpedoes, full speed ahead. On the twenty-second of October 1995, we sold the *Debbie K.* For the first time in sixteen years, I did not own a boat, and was back to having one wife. We charged forward and never looked back.

Selling the *Debbie K.* left a huge void in my life. When it finally sunk in, I realized that probably 80 percent of my waking thoughts had something to do with the boat, or diving. For some reason though, in the back of my mind, I knew that it was the right decision, and within a few days after the boat changed hands, I felt a huge weight being lifted from my shoulders. My future was unclear, but somehow we knew things would work out.

# *Epilogue*

## Epilogue

Those urchin diving days will always be a part of me, and I look back on that period of my life with great fondness. More importantly though, are the wonderful memories of the crazy, hard-working, and fun-loving cast of characters that I've had the privilege of knowing. They are a unique group of individuals and I fill with pride when I think of them.

I tried a few things after retiring from diving, but within a year, realized I was unemployable. After skippering boats, breathing compressed air, and swimming with sea monsters for all those years, I found it impossible to set an alarm clock and go to work for someone else.

We wound up scraping together everything we had and bought some apartments in Santa Rosa, a twenty-minute drive from our house. It was a big change for me and we no longer make the big bucks, but our family is together these days, and I make my own schedule. In some ways, managing the apartments is like diving—every day is an adventure. Most of my days now, though, are spent diving into plumbing or electrical problems, or carpooling kids.

Some of my old pals still make their living sea urchin diving. A few of them moved to New Zealand, and are diving for abalone. A couple of guys parlayed their stakes into the Bristol Bay salmon fishery in Alaska, and some have gotten into the live fish business on the California coast.

Hydroplane Steve Hagen is currently in Norway, acting as a diver consultant. He has traveled the world in search of sea urchins.

Dewey Benton, my skipper on the *Hound Dog*, got out of diving in 1987. He owns and operates a marine supply store in Ventura.

Jerome Betts has five children. After twenty-six years of diving, he's still going strong, and continues to be a fixture on the backside of San Miguel Island. Jerome has personally harvested over fourteen million pounds of urchins.

The bar at Brophy Brothers is where you'll find Jim Cotton. He retired from diving in 1997, but still works on the ocean, commercial fishing for halibut. With no wife or kids, he's Mr. Low Overhead and lives on his boat, which he named after his favorite windsurfing spot—Jalama.

Mark Evanoff (Never off ), is urchin diving in Southeast Alaska, and if I know him, he'll be in the Aleutians in a few years.

Domenic Pasquini, the Italian asshole, is in Chile, exporting fish to China. I hope he stays there.

Matt Chapin, of the *Pisagna*, built his third boat and named it *Fat Choy* (Chinese for "good luck"). Keeping true to his visionary and eclectic ways, he cut a hole in the stern so it would be easier to climb on to. He even painted eyeballs on the bow to help find his way home in the dark!

Robin Brown, with whom Jerome and I had found the Chumash arrowhead, took a brain hit during a deep dive. He went blind temporarily, but has since recovered.

Andreas, The Spaniard, is back on his feet and thinking up new ideas. He's building a new boat as well as trying to start up a restaurant. We had a conversation the last time I passed through Santa Barbara, but I couldn't understand what he was saying.

When the prices on the North Coast took a dump, Ron Elliott tied up the *GW* for several months. But he was lonely—he missed his friends. He bought an underwater video camera, and returned to his home, the Farallon

Islands, where he has spent hundreds of hours up close and personal with Mr. GW himself, making home movies.

Doug Dirkse and I dove together for ten years, and our adventures were some of the best times of my life. Doug took a central nervous system hit in 2005 while diving at San Clemente Island. He was paralyzed from the waist down, but after twelve chamber treatments, he partially recovered, At forty-four years old, he now walks with a limp, and has lower extemity numbness.

Several of us didn't make it financially. One of the more successful divers I knew had two boats, a beautiful home on a golf course, and a prime chunk of land in central California. In the mid-eighties he was pulling in over two hundred grand a year. But when the times got tough, he and his wife couldn't handle the change in lifestyle. They managed to lose everything and got divorced. There are plenty of those stories.

As per the wishes of Weener's family, the *Florentia Marie* was passed to Ward Motyer. He and Steve Stickney worked together for several more years, then parted company. But the terrible events of December ninth created a bond between the two men that endures to this day.

Although I've been retired from diving for several years now, it's still in my blood, and I guess it always will be. When I drive through downtown Sebastopol and see the flag at the library hanging limp, I wonder if the water's clear, and if the roe is fat, and what the prices are.

Surfing has reemerged as a force in my life. I drag my family down to Mexico or Central America every winter for some tropical waves.

Debbie has thirty piano students. She continues to put away a hundred bucks a month and makes me go on a hike with her once a week.

On a recent trip to Mexico, I stopped by Santa Barbara, where, after a few phone calls, I found myself sitting at the bar in Brophy's. I hadn't seen some of the guys for several years. We commented about our gray hair, or lack of it, and our big bellies.

None of us brought up Weener, but when a Tom Waits song came through the speakers, we all looked at each other, silent and misty-eyed. Nothing needed to be said. And it might be my imagination, but it seemed like the whole place, which is usually a madhouse of noise and general commotion, became quiet, as Waits crooned: "What becomes of little boys who never comb their hair?"

As the restaurant was closing and we headed out the door, one of the guys touched my arm, pointing to a wooden plaque mounted high above the bar. "In loving memory of Jim Robinson," it read. A ship's bell sat next to it. "Whenever Weener's name is mentioned, the bell is rung," my friend explained.

The ship's bell, along with a photograph of Jim Robinson, remain to this day, perched on the wall at Brophy's, looking out over the Santa Barbara harbor.

# Appendix

Weener, The Spaniard and the author - 1993

# In Memorium

Glen Brisindine

Billy Bossert

Rod Cochran

Arnie Douglas

Joe Douglas

Ben Espinoza

Kenny Hauser

Gary Hoffman

Tim Johnson

John Lee

Bruce Maassen

Gilbert Mercado

Jim Melhorne

Bobo Moilanen

Bruce Moore

Jim Robinson

Kevin Sears

Andy Smith

Wyn Swint

George Tomlinson

Doug Trimm

Coy White

# Acknowledgements

Without the assistance of Gil Mansergh, who saw possibilities in an early draft, and assisted me with yet another rewrite, this book would not have been possible.

Kathy and Dave Biggs at Azalea Creek Publishing spent countless hours getting things just right. Their patience and knowledge is greatly appreciated; they are the best.

Tom Rissacher, artist and surf compadre. Thanks for the bro-deal.

Scott Hulet, senior editor of The Surfers Journal, encouraged me with his unbridled enthusiasm. He kept the fire burning.

**Manuscript consultation:**
Ken Boettcher, diver, Calif Deptment of Fish & Game Patrol Captain (retired); Gaye LeBaron, columnist, historian; Dr. John McCosker, Aquatic Chair, California Academy of Sciences; Bev Morgan, co-founder, Kirby-Morgan Dive Systems, board member, Historical Diving Society; Christina Slager, curator, Monterey Bay Aquarium; Karen (Tomlinson) Lewis; Reynolds Yater, surfboard manufacturer
**Sea urchin consultation:**
Dr. Thomas Ebert, PhD; Bruce Steele, diver, historian
**Historical diving and technical consultation:**
Lad Handleman, diver, founder, Cal-Dive, Oceaneering Inc.; Harold Shrout, diver, inventor
**Hyperbaric medicine consultation:**
Joel Dovenbarger and Laurie Gowan, Divers Alert Network
**Collaboration on the events of Dec. 9:**
Ward Motyer, diver

# Appendix

. . .

The boats, dive gear and technology for the new sea urchin fishery of the 1970s originated from the California abalone divers of the 1960s. Ron Radon was one of the first abalone divers to use "Light Gear"; that is, wetsuit, fins, and scuba breathing regulator, for abalone harvest. Prior to this time, around 1960, the cumbersome "Hard Hat" gear was the norm. In the next several years, the light gear took over. A few diehards however, stayed with the old ways through the mid-70s.

Abalone divers Bev Morgan and Bob Kirby, combined their talents to become the inventors of the full face mask breathing systems. They went on to form Kirby-Morgan Dive Systems, manufacturing dive helmets that are the current standard in commercial and military use world-wide.

Laddie Handleman, another abalone diver, foresaw the future of mixed-gas diving applications in the offshore oil industry. He founded Cal-Dive and Oceaneering, which went on to become the largest diving contractor in the world.

These men, and many others of their generation, are owed a debt of gratitude by the sea urchin fleet for their contributions, and for "showing us the way."

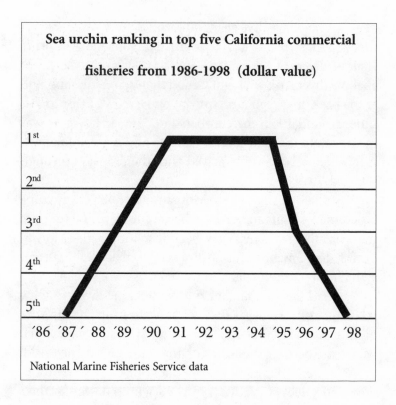

**Sea urchin ranking in top five California commercial fisheries from 1986-1998 (dollar value)**

National Marine Fisheries Service data

Photo by Michael Amsler

Tom Kendrick was in the California Sea Urchin fishery for twenty-two years. He lives in Sebastopol.

Fall, 2006

The California sea urchin fishery is a healthy, sustainable fishery, continuing to maintain a position in the "top five." During the period of time covered in this book, up to 90% of the processed uni went to Japan. Now, however, as the popularity of sushi grows in the U.S., only about 30% goes overseas.

As a result of coordinated efforts of fishermen, processors, and the Department of Fish and Game, policies are now in place to protect this valuable resource, and the thousands of people who depend on it.

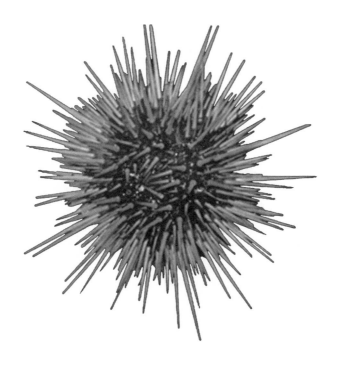

Red Sea Urchin
*Stronglyocentrotus franciscanus*

# To Order

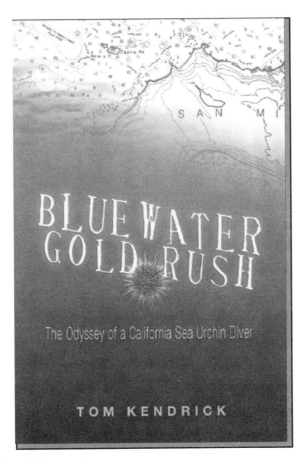

**Website orders:**      **bluewatergoldrush.com**

**Telephone orders:**    (707) 829-7784

**Price:**               $21.00 (includes tax & shipping)